Suburb

by

Steven Kedie

For Gemma, Joel, and Nate.

Prologue

Thursday, 20 May 2004

The Suburbs, South Manchester

I returned home from three years at university to find my parents exactly where I'd left them.

I parked on the kerb outside my family home; semi-detached, identical to its neighbour, stuck in the middle of a cul-de-sac. Slowly, I turned my key in the lock of the front door. Inside the familiar floral décor surrounded me, the smell of Thursday night takeaway curry filled the air. I put my head round the living room door. My parents sat separately; Mum on the settee, Dad in his chair, both staring at the television. *EastEnders* their soap of choice.

'All right?' I asked.

'Hello, Tom,' my mum said.

'All right?' my dad said.

Their eyes didn't leave the screen.

I unloaded my car, storing boxes and bags temporarily in the hallway. My mum appeared as I finished my last trip and offered to

1

cook something for me. I declined, explaining I'd eaten before driving back. She smiled and disappeared back into the living room.

I carried my boxes and bags up the stairs to my brother's old room.

Tuesday, 11 September 2001

The day that shook the world. One of those days that you'll always remember exactly where you were when you heard the news. Like JFK being shot (I wasn't born), or Princess Diana's car crash (I was in a swimming pool in Greece with my brother wondering why the sun beds around the pool were empty, and why my mum was crying in our apartment). I was in my bedroom packing when I saw the first images of the twin towers. I watched repeated news footage of the attacks as I sorted out the clothes I was taking to Leeds uni with me. It felt strange to be quietly preparing to completely change my life, to move away from home for the first time, to finally be independent, while on the television in my room an event was unfolding that would shape the modern world. Echoes of the planes crashing into the New York towers would soon be heard in Afghanistan and Iraq.

I also remember that day for a very different reason. After watching the second plane hit for the thousandth time, I left my house. Some neighbours had gathered on the street and were discussing theories of the goings-on in New York. A large removal van was parked on the opposite side of the road, further down towards the open circle of houses at the end of the cul-de-sac. A woman carried a box from the van to the driveway of number 20 and stopped next to a man I didn't recognise.

I crossed the street and caught the woman's eye. She smiled and I smiled back. The man stood next to her nodded a 'hello'. He was her husband, Stuart, I later found out.

That is the other thing I think about when somebody mentions September 11, 2001, now. It was the day I met Kate Young for the first time. There was nothing special about the meeting, nothing that suggested any significance.

Nothing to indicate we'd eventually start an affair.

Chapter One

I left university with a simple plan. Work, save, go travelling.

I woke up on my first morning home to the sound of my mum shouting to my brother, 'Chris. Get up. It's eight o'clock.'

'I'm up.' His voice matching my mum's for volume.

I lay in what used to be Chris's single bed for a few minutes listening to the sounds of the bathroom. The toilet flushing, the cistern starting to refill, the tap running, Chris spitting toothpaste into the sink. The door opened and his heavy footsteps disappeared downstairs. I squeezed past my unpacked boxes onto the landing.

When I walked into the kitchen my fifteen-year-old brother, who was sat at the small pine table, looked up at me and said, 'All right?' through a mouthful of chocolate Corn Flakes. His school tie hung over the back of his chair and his crumpled white shirt was still un-tucked.

'Morning,' my mum said. She sprayed the kitchen work surface with cleaner, then wiped across the sides, clearing them of toast crumbs and splashes of milk, performing her morning ritual as she had done since I was little. The kitchen always cleaned and tidied before leaving the house; before taking me to nursery, before dropping me at primary school, before I went to secondary school, before taking Chris to primary school, and eventually before she went to work. Clean, tidy, and ready for coming home and starting again.

I bent down in front of the fridge and scanned for orange juice. Standing back up with the carton in my hand I went over to the cupboard with the glasses in. When I opened it a pile of plates and bowls faced me.

'Where are the glasses? I thought they were in here.'

'They were. They're in the next one along now. That one is the bigger cupboard. A couple of plates got chipped when they were being put back in the other one.' My mum glanced at my brother.

Chris stood up, picked his bowl up and left it on the side by the sink, then silently walked out of the kitchen. I poured a bowl of cereal from the box he had left on the table and covered it with milk.

'He's chatty,' I said, as my mum poured the remainder of Chris's breakfast into the bin.

'He's fifteen. He just sits in his room playing his guitar most of the time. You were the same.'

'Sorry about that,' I said, smiling.

My mum began loading the dishwasher. I ate in silence.

AS I JOGGED up the stairs a few minutes later, I heard the loud rev of a car engine followed by the screech of tyres. It accelerated through the gears quickly, the noise carrying as it disappeared down the street. I reached the top of the stairs as my mum came out of her bedroom, transformed from housewife to receptionist.

'That boy is an idiot,' she said. 'He's going to hit someone one day if he's not careful.'

'Who?'

'Paul across the road.' As she answered, she walked into the bathroom, leaving the door open. 'He only passed his test about two months ago. He's already racing down the road every day. No thought for the kids on the road. Only takes one of them to run out of their driveway and that's it. I should say something to his mum.' She carefully squeezed toothpaste onto her toothbrush.

'Don't,' I said. 'You'll only make him worse. He's seventeen. He's not going to listen to his mum, is he? Probably make him go faster.'

'Well,' she spat, running water into the sink to chase away the toothpaste. 'What should I do? Wait until he hits someone?' Her voice had risen slightly, not liking me challenging her.

'No. I'll have a word with him when I see him.'

'Well, do it soon,' she said.

FEELING CLAUSTROPHOBIC AND frustrated, I stood surrounded by half empty boxes. My stuff didn't fit in my brother's old room. I had more CDs than he had shelf space, more clothes than would fit in his wardrobe, more souvenirs of experiences gained away from this house. I reminded myself that staying in this room was only temporary; a means to an end. There was a single bed that ran the length of the room along one wall. A small wardrobe and chest of drawers fitted along the other, leaving a thin corridor of space between the door and the window. My dorm room in my first year at uni was bigger.

Chris stole my bedroom about three days after I moved out. As the first born, I always had the biggest room and he'd always slept in the box room. The first weekend I came home I faced his victorious smile as I opened the door to what was my room. He lay casually on my bed, waiting, surrounded by his things on my shelves, his posters on my walls.

'Keep it,' I said, trying to show I didn't care. 'I don't live here anymore.'

That weekend, and every other time I'd been home since, I'd brought enough stuff to fit in an overnight bag, just to get me by until I went back to Leeds. Now I had everything with me, my life didn't fit.

I managed to get the necessities into some form of order but had leftover things piled on the bed with nowhere to put them. Annoyed, I refilled some boxes with stuff I didn't think I'd need and shoved them under the bed.

It's only temporary, I repeated. Just a means to an end.

I HEARD A key sliding into the front door.

'Hello,' I shouted, from my brother's old room.

I stood up and went down to the kitchen. My dad was filling the kettle.

'You not working?'

'Yeah. I've got to nip and see a job and I left my book here. Thought I'd have a quick brew. Want one?'

'Is there any coffee?'

He clicked the kettle on. 'No. We don't drink it.'

I sat at the table and turned a tabloid newspaper over to the sports pages. It was full of the next day's FA Cup Final: Manchester United v Millwall.

'When did you start drinking coffee?'

'When I had assignment deadlines to meet.'

There was a short silence, broken by the kettle's increasing noise. My dad took two mugs out of the cupboard, dropping a teabag in each one. He slid open a draw and picked up a teaspoon.

'Mum started letting you make it in the cup now?' I asked, nodding to the teapot on the side.

'Your mum's not here.' He laughed. He heaped three sugars into his mug as the kettle boiled. Steam rose upwards. At the peak of the noise my dad said, 'You still take two sugars?'

'One.'

He made the drinks and pushed mine towards me, throwing the spoon into the sink. It bounced around in the bowl and then the noise stopped. Silence again.

'What you up to today?'

'Not a lot. I'm just finishing unpacking.' I glanced at the paper again.

'You got all your stuff from over there?' he asked, meaning Leeds.

'Yeah.'

'Any word on a job?'

'Going to the agency on Monday, see if they can get me any temp work.'

Sips of tea. Silence.

'I should've got you an Evening News last night. It's the job section on a Thursday.'

'I'll be all right. I'll get some temp stuff. See from there.'

More sips. More silence.

'You busy?'

'Always.'

There was a brief moment where I contemplated asking for some hours helping him. He's a landscaper. Long days, hard work. Man's work. I decided against it. I'd been back from uni one day. It didn't seem right going straight for the protection of working with my dad. Instead, I asked, 'You out tonight?'

'Yeah. Some work's meal of your mother's. It's somebody's birthday.'

'Sounds fun,' I offered sarcastically.

'Doesn't it?' He took another a drink of tea, walked to the sink, and poured the remains away. He turned on the tap, rinsed the mug, and left it upside down on the draining board.

'Right, back to it then.' He walked past me into the hall. At the front door, he stopped to put his boots back on. Heavy boots covered in mud. Worker's boots.

'You got your book?' I asked.

'Yeah,' he picked it up from the floor and showed it to me. A black school exercise book, a worn-down pencil sticking out of the end. He opened the door but turned back.

'Where are you watching the final tomorrow?'

Football, our common ground.

'Don't know. Might go out with the lads. You?'

'Here. Your mother's got a list of jobs for me.' He smiled.

I smiled back. 'I might join you. Save you.'

I spent the rest of the afternoon ticking down the hours until I went out. I did some washing, loaded and unloaded the dishwasher, flicked through television channels. It immediately became obvious that I was missing my house mates from uni. The option to combat boredom by going into Sean, Matt, or John's room was gone. In Leeds, I could go to the pub and see someone I knew. Back home, everyone was working.

My mum came home, said hello, then settled in front of the television to watch *Richard and Judy*. I joined her. We asked questions about each other's days, both of us concentrating more on the television. My dad came in, showered the day away and sat in his chair scanning the paper.

I dressed to go out. T-shirt, jeans, and trainers. Uni standard. I re-thought the trainers, undoing them and kicking them off, exchanging them for shoes. I couldn't remember the local pub rules on wearing trainers. Shoes were the safer option.

One quick check in the mirror and I bounded down the stairs.

I got to the bottom step and reached for the front door, opened it about half an inch, and shouted, 'Bye.'

'Tom,' my mum's voice called.

I sighed. 'What?'

'Come here a minute please.'

I closed the door and walked back to the living room. My mum sat on the settee in her dressing gown, her hair and make-up done. 'What?' I asked sharply.

'It's your auntie Linda's birthday on Sunday. She's doing a lunch.'

'OK?'

'She wants us all there. It'll be about three o'clock.'

'Right,' I said. I was aware my tone was questioning why my mum couldn't have asked me this earlier. Or waited until tomorrow. Why wait until I had one foot out of the door?

I shut the living room door, walked back down the hallway, opened the front door, and stepped out into my driveway. Walking past the end of it was Kate Young.

IT'S AMAZING HOW one small detail can change everything. If my mum had not shouted for me, pulling me back from the door at that precise moment, none of this story I'm telling you would have happened. I would have been two minutes ahead of Kate, walking the streets to my night out alone. We might never have had the conversation that was the foundation of everything that happened afterwards. We might have said 'hello' in the street, or seen each other in a local shop or pub and smiled a smile of neighbours; one of recognition for living on the same street, just a few doors apart, but nothing to cause any impact.

In passing once, the previous summer, her husband had invited me to a barbeque at their house. I called in on my way home from a night out and sat for about three hours, drinking, eating cold burgers, talking football with one of her husband's mates. Kate and I exchanged a few words; a joke about her husband's dancing, I think. That night had made us comfortable enough to exchange pleasantries, a nod or a wave when passing in the street.

It made us comfortable enough to say 'hello' when she walked past my front gates.

'Hi,' she said. 'How are you?'

'Very well,' I said. 'Where you off to all alone on a Friday night?'

Side by side we walked together.

'Just local to meet the girls. You?'

'Same. But to meet the lads. It's my mate Jordan's birthday, so we're just having a few beers.'

'Can I walk with you? If you don't mind.'

I laughed when she asked that.

'What's so funny?' she asked.

'Of course, you can walk with me. It'd be pretty shit of me if I just walked off after you told me we were going to exactly the same place. How bad would you feel if I just walked about five yards in front of you the whole way? I'd feel daft with you just watching me walk all the way.'

She laughed softly, and I was glad she wasn't offended that I'd laughed at her.

I changed the subject. 'Is Stuart not out?'

'He's in Cardiff for the Cup final.'

'Nice one. Is he still running the sports company?'

'Yeah. He's off to Portugal for the European Championships in a few weeks.'

'Can't be bad,' I said.

We were on the main road now, walking past rectangular grass verges that were embedded in the wider pavements, trees growing from them.

'Are you going to Portugal?' I asked.

'No. I don't get to go on the trips. He's working. Plus, I'm not that bothered about spending three weeks with all his drunken clients.'

'Not fancy sunbathing for a few weeks?'

'It would be nice, but he has different trips for different parts of the tournament. I think he's coming home about four times during the three weeks. He picks up another group and flies out with them.'

We walked quietly for a few steps.

'Where are you going tonight?' I asked, not wanting the silence to last too long.

'The Boathouse. You?'

'Start in the Silver Moon. Might move on later.'

'Are you back from university now?'

'Yeah. Drove home last night. I've got this last weekend, then I'm officially in the real world.'

'Rent and bills, etc?'

'If my dad has got anything to do with it.'

'Have you got jobs in mind?'

'Not really. I want to go travelling so I just need something to get some money in. Start saving and go from there, really.'

'Travelling? Really? Where to?'

'Everywhere. Thailand, Vietnam – my mate John from uni is in Japan at the moment. He says that's mint. We wanted to go together, but he landed himself a high-paying job last summer and he wanted to go as soon as he could.'

'Why didn't you go?'

'I didn't land a well-paid summer job.'

'Oh. Where else do you want to go?'

'Australia, New Zealand. The usual path. I want to go away for as long as possible. A year, two years if I can get enough money together.'

Her eyes smiled. 'That's brilliant. I wish I'd done it.'

'Me and three mates went around Europe at the end of the first year. Two months we did. Bumming around. *Backpacks and Six-packs*, we called it.'

'I always wanted to do something like that.'

'Why didn't you?'

She shrugged. 'I trained to be an accountant instead.'

'Rock 'n' Roll.'

'Isn't it? It was always one of those things that got put off. I was going to go after university, but I needed to get a job because all the good firms snap people up quickly and I didn't want to miss out. Then I got used to a good salary I suppose. I met Stuart just after university too. Not sure me going away for a year would've done us any good.'

'Where would you have gone?'

'Europe,' she answered. 'Rome, Barcelona, Vienna.'

'We did those when we went. Rome's class. The Colosseum blew my mind. My mate. Matt, kept pretending to be in *Gladiator*. I had to tell him to shut up so I could hear the tour guide. I really wanted to see it, take it all in. And he just kept walking round doing his best Russell Crowe impressions.'

Our walk took me back past the familiar places of home. Past the row of shops that currently housed a fruit and veg shop, Chinese and Indian takeaway places, a cheap booze chain, a Post Office, and a small Spar. Past my old school, its light blue railings that had been painted a deeper dark blue, past the park where we used to play football on the bowling green until the park warden would come and

15

kick us off, past my dad's local, past rows and rows of houses, the same in design, different in colour.

'I haven't seen *Gladiator*.'

Shocked, I said, 'You've not seen *Gladiator*?'

'No. Not really my thing.'

'It should be everyone's thing. It's amazing. Seriously, you've not seen it?'

'Honestly. I wouldn't lie to you, especially considering it's so important to you. I don't think it'd be fair to joke with you about it.'

We laughed.

The conversation turned back to travelling. I recited stories of overnight trains and dodgy hostels from my trip around Europe. She told me about going on a driving holiday in America when she was a child and falling in love with the great open spaces between cities. She wanted to go back and do it again, old enough to understand it all. We agreed how amazing Route 66 would be to drive in an old drop top American car.

I was surprised when our destination appeared in front of us.

We stood outside the Boathouse pub. 'Thanks for letting me walk with you.'

'No worries. I might see you later if I come in there. Might even let you buy me a pint for getting you here safely.'

'No problem.'

She turned and walked into the pub. I went to meet my friends.

'ALL RIGHT?'

Jordan stood at the bar of the Silver Moon with his brother, Sam, and our friend, Neil.

'Happy birthday, you old twat.'

We shook hands, patted each other's arms, and smiled at seeing each other for the first time in three months.

'How are you finding the joys of Manchester? You happier now you're away from the land of the sheep shaggers?'

I laughed. Jordan always did this – insulted Leeds, tried to reinforce the Lancashire/Yorkshire divide. Leeds was all right for him when he'd come over for a night out.

'What took you so long?' he asked.

'Nothing, just walking with a neighbour. What you having?'

'Carling.' Sam and Neil nodded, indicating they wanted the same. I moved to the bar. It wasn't busy, as it was still early. A girl who was a few years above me at school wrestled with the change in her purse. Julia, I thought her name was. She looked like she'd been drinking since she'd finished work, probably a couple of hours before. She caught my eye and smiled, knowing she knew me but unsure where from. I smiled back but was glad when the barman appeared, helping me avoid an awkward conversation.

I gave him my order and waited, looking around. The pub was a typical glass fronted modern chain pub. It had been refurbished since the last time I'd been home, the second time in the three years since I'd been away. The walls were painted a deep red, the floor a dark varnished wood. Slim television screens were mounted on the wall advertising drinks offers that could be found at the bar that took up the whole left-hand side of the pub. A jukebox stood in one corner, next to a computerised pub game machine and a fruit machine.

Passing the drinks out to their owners, I said to Neil, 'I'm surprised you're out. Thought you'd be under lock and key now. How long has she got left?'

'Four weeks,' Neil said, referring to his pregnant girlfriend, Lisa. 'I played the Jordan's birthday card. She was all right about it. Just kept telling me to not spend too much money. Apparently, this is my last night out. As of tomorrow, I'm on driving duty in case she drops.'

Neil and Lisa had been together about six months when she fell pregnant. Within the last year he'd gone from a twenty-one-year-old joiner whose life revolved around Friday and Saturday nights out and attending as many football matches as possible, to becoming an expectant father living with his girlfriend at her parents' house, saving as much money as he could. Even before the pregnancy they argued more than any couple I'd ever met. Most of us had said they wouldn't last. The day Neil told us Lisa was pregnant he looked like the life had been sucked out of him. It was a sad sight to see.

'How's she feeling?'

'Not too bad. She's tired and struggling to get comfortable in bed.'

'That's probably because you're taking up all the room, you fat bastard,' Jordan said, laughing at Neil's sizable frame.

Neil ignored him and said to me, 'You still looking to go travelling?'

I nodded yes as I drank a large mouthful of lager.

'When?'

'Not sure yet. I'm going to work for a bit, save up as much money as possible and just go. The more I save, the longer I can be away.'

'You going on your own?'

'Yeah. One of the lads from uni has just gone so I might meet up with him. But I'm not bothered about going on my own. If I'm on my own I'm not tied to anyone else's plans.'

Jordan finished his drink with one long tilt of the glass. 'Another?'

We spent the next couple of hours, joined by a couple of other friends, stood in a tight circle talking, laughing, and drinking. It was nice to be back with the lads I grew up with. Seeing them was never difficult. If weeks or months passed between my visits home no one ever questioned why it had been so long. When we met up again everything just went back to how it was the last time we had seen each other, especially with me and Jordan.

'You out for the Cup final tomorrow?' Jordan asked me as our eyes followed a blonde girl as she strolled across the pub, aware she had the attention of most of the male eyes in the room.

'Not sure yet. My dad mentioned about watching it. I might just watch it at home with him.' I showed him my nearly empty pint glass and said, 'Fancy having a couple in the Boathouse?'

WE NODDED TO the middle-aged doorman and entered the Boathouse. The interior was a complete contrast to the Silver Moon's modern look. Large leather chairs and couches placed around low oak tables created a more relaxed atmosphere. The main room was lighter and the music played underneath the humming noise of conversation from customers whose average age was higher than the pub we'd just been in.

We walked to the bar and waited to be served. My eyes glanced around for Kate. I noticed her sat with two other women. A bottle of red wine was placed in the middle of the table and each of them had a large, half full glass. Kate sipped on hers when she looked up and spotted me.

I smiled and gave a small wave, then turned back to the bar.

'Who's that?' Jordan said.

'My neighbour. The one I walked here with.'

'She is fit.' He emphasised the last word.

The word I would've used is beautiful. Fortunately, the barmaid interrupted us and asked for our order.

Later, as I walked out of the men's, the door to the ladies' toilet opened. Stephanie Pearce, my ex-girlfriend's best friend, walked out and looked at me. Her face broke out into a huge smile.

'Hiya,' she shouted. 'How are you?' The words were drawn out, and I realised she was drunk. High heels raised her tiny frame. She leant forward and gave me a kiss then wrapped her arms around me and hugged me tightly.

'What you doing here? I thought you were in Leeds.'

'I got back yesterday.'

'For good?'

'I've finished uni, if that's what you mean.'

'Have you seen Melissa?'

'No,' I said, and to change the subject, added, 'What are you up to?'

'Nothing much.' I tried not to wince at the volume of her voice. Even though I'd known her for years, it had always taken me by surprise. 'Just getting drunk. I'm out with the girls from work. We're going into town soon.' She started describing her plans for the night in detail, explaining about meeting up with one of her colleague's boyfriend at a new bar, but she wasn't sure if that was happening because the girl and the boyfriend had had an argument. She started telling me about the argument. She spoke at such speed I struggled to keep up.

Stephanie kept talking for a few more minutes, punctuating her stories with questions about my life. I answered in short responses.

'Is Melissa out of with you?' I asked.

'No. She's in with her new bloke.'

'New bloke?'

'Don't you know about him?'

I shook my head.

'He's called Andy. She's not been with him long.'

'What's he like?'

'He's a dick,' Stephanie said. Her eyes glanced over my shoulder. 'Sorry,' she said as she moved herself and me out of the way of the ladies' toilet door. I turned to see who we were moving for. It was Kate.

'Hi,' I said.

'Hi,' she said, before disappearing through the door.

'Who's that?' Stephanie asked.

'My neighbour.'

'She's so,' she held onto the word again, 'pretty.'

We realised we were blocking part of the small corridor, so walked to the main area of the pub.

'Why's Andy a dick?' I asked.

'He just is. I can't take to him.'

'There must be a reason?' I pushed.

'It's a long story. I'm not going into it.'

AT THE END of the night, Jordan slung his arm over my shoulder and said, 'It's been good to see you dude.'

We were standing in a takeaway waiting for Jordan's pepperoni pizza to cook. I held a portion of chips, waiting for them to cool down.

'You too,' I said.

Jordan was drunk. It was obvious by the way he leant on the counter, watching the staff as they prepared pizza toppings and filled pitta bread with reheated kebab meat and salad.

I faced the other way, watching five lads mock fighting in the taxi queue across the road. They pushed and grabbed at each other's clothes, trying to force their arms around their friends' necks and hold them in headlocks. Only their laughter gave away the fact they were joking. The six others in the queue stood statue like.

Kate joined the queue alone. I could see through the backward telephone number advertised on the takeaway window that she was uncomfortable. The dark orange glow from a street lamp highlighted her face. She stared forwards, desperate not to catch the eye of anyone in the fighting group.

Instinct took over me. 'I'm getting off, mate,' I said to Jordan. 'My neighbour's over there,' I said, pointing to the outside. 'You're walking the other way. Enjoy your pizza.'

Jordan reached out his hand and I shook it. 'Speak to you tomorrow.'

I walked out into the night, quickly glanced across the street and jogged over the road to the queue of people.

'Hi,' I said, snapping Kate's attention into the present.

She looked surprised to see me at first, but then her face broke out into a smile.

'You OK?' I asked.

'Yeah,' she said, her voice quiet.

The lads stopped their game and were now straightening shirts and repositioning haircuts.

'You want someone to walk home with?'

Kate looked unsure. 'I told Stuart I'd get a taxi.'

'We could get home before a taxi gets here. And' – I pushed the white polystyrene container towards her – 'I've got chips.'

'Go on then,' she said.

We walked away from the queue as a police car drove past slowly. One of the lads made a wanker sign at it, as one of his mates pushed him onto the road. He stumbled and nearly fell over, regaining his balance enough to run at his mate and half rugby tackle him at waist level. They fell backwards, nearly crashing into a black concrete bin.

'Pricks,' I said quietly to Kate, who laughed.

'How was your night?' I asked.

'Good. We had a nice catch-up.'

'Are they your friends from school?'

'No. I used to work with them.'

I offered her another chip, which she accepted.

We walked out of the main part of town, leaving the lights of takeaways, the grey shutters of closed shops, and the noise of drunks behind us. We were on a long road with large houses on either side. Lights from sporadic televisions lit up lounges as we passed.

'Who was the girl you were talking to?'

'Stephanie. She's my ex-girlfriend's best mate.'

'She didn't like someone,' she said, reaching over to take a chip.

'Yeah,' I said. 'My ex's new boyfriend. Apparently, he's a dick. She's didn't give me a reason why though. She was a bit tipsy.'

'She didn't seem it,' Kate said sarcastically.

We finished the chips and talked about our days. Kate's had been boring. The most exciting thing to happen was dress down Friday so she could wear jeans.

'Is your office like *The Office?*'

'The programme with Ricky Gervais?'

I nodded.

She paused, thinking through the characters, comparing them with her work colleagues. 'Elements of it I suppose. Now that you mention it a few of the people have similar traits to some of the characters.'

'Come on, don't be shy.'

She looks embarrassed. 'They're my friends.'

'So? They're not here.'

A few stars were scattered throughout the clear sky above. I noticed, despite the cool night air, our walking pace was slow.

'Well, there's one guy who's a bit like Gareth. He sucks up to the boss a lot. And he's got a really bad haircut. His hair is dark though, not blonde. But it looks like his mum cuts it.'

'How old is he?'

'About my age.'

'Which is?' I paused. 'Sorry, I'm not supposed to ask that, am I?'

'I don't mind. I can't change it can I? I'm thirty-one.'

'What's your boss like? Is he like David Brent?'

'Not really. He doesn't come around the office trying to impress us with how great he is. He just sits in his office all day. He's pretty good to us. Lets us finish early if the work's done. He appreciates us. Takes us on nights out every now and then. Puts money behind the bar and stuff.'

'Do you like working there?'

'Yeah. It's OK. It's a smaller firm than the one I used to work at, with the girls from tonight. But it's more money, more responsibility. Career wise it's been a good move.' She tucked a bit of her hair that had fallen across her face back behind her ear. 'What did you do at uni?'

'Sports Science.'

'Will you use the degree for work?'

'When I come back from travelling, yeah. But not now. Just need something to get some money in first. I can't wait to get away.'

'Why?'

'Just the buzz of not being here. No responsibility. Not being tied to anything or anyone for a bit. Freedom to do what I want, go where I want. I'd like to see as much of the world as I can before settling into a job.'

'Do you think you'll miss uni?'

'I already do. Well, I mean, not uni exactly. I'm going to miss my mates, I think. More than I realised. I had a proper boring day today, just hanging around the house. Made me realise I can't just go to the pub with my mates. Or grab a ball and go and play five-a-side or something.'

'Did you play five-a-side a lot?'

'About once a week. Not a regular league or anything.'

'Stuart plays five-a-side every week. He gets sick of his mates letting him down, ringing him to tell him they can't play an hour before.'

'Well, tell him if he wants me to play, I'll help out.'

We stopped at a crossroads and watched a dark car pass. There was a couple arguing in the front seats. The female driver banged on the steering wheel, turning to face her male passenger, and continued to shout. The car disappeared into the distance as Kate said, 'Someone's in trouble.'

'He probably forgot to buy milk or something.'

Kate laughed out loud, half snorting. 'I'm sorry,' she said, covering her mouth with her hand.

'Don't apologise for laughing,' I said, catching her infectious laugh and starting myself. 'I'm just glad I didn't have to resort to the David Brent dance.' I started doing the dance, kicking high in the air, arms outstretched, straight to the elbows then moving left and right. I clapped out of time and moved around Kate, who laughed hysterically.

We approached home. A cat watched us from underneath a parked car as we turned into the quiet of the cul-de-sac. It darted across the road and we watched it scale a fence before disappearing into the night.

'Well, thanks for walking me home,' Kate said as we reached my gate.

'My pleasure,' I said.

I'm unsure why I did this, but then I put my hand out and said, 'Firm handshakes.' She returned the gesture. 'Firm handshakes.'

'You going to be OK getting home the rest of the way?' I asked, nodding towards her house, a short distance across the road.

We let our hands go.

'Not much of a gentleman, are you? Only walking me part of the way home. Let's hope that cat doesn't attack me.'

'I reckon you can take it.'

She lifted her right arm and pretended to tense her muscles. 'Do you think?'

'Well, maybe not with those things. Just run the rest of the way, you'll be fine.'

'I think I'll be OK.'

'I hope so. I don't want it on my conscience.'

'Good night, Tom.' She smiled a beautiful smile, her white teeth framed by her bright pink lipstick. She walked down the road, passed under a street light and out the other side into the dark. When she turned into her driveway, I took out my keys and let myself in to my house.

Chapter Two

My phone rang, increasing in volume as my body dragged itself from sleep. I reached out for it and pushed the answer button. My head stayed on the pillow, my eyes remained closed, and I mumbled 'hello.'

The voice on the other end said, 'I heard you were back.'

'Hi,' I said, opening my eyes to the light of the morning. The dull ache of my head and stale taste of my dry mouth reminded me I'd been drinking the night before.

'Have I woken you?'

The soft voice belonged to Melissa, my ex-girlfriend.

I sat up in bed and looked at the clock. Half-past nine.

'What's up?' I asked.

I started to put together the chain of events that would have led to this phone call. Me talking to Stephanie, followed minutes later by a text message or phone call from her to Melissa saying, *Did you know Tom was back?* The ever revolving information machine of women in full operation.

'Nothing,' she answered. 'I just wanted to see if you wanted to catch-up.'

'When?'

'Tonight. My mum and dad are at the cottage. The house is free.'

At that exact moment, last night's walk home with Kate popped into my head. I spun my legs out of bed and walked to the window, peering through the curtains, down onto the street. A postman pushed a letter through the letter box of the house opposite. Another neighbour was clearing out their garage. My eyes settled on Kate's house. Her bedroom curtains were open, her car was in the driveway.

'What do you think?' Melissa's voice pulled me back into the conversation.

'What about Andy?' I said.

'He's on a stag do,' she answered quickly.

I thought about it for half a second while I closed the curtains. 'Sounds good. What time?'

'Half seven. We'll get Chinese.'

The call ended. I bent down in front of the pile of DVDs I'd stacked the day before and ran my finger down the titles. I stopped at *Gladiator*, pulled the box out, and threw it on the bed.

I had a shower and spent the whole time wondering whether I should walk across the road and give Kate the DVD. I imagined telling her I couldn't let the injustice of her not seeing it go on a day longer. I wanted an excuse to see her again, to talk to her and see if we'd laugh the way we had done the previous night. I played the conversation we would have, the jokey references to our walk home. I imagined her offering me a cup of tea, which became three cups and a bacon sandwich, while we talked about the headlines on the front of the broadsheet newspaper in her kitchen.

I knew the whole thing was stupid, but I had butterflies in my stomach at the thought of being near her.

Still wet, wrapped in a towel, I looked out of my bedroom window to her house again. Disappointingly, her car had gone from the driveway.

I know the scene I've just described is childish. My head was role playing a fantasy. After a brief encounter on a walk home, my mind imagined a 'what if' scenario about somebody who was unobtainable.

Kate was thirty-one. I was twenty-one. She was married.

I fancied her like a teenage boy with a crush on a teacher. Taking her the *Gladiator* DVD was no different to staying after class to ask about homework I already understood just to have a few seconds alone with Miss Belfry, the science teacher who all the lads at secondary school thought was fit.

My phone's ringtone snapped me back to reality.

'Morning,' Jordan said loudly.

'Morning. You all right?'

'Yeah, man. Great night. Remember Julia Hayes from school?'

The image of a drunk Julia stood at the bar the previous night, scrabbling through her purse for change came into my mind.

'She walked into the pizza place about a minute after you left. Ended up going back to hers.'

'And?'

'I don't kiss and tell.'

'No, but you do fuck and phone a friend.'

Jordan laughed. 'Yes, I do my friend, yes I do.'

He continued his story, giving me details from the pizza place all the way back to Julia's bedroom. I made jokes in the right places and sounded impressed when I was expected to be.

'How did you get on with the old bird?'

'She's not old,' I said, defensively.

'Well?'

'No, Jordan. I did not sleep with the married women from across the road.'

KATE'S CAR REAPPEARED later in the morning. I noticed it as I walked to the newsagents to buy instant coffee.

I walked through the back door of our house, collected the *Gladiator* DVD from my room, and headed straight across the road. I decided to just knock on the door, hand it to Kate, say a quick 'hello' and leave.

I reached the end of her driveway and as I opened the gate her front door opened. I stopped dead. She was digging around in her handbag for keys. When she looked up, she was surprised to see me. 'Hi,' she said, smiling.

Caught off guard, my words, embarrassingly, wouldn't leave my mouth in a proper sentence. 'Hi, I, erm, just thought, erm, I'd, drop this off for you. Sorry.' To make her understand what I was rambling, I held up the DVD case like a lawyer submitting evidence.

She closed the door behind her and locked it. *No cups of tea*, I thought. No bacon sandwiches. She walked over to the gate and examined the box. 'Oh brilliant,' she said. She took the case out of my hand and studied the synopsis on the back carefully. 'I'll watch this tonight.'

'You've not got plans?'

'No. Stuart's not back until tomorrow.'

'Well, I hope you like it.'

'Thanks.' She turned her head slightly towards her red Peugeot 206. 'Sorry I've got to go out. I'm meeting a friend for coffee.'

I turned away from the conversation. A conversation empty of my rehearsed jokes, containing no mention of our walk home the previous night. Any small hope, any ridiculous thought that she might have, even for half a second, fancied me, disappeared.

I was snapped back into the real world by a screech of tyres and the hard pressing of an accelerator pedal. I looked to my left to see a dark blue car race past. Paul, the teenager my mum had ranted about the previous day stared forward, one hand resting casually on the steering wheel, the other clamped his mobile phone to his ear. He passed us before I could signal to him to stop.

'He drives like such an idiot in that car,' Kate half shouted behind me.

I turned back and shook my head. 'I know. My mum wants to say something to his mum. I've said I'll try to have a word with him.'

'Good luck catching him.'

'I might have to let his tyres down.'

'Slice them with a knife. I've got a big one in the kitchen.'

'Oh, you supply the tools, but I have to commit the crime. I see how this works.'

'I'll keep watch.'

We laughed conspiratorially.

I SPENT THE afternoon with my dad watching Manchester United easily beat Millwall in the FA Cup. Watching it with my dad reminded me of when he used to take me to matches. He shouted at the players, swore at the ref, and talked about the old days of football. I joked he was going to start going on about how 'men used to be men.' He told me to piss off.

THE EARLY EVENING sun cast an orange glow over the houses and cars of the suburbs as I walked to Melissa's house.

Here is the background on Melissa and me...

We got together one Friday night at a house party when we were fifteen. It started with a bit of flirting in the kitchen and ended with a nervous teenage kiss in the garden, seconds before Jordan stumbled out of the house, shouting, 'Tom, Tom, do you want a drink?' He realised he'd interrupted something and threw his hands up in the air, spilling lager out of the can he was holding, saying, 'Sorry, mate. My bad. My bad.' He turned quickly and disappeared into the house. Melissa and I laughed, then continued kissing.

Our relationship developed in much the same way most relationships do at that age. We grabbed minutes together between lessons in school, spent endless hours on the phone with each other and weekend days just hanging out.

Melissa was the first girl I slept with. The mutual losing of our virginities was planned for a Saturday night when her parents were out having dinner at a friend's house. We did it because we'd been together for two months and we felt we should. We were both still fifteen.

The sex was awkward and uncomfortable in her single bed, under a light pink duvet, surrounded by posters of boy bands. I continually asked her if she was OK, and she repeatedly assured me she was. Afterwards we lay together unsure how to feel. I wasn't allowed to stay the night, so I left before her parents came home. The following day we went to the cinema.

Melissa was the first girl I ever loved. Over the next couple of years, we grew from being kids to young adults. We went to the same college, went on nights out to pubs where we could drink underage. House parties passed in a haze and we had a summer holiday to Spain with her parents.

We had split up just after I'd started uni. I'd driven back for the first two weekends to see her. I missed the third weekend, staying in Leeds to go out with the lads from my halls. Melissa said she didn't mind, but I knew during our nightly phone calls that she did. She spent the next week telling me it was fine, that me being away wasn't a problem, Leeds to Manchester wasn't far, and we could make it work. The problem was I knew I didn't want to. I drove back on the fourth weekend and told her I wanted to end it. We spent the night in her bedroom, crying. As much as I loved her, she was pulling me back towards the place I wanted to escape from. I loved Manchester, loved my family and my mates, but I needed to see a world outside it, to live on my own and learn about myself. Being with Melissa wouldn't enable me to do that.

WITH THE SOLID brass door knocker, I banged on the heavy blue door of her house. As I waited on the doorstep, I thought about how I used to go down the side of the house, lift the latch on the gate and let myself in the back door. Melissa opened the door, dressed casually in jeans and a plain T-shirt. Her appearance had changed, although not dramatically. She had gained a small amount of weight, a good thing as she looked healthier than the last time I'd seen her the previous Boxing Day. Then, she'd been skinnier than I ever remember. Her hair was different too, lighter and shorter, cut to frame her face, highlighting her eyes. Her eyes, the one piece of her above all others that stayed with me. Deep and dark, they were her most attractive feature. Those eyes paraded her feelings as if incapable of lying. At fifteen, the morning after we got together, I'd woken thinking about them shyly smiling at me from across the kitchen. At eighteen, after we'd split up, it took me weeks to erase the image of them filled with pools of tears. Now, at twenty-one, they smiled at me as if only remembering our good times.

I leant forward to give her a kiss on the cheek. She moved her face slightly and our lips brushed against each other clumsily. We hugged quickly.

Although I'd seen Melissa on my visits home from Leeds, I'd not been inside her house for nearly three years. The hallway had been immaculately redecorated, but the kitchen was the same as the day we split up; a big square room with windows along two sides that gave views to the garden and patio area. There was a small dining room to the right, through an archway. I walked to the island in the middle and pulled a stool out from underneath the overhanging dark granite surface. There was a book that had been turned upside down to mark the page, next to a half-finished glass of red wine.

'Starting early?' I said, referencing the wine.

'I was just passing the time before you got here. Do you want one?'

I nodded and watched her reach up towards the high cupboard where the wine glasses were, and carefully bring one down between two fingers.

As she handed me my drink, I asked where Andy had gone on the stag do.

'Prague. He went this morning.'

'When's he back?'

'Tomorrow night.'

I sipped the red wine slowly. 'How long you been with him?'

'I met him in town on New Year's Eve.'

She opened a drawer and took out a brightly coloured takeaway menu; unfolded it and laid it in front of me. 'What do you fancy?'

My eyes scanned down the list, weighing up the pros and cons of individual dishes.

'You want to share two meals?'

'Half and half?' I said, reminding her of something we used to do when we were together.

She laughed and ran her finger through her hair, moving it from in front of her eyes, placing it behind her ear.

'How's it going with Andy then?'

She broke eye contact briefly. 'OK.'

'You don't sound so sure.'

'We had an argument this morning.' Her voice was quiet. She took a large gulp of wine.

'About what?'

'Nothing.' Her tone told me the conversation was going no further.

In the front room, we settled on the couch, side by side. Melissa switched on the television, flicking through to find a music channel. As we sat and talked, filling each other in on the details of our lives, any awkwardness faded away. There was a relaxed ease to our conversation, a familiar comfort. Wine flowed from the bottle to the glasses to our mouths, in between updating each other on parents and siblings.

At one point she asked, 'How does it feel to be back?'

'It's fine. It's only temporary.'

The food arrived, and we spread out the silver trays on the floor and heaped piles of food onto our plates. We ate and talked, the snap of prawn crackers punctuating our conversation. We finished, pushed the plates to one side and returned to face each other. Music videos played quietly on the television, the colours from the screen flashing endlessly. We were disturbed by Melissa's mobile phone ringing loudly. She looked at the screen, sighed, and apologised before rising from the couch to answer it.

I focused on the screen for a couple of minutes, watching The Killers' video for 'Mr Brightside'. The song finished, and the video was replaced by one from a girl band. I picked up the plates and carried them through to the kitchen.

Melissa stood with her back to me, talking quietly but firmly into the phone. 'You're drunk. Just go and enjoy your night and I'll talk to you tomorrow.' Her voice was strong, but she wasn't shouting. I'd been on the receiving end of this voice before. She was angry. 'Please, Andy.' She broke slightly and rushed to end the conversation. 'Just forget it. I'll talk to you tomorrow when you get back.'

The noise of me putting the plates into the sink surprised her. She flinched and turned. I signalled I was opening another bottle of wine. She nodded her permission as she listened to the voice at the other end of the phone.

'I'm just staying in,' she said in response to a question from Prague. More silence. No mention of my name. 'It's fine.' Pause. 'I'll speak to you tomorrow.' Wait. 'You too.'

She ended the call as I poured our next drink. I handed her a full glass, noticing the tension in her hand as I handed it to her.

'You OK?'

'Yeah,' she answered, drinking quickly from the wineglass, rubbing her forehead, and breathing out heavily. 'Not easy arguing with someone when they're on an all-day stag do piss up.'

'What are you arguing about?'

She looked me straight in the eye and said, 'I really don't want to talk about it.'

'You don't want to talk about it, or you don't want to talk to me about it?'

'Does it matter?'

'Yeah.'

'Why?'

'Because you can talk to me about anything?'

Melissa studied me, assessing whether she believed me. She moved past me, back into the lounge. Silently, I followed. She was sat with her legs curled underneath herself. I sat at the other end, leaving a gap between us. Her eyes were focused on the glass that she slowly spun in her hands. 'We've not been getting on for a week.'

I didn't respond, allowing her to speak.

'He stayed over last weekend. On Sunday I got up and used the bathroom and for some reason, I don't know why, but I weighed myself. The last time I'd weighed myself was before Christmas last year, before I met him. Anyway, I'd put on over half a stone. I got back in bed and was a bit quiet. Andy kept asking me what was wrong. I kept saying nothing, but in the end, I told him. He told me I looked great, and that I was beautiful and all that. We went out with Steph and some of the girls for a few drinks later on and Andy kept joking around, pushing my stomach under the table, calling me chubby. I told him to stop. He laughed and said he was joking.'

Melissa continued to stare into the remains of her wine, avoiding my eyes. 'I went to the bar and got some drinks. When I brought them back to the table he said, "Thanks, fatty".' Everybody at the table heard him. I sat down and was pretty quiet for the rest of the night. Steph knew something was up. Andy went to the toilet, and she moved to sit next to me. I told her about weighing myself and just told her I was feeling a bit shit.'

I thought back to the when she'd answered the door three hours earlier. The extra weight, the healthier figure.

'I had a right go at him on the way home. It was our first proper shouting match. I told him he'd really embarrassed me in front of my friends. We didn't really speak much all week. He stayed last night, but it was awkward. He was trying a bit too hard to be nice. He thought I was in a mood because he was going on this bloody stag do.'

'You're not fat,' I said. 'You weren't anorexic at Christmas or anything, but I could tell you'd lost a bit of weight. It was the skinniest I've seen you for a long time. Certainly, in the last year or so.'

'So, what, you thought I looked stupid?'

'No. No. I'm not saying that. That's not what I mean. I'm saying don't worry about half a stone. It makes you look good. More toned.'

'Really?'

'Yeah. Really.'

Writing this from a position of perspective, I'm aware the conversation could be interpreted as I was trying to impress Melissa, to play on the fact that Andy and she were arguing. I'll admit the sadness in her eyes hurt me, but I wasn't using her vulnerability to rekindle any feelings that had previously existed between us. I can say honestly that was not my intention. I cared about Melissa because of our history and what we meant to each other in the past. Despite the couple of drunken nights of sex between us in the mourning period, friendship was all that survived from the ashes of our relationship. The things I told her about her weight were the truth, not words to manufacture old feelings of love.

I say this because of what happened next.

MELISSA EXCUSED HERSELF to go the toilet and I picked up the remote. Music left the screen and the green of the Millennium Stadium pitch replaced it.

Match of the Day's highlights of the day's FA Cup Final were on. I watched, reliving the game I'd watched with my dad earlier in the afternoon. I slumped back into the sofa and my eyes closed for a moment, aware of how much wine I'd drunk.

'I leave the room for five minutes and the bloody football ends up on the tele.' Melissa's voice pulled my eyes open. 'Were you asleep?'

'No.'

'Just resting your eyes?' Melissa said laughing.

'Something like that.' I put my hands on the arm of the sofa and pulled myself up. 'I think I better go home. I'm knackered.'

I stood and faced her.

Melissa, my ex. Melissa, who I'd left here.

She looked at me.

'You can stay if you want.'

Melissa, who had a boyfriend. Melissa, who I'd left here.

'I don't think that's a good idea.'

Those dark brown eyes locked onto mine.

Chapter Three

I woke in the familiar surroundings of Melissa's bedroom.

I lay still, taking in the room. It had the same feel as the last time I'd woken there two-and-a-half years previously. There were some little differences; the plain lining paper that covered the walls had been painted a lighter blue, and the room was tidier than it used to be with no clothes dumped in piles across the floor, except for ours from the previous night. A heart-shaped picture frame held a photo of her on a night out with her girlfriends, dressed as the Spice Girls, laughing. The photograph had replaced a picture of the two of us in Spain from the summer between our first and second year at college. The frame remained on top of the pine chest of drawers that had been in the room since before I'd met her. I couldn't see a picture of her and Andy. The bed was still in the same position, although the removal of her desk had created space for a second wardrobe. The long metal shoe rack still leant against the wall under the bay window. There were more shoes than could fit on the three levels of racking and she'd lined the additional pairs along the skirting board to her en suite bathroom. The boy band posters had gone.

Melissa moved next to me in her sleep, her warm legs touching mine. Not wanting to move, I stared at the white ceiling, unsure how to act. I knew it would be easy to pull her into me, hold her and pick up where we left off when we were eighteen.

A sense of regret washed over me.

Carefully I moved out of bed and gently put my feet on the floor. I crossed to the bathroom, opening and closing the door quietly, the cold floor tiles cooled my warm body. I leant over the toilet and tried to heave in silence. Nothing came out.

I ran the cold tap, filling my cupped hands and splashing water over my face. I looked in the mirror. My lungs expanded with a large intake of breath which I released slowly towards my reflection.

Trapped in the cold white tiled room, I wanted to be anywhere but there, yet I never wanted to leave. I didn't want to face the situation waiting for me on the other side of the door – the inevitable conversation about last night.

Had it been a good idea? Honestly, no. Not in the harsh light of the morning. The previous night, when we were relaxed from wine, with all the laughter and the talk of old times – I'm not going to lie and say staying was a bad idea then. When Melissa gave me the choice to stay it didn't take my head long to decide that staying was a fucking great idea.

The sex had been amazing. Two people rediscovering each other, comfortable with each other's bodies. It was passionate and the sobering thought that it might be a mistake had never crossed our minds. We fell asleep wrapped in each other, like so many times before.

I heard movement in the bedroom and without thinking, opened the bathroom door. We faced each other. Melissa was wearing the faded oversized Simpsons T-shirt she'd slept in. It just covered her underwear. Her hand self-consciously pulled it down towards her knees.

'Morning,' I said, desperately trying to keep my tone neutral.

'I need to use the bathroom,' she said, walking towards me. I didn't move quickly enough and we spent a couple of uncomfortable seconds trying to negotiate swapping places. 'Sorry,' I mumbled.

I gathered my clothes from the floor and dressed quickly, feeling very aware of putting yesterday's socks back on. As I slipped my head into my T-shirt, the bathroom door opened. We shared a half smile as she sat on her bed and wrapped the duvet around her legs.

'I don't know if I'm uncomfortable or not,' she said, breaking what was becoming a long awkward silence.

'Do you think you should feel uncomfortable?' I asked.

'Yeah.'

'Why?'

'Because of Andy.'

Andy. The name that had gone unsaid. The name forgotten hours earlier when we entered her room, kissing, grabbing at each other's clothes.

'So, what do we do?'

Quietly she said, 'I don't know.'

46

She stood up from the bed and left the room. I collected together my wallet and house keys, putting them in my pocket before taking one last look around the room, making sure I hadn't forgotten anything.

Downstairs in the kitchen, Melissa filled the kettle with a rush of water.

'Do you want a cup of tea?'

'No,' I said. 'I better get off.'

She put the kettle down and switched it on. I stood still, unsure whether to leave.

'I'll see you out.'

Silently we walked into the hallway, stopping as she unlocked the door. We looked at each other. I leant forward to kiss her cheek, she moved to hug me. Her shoulder knocked my chin. I placed an awkward kiss, too loud, with too much pressure on the side of her face, almost on her ear.

I quickly pulled back, 'I'll speak to you soon.'

I stepped outside, the thud of the closing door behind me.

HUNGER HIT ME on the way home and I hoped my mum would be stood in the kitchen cooking breakfast. Toast in the toaster, tea in the pot, bacon under the grill, the smell greeting me as I opened the back door. Instead, I got the sound of my dad shouting at my brother.

'I don't care how many times you say it. You're going.'

'I've got plans.' Chris shouted back.

Judging by the loudness of their voices, my dad was positioned at the bottom of the stairs, my brother at the top, hanging over the banister rail.

'I know you've got plans. You're going to your auntie's for dinner,'

'I'm not.'

My mum walked into the kitchen and jumped at seeing me stood in the middle of it. 'Oh,' she said. 'Hi.'

'Morning.'

'What's going on?'

'Your brother doesn't want to go for dinner this afternoon.'

'And Dad's convincing him otherwise.'

'Something like that.'

Upstairs a door slammed, the noise vibrated through the house.

Entering the kitchen my dad said, 'I've a good mind to drag him through that door. The little shit.' He looked up and caught my eye. He looked embarrassed at being heard speaking about Chris like that. Like I'd witnessed him with his guard down, seeing him as a man, not a parent.

'Morning,' I said.

'Morning. Good night?'

'Yeah.'

'Where did you go?'

'Melissa's.'

'Right.' He picked up the kettle and walked to the sink.

THE SILENT ATTITUDE coming from my brother's face as we drove to my auntie Linda's house showed he had lost a battle in the on-going teenage war. My mum had flowers carefully resting on her lap for the ten-minute drive. My dad and I talked about the Cup final from the day before.

Auntie Linda's was a family affair. We wished her a happy birthday as we filtered through the door. She kissed us hard and hugged us tight. It was smiles all round as my mum handed her the flowers and produced a bottle of wine from her bag.

'We'll be wanting some glasses for that,' Linda said laughing.

It was a typical family Sunday lunch. A scene played out all over the country. Uncle John and Dad talked work in the garden while drinking cold lager. Mum and Auntie Linda prepared and served food, fussing over everyone. I stood in the kitchen with my cousin Hannah – John and Linda's only child – half helping, half getting in the way.

Hot plates were transferred from the kitchen to the dining room by hands protected with tea towels. Auntie Linda announced the food was ready and we gathered around the dark wooden table. Plates were passed under bowls, veg swapped for meat, and potatoes picked from the oven dish they sat in. Wine was poured, we clinked a 'cheers' with our glasses, and wished my auntie happy birthday.

As everyone started eating, the only the sound was of knives scratching plates as they cut through meat, followed by a low munching.

Hannah asked if I'd finished at Leeds.

I nodded, my mouth full.

'What you doing next?'

'I want to go travelling,' I said.

Hannah smiled. 'Me too. Next year hopefully, when I've finished.'

'And who's going to pay for that?' Uncle John asked.

'I will,' Hannah said.

'WH Smith's pay more money now do they?'

'Leave her alone,' Auntie Linda said.

'I'm joking,' Uncle John said, taking a large mouthful of beef.

'Where do you want to go?' Hannah asked.

'Everywhere. Thailand. Vietnam. Australia. Fiji. New Zealand. My mate's in Japan at the moment.'

'Have you booked it?'

'No. I need to save up first.'

'Have you got anything lined up? Work wise?' Auntie Linda asked.

'I'm going to the temping agency tomorrow.'

I took a mouthful of lager from the glass next to my plate.

'Are you not doing something sport related? Like your degree?'

'No. I just need to get money together as soon as possible. I'd like to try to get away about Christmas time. I think if I try to get something to do with my degree, I'll end up liking the job and never go away.'

'Why don't you work for your dad?'

I was starting to feel like a witness on the stand. 'I don't want to work for my dad.' I didn't look up when I said it. Instead, focusing on the gravy covered dinner in front of me.

'Too much hard work for you, is it?' Uncle John asked.

'No.' I resented the accusation.

Uncle John smiled. 'When me and your dad finished school – school, not college or university – we got jobs straight away. Our mothers wanted rent off us. We had to start paying our way.'

'The world's changed, Dad,' Hannah said.

'Tell me about it. Now you lot get five more years of education and then want to piss off round the world to *find yourselves*. You'd find out a lot more about yourself grafting for your dad than you would getting pissed in Thailand.'

My brother laughed at the way Uncle John said it. As if travelling round the world was something to be sneered at. As if the people who travelled, who wanted to see as much of the world as possible, were to be treated with caution, as if they were not normal. Apparently not wanting to be born, live, and die all in the same place was something strange.

'What's the problem?' I said, my voice hardening. 'I want to go away and see the world. I want to experience things your generation couldn't. Isn't that why you work so hard? To give your kids more?' I was starting to shout slightly.

'Tom,' my mum said quietly.

'No, Mum. It's annoying.' I turned back to Uncle John. 'I'm paying for this trip myself. I'm not asking for a penny from my mum and dad. I'm going to see some amazing things. I want to see more of the world than the suburbs of northern English cities.' I looked at Hannah, who understood. She shook her head and smiled at me.

Uncle John looked at me. 'Well, I've obviously touched a nerve.'

I glared back.

Later, after birthday cake and coffee, I stood in the hallway waiting to leave. The routine goodbye hugs and handshakes were being performed. My dad moved to stand next to me. 'I'll give you work if you need work,' he said.

'I don't want a job from you,' I said. The conversation paused. His face hardened just for a second and I couldn't tell if he was hurt or not. I collected my thoughts, trying to arrange the words correctly in my head. 'It's not that I don't want the work or think it's too hard or beneath me or anything. I'd probably love it. But you always told me it's important to stand on my own. I don't think just taking your job, without even trying to get something on my own, well, you know. It doesn't feel right.'

My dad nodded, understanding, pleased with my attitude.

As we left the house, Uncle John shook my hand, holding onto it a second too long, making me stop walking. 'I was only winding you up before. I think it's great you want to get away. Do it now while you're young, free, and single.'

I LAY ON my bed thinking about the previous night. I picked up my mobile and scrolled through the numbers, stopping at Melissa's.

As the phone rang, I adjusted my position on the bed, sitting with my back against the wall.

She answered on the fifth ring. 'Hi,' she said, obviously happy to hear from me.

'Hi.'

'You OK?'

'Yeah. You?'

'I'm OK. I've been thinking about last night.'

'Me too,' I said.

'You first.'

I took a deep breath. 'I think it was a mistake.'

'Oh.' The phone line couldn't hide her surprise. 'Why do you think that?'

'I don't know. It just doesn't feel right.'

'Because I'm with Andy?'

'Maybe. I don't know. It just doesn't feel like something we should have done. Maybe that part of our lives is over.'

She let the words hang between us before saying, 'We've been over for nearly three years.'

'It's never felt that way though, has it? I've always felt like we were just taking a break. Like we'd always just fall back into being together again.'

'And you don't want that?' She was clearly hurt by what I'd said. That made my heart ache. But I knew I couldn't lie.

'No. I don't want that.' I said.

She put the phone down.

Chapter Four

I sat with the whole world in front of me.

It was Wednesday afternoon and I'd spent the last two-and-a-half days roaming from temping agency to temping agency across Manchester, repeating the process of registering my details. All the agencies were the same, over enthusiastic Recruitment Consultants wearing flash suits and fake smiles telling me how 'brilliant' my CV was and how much work they would be able to find me. The two-page document didn't really deserve the false praise. It was padded out office experience from the previous summer at uni, and four years of bar and supermarket work from when I left school. On Monday morning I appreciated their efforts but by Wednesday afternoon I was bored. Each place, like drunken lads after a one-night stand, promised to call.

Having lunch in a café on Deansgate in Manchester city centre I received a loud phone call from Joanne at one of the agencies I'd been to that morning, telling me they'd found me something to start the following Tuesday, Monday being a bank holiday. So instead of continuing my agency tour I went into a large chain bookshop and stood in front of the travel section studying the endless rows of books. Every continent, country, or city, all arranged alphabetically. Africa, Alaska, Australia. I didn't know where to start. I picked books off the shelves and slowly read the backs, excited at the possibilities of all the places I could go.

I bought a thick *Lonely Planet* book on *The World* then sat in the store's café and ordered a massive cup of coffee. I took the new book with its sharp pages and ridged spine out of the bag and placed it on the small round table. It lay there unopened and I felt untravelled. I sipped my coffee and carefully turned the pages, taking in the bright photographs of must-see places. Food markets in Thailand and beaches in Bali drew my eye. New York's towering buildings and an Indian elephant. Transfixed, I opened up a double page map. The continents stretched out across the pages, dipping in the middle.

I started to form a route, a plan of escape.

THAT WEEKEND, MY dad asked me to help him replace the fencing at our house. After another Friday out with the lads I dragged myself out of bed early on Saturday morning. My dad was already up, sliding fence panels out of their grey concrete posts and stacking them against the side of the garage. An empty bright yellow skip sat at the end of the driveway.

'Morning,' I said.

'Morning,' he replied, his eyes on the job.

I stepped off the back doorstep and helped him ease out a panel.

'Your brother not up yet?'

'No. Is he supposed to be?'

'He said he'd help too.'

'Did you offer him money?'

My dad laughed. 'No.'

'Then you must have asked the wrong kid.'

'Piss off.' We spun round. My brother stood in the kitchen dressed in old tracksuit bottoms and an old England football shirt.

'I take it back,' I said.

We started work. As my dad and I ripped up concrete posts, Chris smashed up the fence panels and started filling the skip. My mum appeared with welcome bacon sandwiches that we washed down with hot, fresh tea. As he ate, my brother took out his mobile phone and sent a text message, and then kept his phone out, awaiting the reply.

My dad gulped down the last of his tea, passed his plate to Chris and said, 'Put that inside, will you?'

My brother's phone beeped as the message he was waiting for appeared on the screen. He tried to take the plate off Dad, hold his own plate and cup and read the new message at the same time. His wrist swayed slightly and tea spilt out, splashing on the dirty driveway.

'Careful,' my dad said. 'The message won't go away if you don't read it after three seconds you know?'

'I wasn't reading it,' Chris snapped, embarrassed.

My dad lifted his hands up in mock surrender.

'Come on, back to graft.'

As the morning continued the perimeter of our house reduced to nothing as the skip filled with cracked concrete and broken wood. My dad gave instructions and we followed them, bowing to his knowledge. It was good to watch him work. He planned his next move as we cleared up the mess around him.

My brother's phone beeped at regular intervals and for seconds at a time he'd read the words then rapidly type a reply.

'Is she worth it?' my dad asked eventually.

'Who?' Chris said.

'The girl sending you all them messages.'

My brother looked at me. He was torn. If he told us who the girl was my dad would take the piss out of him for having a girlfriend. If he said it wasn't a girl, he'd get jokes about his mates being more important than the work we were doing. I shrugged, unable to help.

'She's called Laura.'

'Laura,' my dad said slowly, as if holding the name up and inspecting it, seeing what it would reveal. Chris waited for the onslaught. 'Right,' my dad said. He turned and pointed to the wall where a spade leant against it. 'Tom, pass me that will you.'

I reached over and handed it to him. He lifted it above his head, then shoved it into the ground and began digging a hole.

My dad went into teaching mode. He explained that we'd build the new fencing up slowly, taking the time and care to make each section level. I held the concrete posts in place while he poured fresh concrete into the holes or checked the height and laid the spirit level across the base panels.

His eyes studied the bubble inside the spirit level as my brother's phone beeped again. Chris's hand went to his pocket. He read the message and laughed.

'What's funny?' I asked.

'Nothing,' Chris said.

'Come on, tell us. What's funny?'

'Nothing. Leave it.'

My dad and I shared a look.

'Share the joke with the class,' my dad said.

Chris sighed. 'It's just something Laura said.'

'Oh, Laura said it,' I said.

'You like her, this Laura?' Dad asked, leaning on a fence post.

With a slightly bowed head Chris answered that he did.

'You shagged her yet?'

Chris' head shot up, his eyes giving away his shock.

'Come on. You're with the boys today. Working like a man. I'm asking you, man to man,' my dad said.

'No,' he said unsure whether to be ashamed or not.

Softly, with no joking in his voice, my dad said, 'Well, when you do, be careful will you?'

My brother nodded. My dad looked straight at him and said, 'Because if you get her pregnant your mother will find a way to blame me and I'll get a right bollocking.'

We all laughed, breaking the moment.

My dad pulled a crumpled twenty quid from his pocket and sent me across the road to the chippy. Stood in the queue with dirty jeans on, covered in soil and concrete dust, the brown smearing of the fence panels on my hands, I felt a sense of pride at being what other people would see as a worker. Proud to be 'one of the boys'.

I walked back with our food, finding my dad was on his own drinking another cup of tea.

'Where's Chris?'

'In the shower.'

'He's not helping?'

'No. He's meeting Laura. I think he's a bit knackered. Can't hack a bit of work these kids.' I couldn't tell by the way he said it whether he included me in that category. Strangely, it seemed important that he saw me as a grafter.

We worked throughout the afternoon, seeing the new fencing grow down the driveway. Conversation was kept to a minimum, me asking the occasional question about our methods, or my dad giving me instructions. At one point he asked, 'Are you looking forward to Tuesday?' referring to my new job.

'Suppose so. A job is a job right? Money in the bank.'

'Yep.'

Mid-afternoon, a female voice interrupted our concentration. 'Looking good,' it said. I looked round and saw Kate stood at the end of the driveway. My mouth automatically smiled.

'Are you after my mum?' I said.

'No, no. I've come to see you.'

She stepped forward, carefully avoiding the mess.

I walked towards her, out of earshot of my dad who continued to work.

'What's up?' I asked.

'Nothing. I mentioned your five-a-side offer to Stuart and he wanted to know if you could play on Wednesday night.'

'Yeah, sure. What time?'

'He said get to ours about half six-ish. It's at seven, for an hour.'

'OK. No problem.'

She smiled.

'The only thing is I start a new job on Tuesday. It's in Trafford Park. It shouldn't be a problem getting back but I'm not sure how long it'll take to get home. I'll know on Tuesday. If I'm not going to be home, I can meet him wherever the football is.'

'It's in Stockport.'

'OK. Give me Stuart's number and I'll ring him if I need to meet him there.'

She slid her mobile phone out of her pocket, pressed a button and asked, 'What's your number?'

I gave it to her and she programmed it into her phone. 'What's your surname?' she asked, while her fingers spelt out my first name on the screen.

'Fray.'

'Tom Fray,' she repeated, pressing 'call'. My phone vibrated in my pocket for a couple of seconds.

'That's my number,' she said. 'Any problems just ring me. I'll give Stuart your number in case he needs to get hold of you.' She paused. 'What's the job?'

'Just some temp work. Office stuff.'

'All money for the travelling fund though, right?'

I smiled. 'Exactly.'

'I hope it goes well. Good luck.'

'Thanks,' I said, again watching her for a second too long as she walked away.

I STARTED THE temp job on Tuesday morning. It was a boring data entry job that lasted for six weeks and doesn't feature heavily in this story. It was in a small office on a floor full of small offices in a building full of floors full of small offices. The work was easy and the people were all right. My office had five others in. Three middle-aged women talked about their kids, the soaps, and what they'd had for their tea the previous night. The two men talked about football and complained about their wives. During my second week one of the women turned fifty. We all went to the pub at lunchtime to celebrate by eating microwaved burgers and chips.

ON THE WEDNESDAY night I walked across the street dressed in football kit, my socks pushed down to my ankles. I knocked on the door and waited. Stuart opened it. He was still dressed in his suit, minus a tie.

'Hi, mate,' he said, stepping backwards to let me in. 'I'll just get changed then we can get off. Kate's in the kitchen.' He pointed down the hallway then started walking up the stairs, freeing his arms from his jacket as he climbed.

'Cheers. I'm a bit early. Sorry.'

'No worries. Better than you being late.'

I walked into the kitchen. It was very modern, with shiny work surfaces. To the left of the door there was a small round table underneath a window that looked out across the driveway, over a low fence into Mrs Wallace's kitchen. On the table was a fruit bowl containing two bananas and a set of house keys. A football magazine sat on top of the day's newspaper, next to a half-finished cup of tea. Kate, still in her work suit, stood barefooted at the open fridge, studying the goods inside.

'Hello,' she said.

'Hi.'

She took out two red peppers and an onion from the fridge and closed it. 'How did the job go?' She placed the peppers on a chopping board and took out a large sharp knife from a metal knife block and began cutting the peppers into thin slices. 'Don't mind me,' she said. 'Just getting dinner ready for later.'

'No problem. Work was OK. It's getting set up on the system really, introduced to everyone.'

'Are they like *The Office* characters?'

I laughed, not thinking she would have remembered the details of our conversation from the night we walked home together. 'Maybe. Not got to know them well enough yet.'

'What's the work?'

'Data entry. Nothing too strenuous. Like you said, just money for going away.'

'How do you think you did in your degree?'

'Not too bad, I think. I worked my arse off for the last year. Once I'd got my partying out of the way.'

'So, you only went out five nights a week in the last year?'

'Something like that.'

'Oh,' she said, remembering something. 'I left this out or you,' passing me the *Gladiator* DVD case.

'Thanks. Did you like it?'

'Yeah. I thought it was going to be too violent but I really got into it.'

'Did you cry at the end?'

She smiled. 'I'm not ashamed to admit I did. Did you?'

'Can you keep a secret?'

'I can.'

'I did.'

Laughing, she moved around the kitchen opening cupboards, taking out ingredients, and things to cook them in. 'The fencing looks good.'

'Good job too because my dad's a landscaper. That's free advertising on our driveway.'

She laughed and shook her head. She was just about to say something but Stuart burst into the kitchen and moved across it to kiss her on the cheek, picking his keys out of the fruit bowl as he passed it. He talked as quickly as he moved. 'See you later. Let's go, Tom.'

I SAT IN Stuart's car, a black Audi A3 with a McDonald's coffee cup in the holder and CD cases stuffed into the inside of the door, I clipped in the seat belt and Stuart reversed the car off the driveway.

'Sorry about that,' he said putting the car in first gear and accelerating down the road. 'I'd only just got in from work.'

'No problem. Like I said I was a little bit early anyway.'

'Kate said you started a job yesterday.'

'Yeah. Just a temp thing to get some cash in.'

Concentrating on the road ahead, Stuart said, 'It's better to be working than not. Was it OK?'

'Yeah. Not bad.' I paused, thinking of a change of subject as I didn't have a lot to report from my two days in the office. 'Kate said you're going to the Euros.'

'Yeah. Fly out the morning of the England – France game. It's all work obviously,' he said sarcastically.

'What does your company do?'

'We run trips to sporting events. Anything from days at the races to five days at a test match in Australia. We put together the transport, hotels, and stuff.'

'Sounds good. Plus, you've got the bonus of being able to go to the European Championships and tell your wife it's for work.'

Stuart laughed agreement. 'There is that.' He indicated and took a right turn up a motorway slip road, pulling out in traffic, getting into the outside lane as quickly as possible. 'To be honest these championships are a new thing for us. I'm trying to go a bit more up market and I'm using them as a trial run. I've been approaching companies and trying to get them to put together trips as incentives for their salespeople, etc. We've got a car company who've got about fifteen dealerships across the north of England. I'm taking the best salesman from every dealership to the France game, plus the bosses. My company has sorted all the flights, hotels, tickets, and charges the company an all-inclusive fee. They look like good bosses for taking the staff to such a cool event and we make a nice profit for arranging it all. I've got different trips for all the group games, so I'm coming home in between then flying back out. It's going to be a lot of rushing around.' He laughed to himself and said, 'Good job I've got an understanding wife.'

The way Stuart talked, the way he carried himself, even the way he drove, anticipating the road ahead, smoothly passing other vehicles, displayed a confidence I'd never felt in myself. He had the self-belief of someone who knew what he wanted and how to go about getting it. Sat in the passenger seat listening to him speak about his vision for his company made my crush on his wife seem all the more ridiculous.

I FOUND MYSELF in the first proper working routine of my life, not just doing jobs to support education. Every day I got up at seven, timed my use of the bathroom to avoid my mum getting ready for work, danced around my dad eating breakfast in the kitchen, made lunch, straightened my tie, and headed out into the slow parade of morning rush hour. Every weekday I worked in an office with other people who did the same thing every day of their lives with families to support or bills to pay. People who worried about interest rates and performance reviews. On Friday and Saturday night I went out with the lads, recovered on Sunday, and started the cycle again on Monday.

Stuart asked me to keep playing five-a-side so the next Wednesday I walked across to his house, knocked on the door, purposely early. Again, he wasn't ready. I sat in the kitchen and talked to Kate. Again, we laughed. Again, Stuart cut our conversation short.

Mid-June, on the Friday night at the end of my second working week I stood in the Silver Moon with Jordan and Sam. It was busy and loud, the Friday night crowd relaxing and drinking away the stresses of the week. Girls wearing too much make-up sat at tables sharing bottles of wine, eyes on the lads who stood, drinks in hand, in tight circles talking football and trying not to get caught looking back at the girls.

We stood next to a high table and talked about our weeks.

'How's the job?'

'It's a job,' I said, responding to Jordan's question.

I gave details and then we sipped from our pints in unison.

'How's work for you?' I asked. We had gone to college together but as I'd made applications to universities Jordan ended his life in education. He increased his part-time hours to full-time at the supermarket we worked at together, working his way up to supervisor level.

He shrugged. 'Shit. I'm sick of looking at fruit and veg.'

'You thought about doing something else?' I asked.

'Everyone always thinks about doing something else. It's the doing it that's the problem.' He poured the rest of his pint down his neck and showed his empty glass to Sam. 'Your round.'

As Sam faded into the crowd at the bar, Jordan turned to me and said, 'To be honest, mate, I've had an offer at work but don't want to tell Sam about it until I've decided what to do. He'll tell my mum and dad and they'll be pushing me to do it.'

'What is it?'

'There's this management training programme coming up and my boss pulled me to one side the other day and told me to go for it. Said I'd have no problem getting on. In fact, he'd make sure I did.'

'That's good.' I paused. 'Isn't it?'

'I don't know. I thought it was. But then I thought about it and it seems so, I don't know, final.'

'What'd you mean, final?'

'I don't know. Just, I've worked there since I was sixteen. I'm not sure I want to go all the way through the system and stay there all my life.'

'What do you want to do? Travel?'

'No. That's your thing. I'm not interested. Good holidays yeah, but I'm not cut out for backpacking. I want to work. I just want to do something that I enjoy when I get out of bed in the morning.'

'Why not do the course anyway? Get the training, earn a bit more money and if you want to leave then at least you'll be trained to management level.'

'I know you're right, it's just the thought of being there forever fills me with dread. My dad has worked at Jones' since he was eighteen. He looks bored shitless by it.'

'That's just our parents' generation, mate. All the same. Work, mortgages, kids. They don't seem to understand we want a bit more.'

Sam slipped out of the crowd carrying three drinks.

'Don't say anything to him,' Jordan said quietly to me.

Our position in the pub had a perfect view of the main door. Jordan commented on every girl who walked past the bouncers. There was a moment of pause as the younger girls, all make-up and short skirts, cast their eyes around the room to see which lads were paying attention to them. In the middle of the procession a couple caught my eye. Melissa walked hand in hand with a lad I didn't recognise. He wore a plain white T-shirt that showed off his wide, gym-created shoulders. A tribal tattoo peeked out from under the sleeve.

Melissa's eyes met mine. She froze, then smiled. We hadn't spoken since she put the phone down on me nearly three weeks previously. I thought she'd walk past me but she swerved off course for the bar and pulled the lad towards me.

'Hi,' she said. Her voice was too high-pitched and I knew instantly she was being fake.

'Hi,' I said. 'You OK?'

'Yeah. Fine.' She turned to the lad who was just staring at me. 'This is Andy,' she said by way of introduction. 'Andy, this is Tom.'

We stood face to face. Me, the ex-boyfriend. Andy, the current one.

'Hi, mate. You OK?' I offered my hand out to shake. Andy had to let go of Melissa's hand to shake mine.

'Right, I need a drink.' Before we noticed what was going on, Melissa had left us standing awkwardly facing each other. I sipped my drink and tried desperately not to think about that the last time I'd seen his girlfriend was the morning after I'd had sex with her.

'Melissa said you've been on a stag do.'

Images of kissing Melissa in her front room entered my mind.

'Yeah. Prague. About three weeks ago.'

Melissa and I moved urgently up the staircase, struggling with each other's clothes.

'Any good?'

He nodded. 'Very. Just two days on the piss. Well cheap out there.'

'When's the wedding?'

In my mind we fell on her bed and she started to undo my jeans. I looked Andy in the eyes and focused on the present.

'Tomorrow.'

'You an usher or anything?'

'No.'

'Melissa going with you?'

I quickly glanced towards the bar where Melissa was paying.

'Yeah.'

She turned and carried two drinks towards us.

'Here she is,' I said, stating the obvious.

Melissa handed Andy a pint which he gave straight back and said, 'I'm going for a piss. Be back in a minute.'

When I was sure he couldn't hear us, I said, 'Fucking thanks for that.'

'For what?'

Turning away so my friends couldn't hear me, I said, 'Don't give me that. You know what.' My voice hardened. 'Leaving me with him. Was that to make me feel bad for not wanting to get back with you?'

'No.'

'Don't be so childish.'

'Tom, I didn't do it on purpose,' she protested.

'Yes, you did. You wanted me to feel awkward. Congratulations, it worked. Don't ever do that to me again.'

She went quiet. 'I'm sorry. I'll see you later.' She walked away, deep into the crowd of people.

'You OK, mate?' Jordan asked.

'Fine. Can we go somewhere else?'

THE FOLLOWING WEDNESDAY, I opened the back door of my grandparents' house, and stepped into the 1970s.

'Hello, Granddad,' I said.

He sat at the kitchen table, reading the Manchester Evening News, cup of tea in front of him. He raised his eyes from the article, folded the paper to mark his place, and laid it on the table.

'You OK?' I asked.

As he nodded, his bald head wrinkled. 'Not bad.'

'Nana in?'

'She's at Mary's.' He put his hand on the back of the chair and carefully pushed himself up. 'You want a cup of tea?'

'No thanks. I can't stay. I've got five-a-side. I just wanted to see if you need anything. You want me to take you food shopping on Saturday morning or anything?'

He shuffled across the kitchen – a room of faded brown cupboards and a stand-alone cooker – unchanged since before I was born – with his mug of tea, and poured the remainder away. He still had the broad shoulders of a man who had worked manual jobs all his life, only now they hunched forward causing him to look smaller and less imposing than when I was a kid. 'No thanks lad. I'll get the bus tomorrow.'

'You sure?'

'Yeah.' He paused and breathed in and out. 'Did you watch that lot the other night?'

He was talking about the England v France, Euro 2004 game. 'Yeah. In the pub, with Jordan.'

'Bloody rubbish. Two goals in the last two minutes.' Disgust disabled his ability to talk so instead he just shook his head. A few seconds later he added, 'You shouldn't concede two goals in the last two minutes. We always got taught to play until the whistle. Not switch off before the end.'

'I better get ready for football. I'll see you soon, Granddad.'

He sat back at the table and unfolded his paper. 'I hope you're better than that lot.'

I laughed, thinking about how he sounded like my dad, his son.

I LIFTED MY hand up to knock on Kate's door but froze at the sound of loud voices on the other side.

'You told me you weren't playing,' Kate shouted.

'I wasn't going to,' Stuart responded, his voice a level higher. 'But they couldn't get anyone else to play.'

'So, you'd rather let me down than your friends?'

The clarity of their words placed them in the hallway, stood face to face; Kate shouting towards the front door, Stuart away from it. Conscious I couldn't stand in the driveway until someone came out of the house, I faced a choice. Knock or don't knock?

Their voices went quiet, and I heard only mumbling. I imagined Stuart on the other side of the door, his hands held high in the air, palms open, pleading for calm.

Knock or don't knock?

Kate's voice went back to a shout. 'Don't pull that with me. Don't make out I'm being unreasonable because you were working.'

I'd stared at the white front door for too long. I counted to five and then knocked.

Stuart opened the door but didn't invite me in. 'One second, mate,' he said. 'I'll just get my keys.' He ran up the stairs.

The door remained open, and I looked down the hallway into the kitchen. Kate stood leaning against the sink at the far end, arms folded across her chest.

'Hi,' she said, acting politely.

'You OK?' I said, trying to sound casual.

'Good,' she said. 'You?'

'Yeah. Good.'

Silence fell between us.

I offered a smile and got one in return.

IN THE CAR, Stuart moaned that 'the wife' was giving him shit. Shifting the course of conversation, I asked how his trip had gone.

As we stood warming up before the game, Justin, one of the regular players, asked, 'What did you do after the game in Portugal?'

'The people I took were all sales guys. All mid-forties and married. They were all off the leash, so they wanted to enjoy every minute of being away. Win or lose.'

'Strip club then,' one of the other players said.

'Of course. Salespeople and the boss's credit card. Would've been rude not to.'

Justin asked, 'Did it take your mind off the match?'

'What match?' Stuart said, laughing at his own joke.

THE NEXT DAY I answered my ringing mobile.

There was a long pause from the other end. 'All right, pal? How are you?' I realised the pause was because it was an international call.

'I'm good, mate. How are you?'

It was John, my friend from uni, who was away travelling.

'Can't complain.'

'Where are you?'

'Sydney.'

'Nice.'

'It's fuckin' boss, mate. Better than Leeds, put it that way.'

'You loved Leeds. Leeds made you a man.'

'Yes, but Sydney's making me a better man.'

I laughed, and seconds later so did John, the banter slower between us because of the delay on the phone line.

'Have you been getting my emails?' he asked.

'Yeah. Just what I want to read on a cold day in Manchester.' He laughed again. 'What's your plan at the moment?' I asked.

'I've done Japan which was cool. Got to Oz about a month ago. I'm travelling around here in the summer, then coming back to Sydney to work for about eight months. Save up a bit of money then I'm going to New Zealand for a bit. I'll work there too if I can. Then hopefully come back via Asia about November next year. Might spend a few months in Asia though. It's well cheap so seems better to do it on the way back.'

'So, you're away a while then?'

'Yeah. The longer the better.'

Another long gap.

'When are you coming to join me?' The question I asked myself every day.

'I'm working and saving at the moment. I want enough money to not have to work while I'm away.'

'So, what are you doing?'

'Temping in an office.'

'Sounds fun.'

'It's shit. But I've started saving which is the main thing.'

'Well, soon as you've got enough let me know and you can come meet me.'

'Love to, mate. Can't wait.'

THE FOLLOWING MONDAY, I parked my car outside my house. I got out, tie loose around my neck, shirt un-tucked. Kate stood in her driveway talking on her mobile. I'd see her regularly after work like this and would usually walk across for a brief chat, but on this day because she was on her phone, I was unsure whether to approach. As I locked my car, she put her phone into her bag. I crossed the road and said, 'Hi.'

She didn't respond. Tears streamed down her face. I quickly opened the gate and approached her. She collapsed in my arms like a dead weight.

'Hey, what's wrong?' I asked, holding her up.

She continued to cry and I felt very on show to my neighbours.

'Come on, let's get you inside.'

Kate walked towards the house. I shut her car door and followed.

Inside she sat on the stairs and a large burst of noise erupted from her as a new wave of crying began.

I closed the front door. I wanted to sit next to her, pull her close, and kiss away the tears that stained her face. Instead, I stood rigid against the front door, unsure what to do. 'Kate,' I said softly. 'What's wrong?'

The words snapped her back to reality. She sniffed, her nose making a noise like paper being torn. She looked at me. Her eyes were dark from where her make-up had run. 'I'm sorry.' She wiped her eyes and a black line smudged across her face.

'You don't need to apologise. Do you want to talk about it?'

'I'm not sure where that came from.'

I let silence fill the air for a few seconds while she took three deep breaths.

'My friend Amy is pregnant.'

'OK,' I said, carefully.

'And I'm really happy for her.'

'I've got to be honest, Kate; it doesn't look like it.'

I regretted the joke instantly. Thankfully, she laughed, causing some snot to escape from her nose. Embarrassed, she quickly wiped it with her sleeve. 'I know this must look ridiculous.'

'It's fine. You don't have to tell me anything. I just want to make sure you're OK.'

She gathered her composure and looked up at me. 'Six months ago, I had a miscarriage.'

I searched my mind for words of comfort but could only find 'Oh.'

She started to cry again, her elbows digging into her knees, palms pushed tightly against her eyes. I moved from my position at the door and squatted in front of her, letting her cry. The noise stopped, but her eyes were filled with tears.

'Kate, I'm sorry.'

'When Amy told me about her pregnancy it just all came back to me.'

'Do you need me to ring Stuart?'

'No. I just need to,' she made a non-committal noise, turned, and ran up the stairs. Her step got quicker as she reached the top, before disappearing into the bathroom.

I stood alone in the hallway. I thought about leaving. I wondered if it would be less embarrassing for Kate if I wasn't there when she came back down the stairs. It seemed rude to not check she was OK though.

Eventually Kate came back downstairs. The black marks around her eyes were gone and her freshly washed face glowed.

'Are you OK?'

Composed, she said, 'Yeah. I'm sorry about that. I hadn't really thought about how I would feel if someone else told me they were pregnant. Obviously, I wasn't really ready to hear that.' She walked towards the kitchen and offered me a drink.

'No thanks. I better get home.' I paused. 'If you're OK, that is?'

'No, no. You go. I'll be fine.' Water rushed into the kettle. 'What are you doing tonight?'

'It's England – Croatia.'

'Oh God. I forgot. I'm keeping you from it.'

'It's not kicked off yet. Don't worry.'

'If it was kicking off, would you have left me crying on the street?' She laughed a bit too loud, trying to emphasise she was joking.

'Maybe,' I said, playing along. 'Will you watch it?'

'Yeah. Probably. Are you going to the pub?'

'No. I did for the last two games. I'll just watch it at home.'

She opened a cupboard and took out a mug and placed a tea bag inside. 'OK. You sure you don't want a drink?'

'Honestly, it's fine. Are you OK now?'

'Yes. Thank you.'

I SAT IN one of the two armchairs in the lounge; my dad was in the other, a bottle of lager on a small side table next to him. My brother was lying across three seats of the settee.

England's footballers stood still as the camera panned down the line, providing shots of concentrated faces. The national anthem played loudly in the stadium.

'Can I have a beer?' Chris asked.

'Yes. But you'll have to get more from the garage because there aren't many in the fridge.'

Chris heaved himself off the settee with a sigh. He walked to the door and opened it.

'Hold on, hold on,' my dad said.

'What?' Chris said, frustrated.

'What about your brother?'

Chris turned to me. 'Do you want one?'

'Nice of you to ask. Let me think.' I made a long show of thinking.

'Don't take the piss. The game's kicking off.'

'Go on then.'

The game kicked off. My mum came in the room and made Chris sit up properly so she could sit on the settee too. She read her book, one eye on the game.

The communal family watching of football followed its usual pattern. My dad complained about the players, my mum made general comments about 'things not being very good', and my brother swore occasionally, each time increasing the harshness of the words to push the boundaries of what he could get away with. My mum would then tell him to watch his language. Within five minutes England were losing one-nil.

My mobile phone beeped with a text from Kate.

I'm guessing that wasn't supposed to happen.

My fingers typed out a response.

Not part of the plan. I think my dad is going to punch the tele.

People get very angry, don't they?

They do.

I went back to watching the game but my mind couldn't focus. I picked up my phone and typed a message.

How are you feeling? My finger hovered over the send button, wrestling with whether it was a good idea to ask the question.

Tearing me from my concentration my dad jumped off his seat, throwing his hands in the air. England had scored.

My phone beeped. *That's better*, Kate had written.

I deleted what I'd written and replaced it with, *My dad has just kissed the tele.*

I waited a few minutes and no response came. I retyped my message asking how she was feeling and sent it.

Feeling a bit better. Thank you for before x x she replied.

My dad's voice pulled me from re-reading the message. 'Who keeps texting you? You're worse than your bloody brother.'

'Jordan,' I lied, putting my phone down.

Another eruption of noise came just before half time as Wayne Rooney smashed the ball past the Croatia goalkeeper to put England in the lead, my entire family jumped around the room.

The half time whistle blew and the lounge was evacuated. Chris went to the toilet, my dad to the fridge, my mum following him into the kitchen to put the kettle on.

'Tom, do you want another beer?' Dad shouted.

I stood up. 'No,' I answered. 'I'm going out.'

I walked down the hallway to the front door.

'Out? What about the match?'

'I'll still watch it.'

Chris ran down the stairs. 'Can I have another one?'

'No. One's enough. You're only fifteen. Don't push your luck.'

I closed the front door and walked across the road. I knocked on her door and waited, unsure why I was there. I guessed she was texting me because she didn't want to sit alone thinking about what had happened earlier. Even though I could be the only person who knew how upset she was, standing on her front step in the hollow seconds before she answered, I felt uncomfortable at being the one to keep her company.

She opened the door dressed in baggy pyjama bottoms and an old football top.

Before she could speak, I said, 'I thought I'd save your phone bill.'

What seemed like a genuine smile appeared on her make-up free face. 'Come in.'

I followed her down the hallway.

'Would you like a drink?'

'What have you got?'

'I'm having wine but Stuart's got some beer in the fridge.'

'Beer would be good.'

She handed me a beer and we went in to the lounge, sitting down on the couch. The half time football analysis was happening on the television.

We chatted, ignoring the obvious conversation about earlier. She asked me about work and if I'd made travelling plans. I told her about my conversation with John in Sydney and how it made me wish I could go tomorrow. The game restarted, and we watched it while talking.

After celebrating Frank Lampard's goal that made the game 4-2 to England, we fell silent. I sipped my beer; she drained her wine.

'Any plans for tomorrow?' I asked to fill the silence.

'I need to buy Amy a congratulations card.'

Silence.

'I'm sorry about before,' she said quietly into the glass.

'Stop apologising. I'm just glad you're OK.'

'Amy is the first friend of mine to get pregnant since I, well, you know.' She couldn't bring herself to say the word again. 'I guess the emotion that came out has been building for a few months.'

'Did people know you were pregnant?'

'Some did. Not Amy. My parents and my sisters did. The whole thing was a bit of a shock, really. We hadn't been trying to get pregnant. It just happened. A happy accident, I guess you'd call it. We were pleased and just getting used to the idea when, just before the twelve-week scan, I started bleeding heavily and it turned out I'd lost it. I was upset for a few weeks but eventually normality returned. After a month or so, Stuart booked a trip to the Lake District, and we just went away and got very drunk, talked about how gutted we were. We then came home and got on with life. Until today.'

She looked at the television. The natural question to ask was if they were trying to get pregnant again, but I could see she looked so drained from the subject that instead I asked, 'How many sisters have you got?'

She turned back to me and said, 'Two. One older, one younger.'

'How old?'

'Thirty-three and twenty-four.'

'Is the younger one single?' I asked.

'She is, but she's also a bit mental when it comes to men. I think lads would call her needy. So, I won't set you up.'

'Thank you for considering my feelings.'

'You're welcome. You'd only blame me when she's ringing you every twenty minutes even after you've split up.'

'I've got enough ex-girlfriend problems at the moment. I don't need any more.'

She turned her body slightly on the couch to face me instead of the television. 'Sounds interesting.'

'It's not.'

'Come on, do tell.'

'It's a long story,' I said, before finishing my drink.

More seriously, she said, 'Want to talk about it?'

I shook my head. 'Not really. Can I use your toilet?'

'Sure. Straight upstairs.'

I stood up and walked upstairs as the house was filled with the sound of a ringing phone.

It stopped, and I heard Kate say, 'Hello.'

I entered the bathroom and used the toilet, washing my hands and drying them. As I walked out of the bathroom, I heard Kate's voice, louder than before.

'What if they win the quarter final? Will you be staying on for the semi-final too?'

She was quiet while she waited for the answer.

'I'm not angry. I just wondered why you didn't tell me this was a possibility before you left yesterday morning.'

Another pause.

I stood on the stairs, not wanting to listen, but not wanting to move and draw attention to my presence.

'Stuart, the game finished ten fucking minutes ago. Don't make out like you've just thought of this.'

Pause.

I moved a step down, placing my feet softly.

'Stuart, I understand.' Her voice was hard. 'You don't need to explain it. You want to have a few days away with the boys. I'm not stopping you. Have fun.'

Pause while Stuart spoke.

I moved again. This time, the floor creaked.

Kate's manner calmed. 'I've said it's not a problem.'

Stuart spoke again. I moved forward to the bottom step and walked down the hallway and stopped outside the open doorway.

'It was OK,' Kate said in response to a question from her husband.

It felt more uncomfortable to wait in the hallway, so I walked into the lounge as Kate said, 'Amy is pregnant.'

Her face exposed her feelings. She looked angry and tired. 'I'll speak to you tomorrow.' She replaced the receiver and let out a large deep breath. 'Well, that was fun.'

'Are you OK?'

'Not really.'

'What's wrong?'

She moved back to the couch. I followed, facing her but sitting a cushion's length apart.

'My husband is staying in Portugal for the next match, which I have absolutely no problem with. But he's ringing ten minutes after the game has finished and is making out this is an impulse decision.'

'And you don't think it is?'

'Not really. I just don't understand why he feels he can't tell me what he's got planned? What does he think of me? That I'm going to stop him from doing it? Am I some kind of ogre?'

'I don't think so.'

'He did this the other day, too. Before you came around for five-a-side.'

My senses heightened. 'What do you mean?'

'He told me he wasn't playing football and then tells me as I walk through the door from work, that they couldn't find a replacement and that he's going out. It was annoying because he was going back to Portugal with another group of customers the next morning, so I barely got to spend any time with him.'

I didn't reveal that I'd heard the argument.

'What I hate is that he's turned me into this shouting wife who gets annoyed when her husband plays five-a-side. I hate it. I was thinking I'd get to spend a night with him before he went back to Portugal and he came home and played bloody football. He could've missed it for one week.'

She looked at me, realising she was exposing an intimate layer of their marriage, and apologised again. 'I'm just dropping all my shit on you today.'

'I don't mind.'

'I have no problem with Stuart working away. No problem with him trying to build his business. I think it's great. For both of us. But he annoyed me because he makes out I'm the bad guy because I want to spend time with him when he's home.'

'Do you think he could've genuinely just decided to stay? Tonight, I mean.'

'Maybe,' she said, shrugging. 'But the way he was last week with football, it's just making me second guess it. The annoying thing is I honestly don't mind him staying out there. He works really hard. His business is starting to do well and he deserves to have a few days off. It's not like we've got kids.'

The last sentence hung in the air.

We looked at each other for a second too long.

I broke the look by saying, 'I should go.'

We stood, our faces appearing in the mirror above the fireplace, framed in black. She touched her face, pushing her finger into her chin and said, 'I look like shit.'

'Don't be stupid,' I said. Instinctively, my mouth added what my mind was thinking, 'You're beautiful.'

She kissed me. It was hard and took me by surprise. I kissed her back, and she pulled me towards the couch and we fell to the floor. Her hands reached for the button of my jeans. The way we were laid on the floor made the angle impossible for her to undo them. I moved back and started to open the button and yank down the zip. She took off her pyjama bottoms and her underwear in one move. Half clothed, she pulled me down inside her.

Everything was hazy.

She put her hands on my chest and pushed me off her. 'No. I can't, I can't. No.'

As I stood up as she reached quickly for her clothes, turning away from me as she stepped back into them. I grabbed my jeans and did the same. I looked at her sat on the couch staring into nothing, bent over, arms wrapped tightly across herself.

'Kate, I...' Words failed me.

'I think you should go.'

I DRIFTED BACK across the road on autopilot, put the key in the door, ignored the noise from the television in the lounge, and walked straight upstairs. I closed my bedroom door, lay on the bed, my heart and mind racing. What had just happened? I thought of Kate, sat on the couch, her face white with shock. I wanted to hold her, tell her I was sorry, that it would all be OK. But I didn't know if that was true because we had overstepped a line, and no matter what we did from this point on we could never cross back and erase what we had done.

Chapter Five

Running late, I arrived in the Silver Moon just before kick-off. England are playing Portugal in the Euros quarter finals. People were packed tight in a sea of red and white. St George's cross flags hung from walls and behind the long wooden bar. The bar staff all wore England tops. I pushed my way through the crowd, repeatedly saying 'excuse me' and 'sorry,' and found Jordan and Sam in the corner with a few others.

Jordan handed me a pint and gave me team news.

'Cheers,' I said, taking a long drink.

'You got Neil's text?'

'No,' I said. 'I've not checked my phone.'

'Lisa's gone into labour.'

'Nice one. How long?'

Jordan moved his pint glass from his mouth and said, 'No idea. Just said he'd text when she'd had it.'

The game kicked off and we stood with our eyes fixed on the television that was attached high on the wall in the corner of the pub. Shouts of response to the action could be heard from different sections around the pub. Staff leant on the bar, hoping no one would want serving.

'Where've you been the last few of days?' Jordan asked. 'I rang you.'

'I had to work late.'

It was a lie.

After what happened with Kate, I'd spent the next few days shut off from the world, wondering what to do. I hadn't heard from her and didn't know if she wanted me to get in touch with her. I phoned in sick from work on both Tuesday and Wednesday but had to go back because I didn't get paid for being off. I'd barely eaten anything and still had a tight knot in my stomach. I'd typed out several messages to Kate but had not sent them. No words seemed right. I'd gone to her number in my phone book many times but couldn't find the courage to press 'call'.

Michael Owen's goal rescued me from explaining any of this to Jordan.

The pub was an eruption of noise. We grabbed each other, jumping up and down, hugging and shouting. Beer spilt; strangers smiled at us and shook their fists in the air.

Calm spread as we watched the replay.

'If Neil has a boy, he'd better call it Owen,' Jordan said.

The game continued. We drank our pints, studied players' movements, drank again, shouted, groaned, and kicked every ball in our minds. I could see people's bodies in front of me reacting to the movements on the screen.

After twenty-five minutes, I felt my phone vibrating in my pocket as I watched in disbelief as Darius Vassell stood on the touchline waiting to replace the injured Wayne Rooney. I looked at my phone's screen and saw that Melissa was calling me. The crowd in the pub started applauding Rooney as he limped heavily towards the side of the pitch.

'Hello,' I answered.

'One Wayne Rooney, there's only one Wayne Rooney,' the pub chanted.

'Mel, I can't hear you.'

'One Wayne Roooooney,'

'What?' I shouted.

Frustrated, I gave up. 'I'll ring you back at half time,' I said loudly, hoping she'd hear me. We hadn't spoken since she'd left me talking to Andy and I couldn't understand why she was phoning me now.

The half time whistle blew, and the pub seemed shocked into action. The bar staff started to serve people, quickly exchanging money for drinks and moving on to the next waiting customer who shouted orders and passed pints back to friends behind them.

'Where you going?' Jordan shouted to me as I moved towards the door.

I turned back. 'Got to make a phone call.'

'I'll come with you. I need a cig.'

He followed me through the crowd. Outside, other fans stood around smoking, talking to the bouncers. Jordan lit a cigarette as I took out my phone and dialled Melissa's number.

As it rang, Andy walked around the corner with a friend of his. I remember thinking it was a strange coincidence, almost funny that I was ringing Melissa as her boyfriend appeared in front of me.

'Andy knows,' Melissa's voice said at the other end of the phone.

Andy punched me hard in the face.

I'd love to write that I took the punch, laughed at him and went on to easily win the fight, but that's not the reality. The reality is I dropped my phone as I fell backwards into Jordan. Andy went for me again, swinging wildly as a bouncer expertly positioned himself between us and pushed Andy away.

Jordan tried to get to Andy, but the second bouncer stopped him. Andy casually walked away with his friend as Jordan shouted useless insults at them.

The bouncer checked I was OK and asked, 'What was that about?'

I took my hand off my mouth and saw blood all over my fingers. 'I had sex with his girlfriend. I guess he found out about it.'

'So, you deserved it then?' the bouncer said. The sympathy drained from his face.

'Yeah. You could say that.'

'When did you shag Melissa?' Jordan asked.

I looked at him, blood running from my lip down my chin and snapped, 'Can we talk about this later? I need to sort my fucking face out.'

In the toilet, I stared into the large mirror above the sinks and pressed a fist full of toilet paper against my swollen lip. The bleeding had slowed. I took the mostly red paper off and ran the cold tap. The water stung as I flushed the blood out of my mouth. I used more toilet roll to dry it off and studied my reflection. My lip was cut and had ballooned up. I could feel a low dull ache as it throbbed.

I took my mobile from my pocket and assessed the damage. The screen was scratched but not smashed. I rang Melissa.

'What the fuck did you tell him for?' I shouted as she answered.

'What happened?'

'He fucking punched me.'

'I'm sorry.'

'You're saying that to me a lot recently.'

'I know,' she said, then repeating the words a little bit quieter.

Her explanation followed. She and Andy had been arguing, which had been happening more frequently. He'd become controlling, she explained. 'Where are you?' 'Who are you with?' More fights than fun, she said. He was moody if she went out with the girls, annoyed if she didn't make an effort to see him every day. 'I was tired,' she said. Earlier, they'd shouted back and forward. She'd told him she wanted him to leave. Leave or split up? He had asked. Split up, she answered, surprising them both. He said he loved her. She screamed for him to get out. He wouldn't go. Angry and crying, she told him to just fuck off, leave her alone. No, he said, moving towards her. He tried to hold her but as he touched her, she shouted into his face, 'I slept with Tom.'

'He just left,' she said.

The rest I could fill in. He'd come looking for me and I wasn't hard to find. Try all the pubs. And I'd just stood outside, oblivious, his prey waiting.

'Why did you tell him it was me? Why not just say you slept with someone?' I asked.

'I don't know, Tom. It just came out. I'm sorry,' she repeated.

Silence.

I could hear football chants coming from the main bar.

'I miss you,' she said.

The words hit me harder than Andy's punch.

I missed her too. I missed her laughter, the silly faces she'd make when no one else was looking. I missed the fun we had and the fact I knew that even if no one else in the world knew I was having a shit day, she understood. I missed Friday nights out and Saturday mornings in. I missed her hair, her face, the old scar on her arm from when she'd fallen off her bike as a kid. I missed all the other million little reasons why I loved her.

But I didn't miss being with her anymore.

And that was the only thing I chose to tell her at that moment.

She cried. And now it was my turn to say sorry.

I looked at my face in the mirror. My wounded face and my wounded pride.

Back in the bar I watched the rest of the second half in a haze. I focused on the screen and tried to rid my mind of everything that had happened in the past few days. Melissa, Andy, and especially Kate. The adrenalin which flowed through me after being punched had worn off and I was starting to feel sorry for myself. I stared at the screen silently, barely touching the pint Jordan had bought for me. I hardly moved an inch when Postiga scored for Portugal with seven minutes left, to make the score 1-1.

Between full-time and extra time Jordan said, 'Why didn't you tell me you slept with Melissa?'

'It wasn't something I wanted to talk about.'

'When was it?'

'Just after I got back from Leeds.'

'Didn't waste any time, did you?' Jordan had a jokey tone to his voice that I wasn't in the mood for. My mouth and jaw were throbbing constantly.

'Jordan, I'm not being funny, mate, but I don't want to talk about it. Shut up or fuck off.'

Sam laughed, and I threw him a look, trying my best to look intimidating, which was laughable with my swollen mouth.

I turned back to the screen and watched the England team line up for extra time. My head dropped again when we went 2-1 down. People in the pub shouted at the screen, swore at the players, made frustrated gestures to friends. Girls held their heads in their hands. Most of them looked like this was the first football match they'd ever watched. They were dressed in Top Shop England shirts, drank pints, and pretended to be one of the lads. If I hadn't been so pissed off, I would've been laughing with Jordan about it.

'You OK, mate?' Jordan asked in the second half as Gary Neville received a pass.

'Fine, mate. Just pissed off.' As much as I wanted to, I couldn't bring myself to confess my sin of what happened with Kate to Jordan. I kept up the pretence that the only weight on my mind was the situation with Melissa. Gary Neville tried to cross, but the ball deflected for an England corner. 'I shouldn't have let it happen. I knew it was a mistake the morning after. Didn't think she'd tell him though.'

'It was a good punch.'

'I probably deserved that. Fucking hurt, though. I just...' I paused as David Beckham prepared to take the corner.

'Come on,' fans shouted in the pub.

I continued over the noise. 'It's Melissa isn't it? I love her to bits, but I don't want to get involved again. Sleeping with her is only going to hurt her because I'm not going to get back with her. I just wish I hadn't done it.'

A wall of noise surrounded me and I was pulled under a wave of people. Everyone was jumping up and down and pushing me in different directions at once. I managed to regain my balance and my eye caught the television screen. A replay of Beckham's corner was being shown. It was headed down and Frank Lampard stopped the ball dead with his left foot, turned and hit it with his right. 2-2.

'Ing-er-land…' was the pub's repeated chant all the way through to full-time.

I stood, half smiling again, with Jordan and Sam waiting for the drama of penalty shoot-out.

'We can't lose another one,' Sam said.

'We'll be OK,' Jordan said. 'We're not playing Germany.'

'Thank fuck.'

Sam turned and started pushing his way towards the toilet.

'I understand what you mean about Melissa, mate,' Jordan said. 'But you can't let it worry you. What's done is done. She's a big girl. It takes two of you.'

'I know,' I said. 'But she was gutted when I didn't want her back. It seems to be becoming a habit in my life, telling her I'm not interested in getting back together.'

'Why aren't you? You two were amazing together.'

He was right. We were amazing together – three years ago. I wanted different things now.

A roar went up as David Beckham carried the ball towards the penalty spot.

Hands clapped; people shouted. Our captain, our hero, filled the screen. 'Come on, Becks.'

'Here we go,' Jordan said.

I felt my mobile phone vibrate in my pocket. I took it out, one eye still on the screen as Beckham placed the ball on the spot and began to walk towards the eighteen-yard line.

On my phone was a message from Kate.

I looked at the television. Beckham started his run up.

I clicked the message open.

I watched Beckham kick the ball, which flew widely over the bar.

My head dropped towards my mobile and I read the words. *I think we need to talk.*

I felt sick.

Beckham was pointing at the penalty spot, gesturing about the ground. As the television replayed the penalty miss, I re-read Kate's words. My body went dizzy, knowing there was nothing I could do to change the situation. No second chance to go back and not cross the line.

On the television, the replay changed angles showing the same result. No goal.

Life moved on. Portugal scored their first penalty. The feeling of regret and disbelief remained.

Owen and Lampard scored for England either side of a Portugal goal. It was 2-2, but Portugal had taken an extra penalty. More heads rested in hands; more people watched through the gaps in fingers.

My phone vibrated again. It was from Neil. I nudged Jordan, showing him. I opened it and we read the message together.

Alex Thomas Johnson. Born today. 7 pounds 3 ounces. Lisa tired but doing well. My son is the most amazing thing ever.

Jordan and I looked at each other and smiled. We turned back to the screen just in time to watch Rui Costa smash the ball over the bar. Still 2-2. England were back in the game.

England goal, Portugal goal, England goal, Portugal goal, England goal, Portugal goal.

England miss.

The pub emptied of hope rapidly, like water running down a drain.

Portugal goal.

England were out of the tournament. Lost on penalties. Again.

I STOOD OUTSIDE the pub. England-shirted people filtered past with disappointed looks on their faces. I shook Sam's hand, and he said, 'Make sure you get some ice on your lip.'

Walking home, I took out my phone and re-read Kate's message. She was right. We did need to talk. The question was what to say to her. I'd thought about nothing else for the last three days and was still no closer to an answer.

I sent a response to her that read: *You're right. We do need to talk. Where and when?*

My phone rang immediately. Kate's name flashed on the screen.

Cautiously, I answered, 'Hello.'

'Where are you?'

'Just walking home from the Silver Moon.'

'I'll come and pick you up.'

WE DROVE IN silence from the moment I clipped in my seat belt. After five minutes or so, we pulled into a supermarket car park. Dim lights from the store glowed over the rows of trolleys lined up at the entrance. We drove past a few scattered cars and parked in a dark corner, away from the view of the world.

Kate switched the engine off and the noise from the car disappeared. We stared forward into the night.

'What happened to your face?' Kate asked.

I almost laughed. 'You really want to know?'

'Yes,' she said. 'Are you OK?'

'Do you remember my ex-girlfriend Melissa, I told you about?'

'Yes.'

'Well, I had sex with her. Her boyfriend found out about it and did this to me.'

Another silence as we both contemplated the parallels to our own situation.

'It's almost laughable,' I said eventually.

'What is?'

'This whole situation. I'm sat in a car in a supermarket car park with a married woman who I should not have had sex with, telling her that my face is swollen because the boyfriend of another girl I should not have had sex with, punched me. We should be talking about what happened between us and yet my other...' I stumbled into a pause as I tried to think of the right word, 'indiscretion, is the main topic of conversation.'

We turned to look at each other for the first time since getting into the car. She looked tired, her face showed no traces of make-up, and yet I remember how inappropriate it was that I wanted to tell her that she was beautiful.

'I'm not really sure what to say,' I said, turning to face the windscreen again. 'I suppose I should start with I'm sorry. The other night should never have happened. You're married, your husband is a mate of mine. I'm so sorry.'

'It took two of us,' Kate said. 'But it was a mistake. It is something I regret deeply and I needed to tell you that it cannot happen again.'

I was overcome by feelings of guilt and shame. Not just for what happened with Kate, but also with Melissa and Andy. I started to cry. At first tears welled up in my eyes and slowly rolled down my cheeks, but I began to feel overwhelmed by emotion. I leant forward, my arms resting on my thighs and cried loudly. After a minute or so, I tried to regain my control and sat upright again.

My body shook uncontrollably. 'I'm so sorry,' I repeated several times. I took a deep intake of breath, desperately trying to compose myself. Words started pouring out of me. 'I don't know when I became this person. This is not me. I'm not like this.'

'What do you mean?' she asked, her hand reaching out to comfort me.

'I don't know. I don't know how I let this happen.'

'Me neither,' she said softly.

Feeling embarrassed and stupid, I wiped my face with my hand. The dull ache in my mouth continued. I couldn't bring myself to look at Kate or at myself in the dark reflection of the windscreen. I let my head drop and tried to pull myself together.

'Tom, listen to me,' she said. 'What happened should never have happened. But it did and we cannot take it back. I wish we could. I'm married and I love my husband. I've spent the last three days trying to see the best way out of this situation. It was a mistake. A stupid, stupid mistake. Stuart and I have been having issues but that's no excuse for what happened. I do not want to lose my husband, so I need you to promise me we can keep this between us.'

I looked at her. 'I think that's a good idea.'

Chapter Six

Following our conversation, Kate and I said goodbye, took our secret and went back to our lives.

After the drama of those few days, things returned to normal fairly quickly. The swelling in my lip reduced. People stopped asking how it had happened, so I could stop repeating a lie about a drunken England fan and an argument about penalty takers. Melissa and I started rebuilding a friendship through text messages and phone calls a few times a week and I continued to play five-a-side with Stuart, although I made vague excuses about running late for a couple of weeks so I didn't have to go to their house before the games.

By the middle of July, my temp job came to an end and I found myself unemployed. Again, I sat in front of the same smiling Recruitment Consultants, answering the same questions, going through the same process of being given the same promises of employment. By the time of my graduation a week later, no one had called back with a new job for me.

The morning of my graduation my mum dressed in her new outfit, my dad put on his only suit, minus the tie which he told my mum during the discussion – and I use the word loosely – that wearing it made him feel uncomfortable and he'd put it on when we got there. I dressed in the new suit I'd bought for the occasion and we drove to Leeds.

We arrived, parking with lots of time to spare, and walked with all the other families heading for the auditorium where the ceremony was taking place. Outside, crowds of graduates stood dressed identically in black gowns and graduation caps, smiling at each other and introducing friends to parents, parents to friends.

'Thomas,' came the shout, in the form of an impression of the woman from the cartoon *Tom and Jerry*.

I turned around and saw my friend Sean with a big smile on his face. We shook hands and hugged. Sean kissed my mum, shook my dad's hand, and introduced his parents and twin sister, Helen. Small talk about the weather and journeys to Leeds started between the adults.

'Have you seen Matt?' I asked.

Sean shook his head. 'He called me five minutes ago. He's meeting us here.'

As Sean spoke, we looked up and saw the tall, solid frame of Matt Jones walking towards us, hand in hand with his girlfriend of three years, Michelle Stevens. Both were dressed in graduation gowns and freshly tanned from their recent holiday in Greece. Matt's mum and dad walked slightly behind with Michelle's parents. Matt let Michelle's hand go and shook hands with me and Sean. Another round of parent introductions began.

Sean slipped his hand into the inside of his suit jacket and produced a small bottle of tequila. 'Gentlemen,' addressing us as he always did when we stood collectively. 'I thought we could end this journey the way it began.' He unscrewed the top and took a drink from the bottle.

'Sounds like a plan,' I said, taking a drink and avoiding my mum's watchful eye.

I passed the bottle to Matt who said, 'To our absent friend,' as he raised the bottle.

'He's only travelling,' I said. 'He's not dead.'

The day I arrived at Leeds uni I walked down the long neutral painted corridor in my halls, plain doors on either side, carrying my belongings in a box and my clothes in an Adidas holdall. Inside the room that would be my home for the next year, I started putting my clothes in the single wardrobe and unpacking the box, placing items on the small bedside table and desk.

There was a loud knock on the door, followed by a lower knock on a different door. The knock on my door repeated, followed again by a lower one.

I opened my door to find a lad stood with arms outstretched in the middle of the corridor. The opposite door opened, revealing another guy who looked as confused as I did.

'Hello, gentlemen,' said the knocker. 'I'm Sean. This,' he said holding up a bottle, 'is my friend tequila. Have you met?'

Smiling, I said, 'He's an acquaintance of mine.'

'We're old friends,' the other lad said in a light Scottish accent.

'Good,' Sean said. 'Shall we get this party underway then?'

I shrugged. 'Sounds like a plan.'

Sean's room was next to mine. Inside, he cleared a space on his desk and pulled three mugs from a box. As he poured large measures of tequila into each one, I introduced myself to the Scottish guy.

'Matt,' he said. We shook hands.

Sean passed out the mugs and we raised them up before knocking back the drink.

Through the open door, Sean noticed another lad walking down, struggling with bags the corridor. 'You OK with those?'

'I'll be all right. This is my room,' nodding at the door next to Matt's.

'Well, dump them in there and grab yourself a mug.'

Two minutes later John joined us.

Matt was from Edinburgh and was in Leeds to do the same Sports Science course as me. John, from Liverpool, was doing English. We found out later he'd got all As in his A Levels and he was our resident genius. Sean was from Bath. He told us his dad owned a property company and he had a job waiting on the condition he got a business degree. We went to the Student Union and got drunk, shared stories and life histories. That night we laid the foundations of the friendship that would take us through to standing outside waiting for graduation with our families.

'Has anyone spoken to John?' I asked.

'Yeah,' Matt said. 'On Monday. He's met some American girl and is travelling around with her.'

We made our way into the auditorium dressed in our gowns, sat uncomfortably through speeches, watched hundreds of students stand on stage, wave at family members, and smile relieved smiles at the moment of finally graduating. We did the same as we walked across the stage, basking in the applause.

Back outside we posed for photographs with parents and each other before shedding our gowns. I walked back to the car with my mum and dad, took an overnight bag out of the boot and shook my dad's hand as he said, 'Well done, son. Have a good night.'

My mum gave me a tight hug and kissed me on the cheek. 'We're really proud of you.'

They got back into the car, my dad ripping the tie from round his neck as he slid into the driver's seat. My mum waved as they pulled out of the parking space and drove off into the traffic.

I stood alone for a few seconds, took in the crisp blue sky and enjoyed the feeling of graduating. There was a huge sense of achievement and pride in finally being done with something as big as uni, although that feeling was tinged with the sadness that the experience was over. I picked up my bag and walked back towards the university.

Matt and Michelle sat on stone steps next to Sean's twin sister Helen, a small suitcase at their feet. Sean stood away from them talking rapidly into his mobile phone.

'Who's he talking to?' I asked.

'Mike.'

Sean ended his conversation. 'Right,' he said. 'Mike said he and a few others have checked in already. Shall we?'

'Let's go,' Matt said, standing.

We walked for about ten minutes to the Travelodge we had booked for the night, checked in and dropped our bags in our rooms. I was sharing with Sean. We kept our suits on and headed back into the reception area.

'Mike says they're in the Black Dog.'

'Where is that?'

'Don't know.'

I asked the receptionist for directions and she pointed across the road to a pub we couldn't miss. We walked over the road laughing.

The Black Dog was an old man's pub. One barman leant on the bar talking to a man who was nursing a pint of bitter and reading a newspaper, folded at the racing section. Small round wooden tables surrounded by short stools were spread across the pub. It was dark inside, despite the day's sunshine. The only noise in the room came from a group of six newly graduated students dressed in crisp suits and new dresses. We walked over and joined the group.

Mike stood up and shook my hand. We had known Mike since early on in our first year. He had landed an elusive job behind the bar at the Student Union and we got to know him during the many hours we spent in there. It had been his idea, arranged through a series of send-to-many emails, to get a group of people together after graduation and stay over in Leeds for a night out.

Drinks were bought, ties loosened, and stories swapped about our brief time since finishing uni. I laid out my plans for travel again, playing down my current unemployed state.

After a couple of drinks, we moved on into the city centre into a chain pub and ordered food. Plates of chips and burgers appeared, which we ate quickly.

I was sat next to Helen, Sean's sister. She had gone to Newcastle for university to do English, but after spending weekends at Sean's parents' house we all knew her well and were happy for her to come on our night out.

'When's your graduation?' I asked through a mouthful of burger.

'Next week.' She drank from a glass of red wine.

'How's Phil?' referring to her long-term boyfriend.

'Good. Working hard. How's your love life?'

I laughed, my mind replaying the night at Kate's.

'What's so funny?' Helen asked.

'My love life,' I said, screwing my face up as I said the last two words.

'Come on, Tom. No stories to tell?'

My mobile phone vibrated in my pocket, giving me an escape from the conversation. 'Excuse me,' I said, reading the message from Melissa that appeared on the screen.

Hi, hope today went well. It's funny I always thought I'd be with you when you graduated. Have a good night out. Speak soon. M xxx

I shook my head at the reference to us not being together anymore.

'What's wrong?' Helen asked.

'I suppose you could say it's my love life.'

Sean picked up on my words and turned towards me. 'What's up my friend?'

'Nothing, mate.'

'Come on. Don't be shy. Girl trouble?'

'Fuck off, Sean,' I said.

Sean took exaggerated mock offence.

'Leave him, Sean,' Helen said.

'It's all right,' I said. 'It's nothing, mate. Just Melissa.'

Sean downed the end of his pint. 'Melissa, the former love of your life, Melissa?'

'You know who Melissa is.'

Sean stood. 'I think we might need more drinks for this. Do you want one?'

I nodded.

Sean took orders and disappeared to the bar. He returned minutes later and handed out the new drinks.

I explained Melissa's text and her dig about us not being together.

'Does she want to get back with you?' Sean asked.

'Yeah, I think so.'

'And you don't want to get back with her?' asked Helen.

'No.'

'You guys have not been together for three years. Why does she want to get back together?'

I sipped from my pint. 'We sort of had sex.'

Sean smiled. 'Sort of?'

'We had sex.' I went back to the beginning of the story and told them everything, including Andy's punch. 'We have been sorting it out over the last few weeks. I'm up for being mates, but now and then she drops little hints about getting back together. It winds me up.'

Helen sipped her wine. 'Why don't you want her back? You were happy, weren't you?'

'We were happy. Then. But I don't want to get back with her now because it'd feel like a step backwards. I want to go away and see the world. If I get back with her, I don't think I'd go.'

'Why can't she go with you?' Helen asked.

'Because I don't want her to.'

'Well, that'll do it,' Sean said, laughing.

LATER, IN A small dark sweaty club, as we danced drunkenly to cheesy pop music, Sean threw his arms around my shoulder, shouting, 'Are you OK?'

'Yeah. I'm good,' I said, pushing my fist into the air. I watched Matt dancing behind Michelle, laughing and smiling.

Sean stopped dancing and looked me in the eye. 'I'm serious. You seem a bit down.'

'I'm OK,' I said.

'Well, if you need me, just ring me. OK?'

I nodded, but softly protested. 'I'm all right, mate. Just a bit bored with life at home.'

I looked at Sean, the person who knew the person I was now better than anyone in the world. Better than Jordan or anyone else in Manchester. I wanted to take him into the corner and tell him about my frustration with not being in work, about not being away, about living at home and watching my parents go through the same routine day after day, week after week. Most of all, I wanted to confess what had happened with Kate. I wanted to pour out my soul and unlock the secret I was carrying with me.

'You'll be OK once you get away,' he said reassuringly.

I wanted to tell him I was starting to feel like that might never happen, but instead I downed my bottle of lager and carried on dancing.

Chapter Seven

Boredom visited me, then outstayed its welcome.

I was still unemployed when my brother finished school for the summer at the end of July. A week later, I drove him and my parents to Manchester Airport for their flight to Turkey. I'd been invited on the holiday six months earlier when they'd booked it. My mum rang me and offered to pay for my flights and accommodation, but I'd turned her down, assuming I'd be working, saving any money I earned for travelling.

Instead, I spent my days in a quiet house. I slept late, unsure if my first meal was a late breakfast or early lunch. For the first few days, I regularly rang the temping agencies, checking on work availability. It was a constant battle to get people to ring me back with updates and as the days dragged on my hunger for the chase faded.

I started taking baths instead of showers to kill more time.

For the first time in weeks, I did my own washing again. On my return from uni, my mum had tried to come in my bedroom and take any washing I had. Firmly, I told her I was capable of doing it myself. This went on for a couple of weeks; her telling me it was no trouble; me keen to hold on to the independence I gained while living away. Starting with the odd washing of football kit, or just putting some work shirts in with my brother's school uniform, my fight eroded. By the time they went on holiday, we were back to the setup we had when I was at school.

On Friday, six days after my parents went away, John emailed me from Sydney. I replied, then sat around waiting for his response. I read his messages several times, digesting stories of his travelling life. With intense feelings of jealousy, I checked my online savings account. I stared at the balance and felt my shoulders slump. The figure wasn't even enough to cover the round the world plane ticket I had intentions of buying. I wasn't expecting tens of thousands in my account, but the figure was lower than I'd anticipated.

In my mind, I went through all the things I spent money on. When I was temping, I'd been paid weekly, so I made sure I had enough money for petrol, five-a-side, lunchtimes, and Friday and Saturday nights out. The rest I transferred straight into my travelling account. My car had needed an MOT and service. New brake pads had made the final price about three hundred quid. The night out in Leeds after graduation had cost over a hundred quid, including the hotel and price of the train home. The obvious realisation hit me that if I was serious about going away, I needed to get serious about saving.

I rang all the agencies I was registered with and, filled with a renewed sense of determination, put more pressure on them to find me a job.

Jordan called.

'What's up?' I asked.

'Nothing's up. Not seen nor heard from you all week. Just checking you're not dead.'

'I can assure you I'm not dead.'

'What you been up to then? Thought you'd be out every night, your mum and dad away and all that. Why are we not having a party?'

'Because I'm not fifteen.'

There was a crackle on the line, the wind blowing down Jordan's mobile.

'Where are you?' I asked.

'Just finished work. I'm walking across the car park.'

'You going home?'

'No, to the pub. You coming out?'

Decision time. 'No. I'm skint.'

'Come on, man, it's Friday.'

'Doesn't matter what day it is, I'm skint.'

'I'll sort you out for the night.'

'No thanks, mate.' My newfound resolve to start saving properly was being tested, and I was passing.

'Come on. We'll get pissed, go to town, try to finger girls in some dark and dingy club. Just like the old days.'

I laughed. 'As tempted as I am.'

'You're out tomorrow, though, right? It's the wetting of the baby's head night.'

I paused before answering.

Jordan pounced. 'You can't miss it. The kid is five weeks old. Neil hasn't had a proper night out. If we wait any longer, Alex will be old enough to buy the first fucking round.'

'I know. I'll be out tomorrow. Don't worry. I just can't do tonight as well.'

'Fair enough. I'll leave you to your own company then. I'm off to get pissed.'

I hung up the phone and went to my DVD collection to decide which film to watch again on a Friday night in alone.

REFRESHED AND FULL of purpose, I got up early on Saturday morning. I cleaned my car, inside and out, half filling a bin bag with all the chocolate wrappers and old McDonald's drink cartons that I found under the seats.

A car horn made me jump while I was polishing the steering wheel.

I looked through the windscreen and saw Stuart's car stopped in front of my house. I waved, thinking he would drive off. He didn't. I got out of my car and walked over to his. Stuart leant over the seat towards me. 'OK?' he asked as the electric passenger side window slid down.

'Yeah. You?'

'Very good. Out last night?'

'No. Stayed in a watched *Gladiator*.' I looked on the passenger seat and noticed an overnight bag. 'Off somewhere?'

'Newcastle for Anthony's thirtieth. Just until tomorrow.'

'Is that today? He mentioned it at football a couple of weeks ago. He invited me.'

'How come you're not coming?'

I shook my head. 'Not the best month money wise.'

'I'll sort you out for the weekend if you want.'

The offer surprised me. It was the second time in twenty-four hours somebody had offered to pay for me to go out. Was I that much fun? 'I can't, mate. We're wetting my mate's baby's head tonight.' I was glad of the excuse. The truth was my original decision had been based on the fact a weekend away with Stuart and alcohol would be uncomfortable and potentially dangerous.

I leant back towards my car and said, 'I'll leave you to it. Have a good weekend.'

'Cheers, mate. Have fun tonight.'

He turned the volume up on his stereo, slid the window shut, and drove off, leaving me standing on the pavement.

TEMPING HAD BEEN the obvious answer for employment at the beginning of the summer. Regular work I didn't care about or get attached to, weekly pay and the ability to leave on short notice. Now, though, the agency's lack of quick response was making me feel like the source was drying up.

After lunch on Saturday afternoon, I sat in front of the computer in the dining room and started looking at the endless number of retailers in the city centre and the Trafford Centre, the huge

American style shopping centre on the outskirts of Manchester, for full-time jobs. I figured if I could get a job in a shop before all the students came back to Manchester I'd be set until Christmas. My hours might even increase in the build-up to the festive season. Long retail hours would mean I could get loads of overtime in too.

I trawled through website after website, filling in forms, downloading application packs. I applied for everything; music shops, clothing stores, coffee places. Hours passed productively. I felt positive about finding something for the first time in a couple of weeks.

I put the words 'full-time employment Manchester' into a search engine. Hundreds of web pages were instantly listed on the screen. I read through them slowly, making notes of the ones I thought I could get. I decided that on Monday morning the job hunt would get back to being full-time.

The clock in the corner of the computer screen told me I was running late.

I put a pizza in the oven and ironed a shirt in the hallway while it heated. I ate quickly, leaving my empty plate on the kitchen side, next to the plates and cutlery from the day's meals that seemed to be breeding and spreading across the work surface. I'd planned to empty the dishwasher and restack it at some point, but the job hunting had distracted me.

In the hallway, I walked past the ironing board and decided to clean up the next day, again giving me some purpose and providing me with something to distract me from spending money.

THE SAME FACES stood in the same spots with the same friends drinking the same drinks.

We quizzed Neil about fatherhood. He looked knackered; his eyes framed with dark rings put there by lack of sleep. He explained the night time routine, the little changes in the baby since he was born, and showed us a couple of photographs from his wallet. We'd all been around to see the baby a couple of times but no one would deny him the sense of pride that glowed from him during the conversation.

Jordan carried drinks back to the group on a tray. Next to each pint stood a shot glass. We all took our drinks and Jordan said, 'This is fucking weird. Not only to think one of us is actually a dad, responsible for the life of another human being, a poor innocent human at that. But what's weirder is that it's Neil. Who knew he could even take care of himself?'

We all laughed, including Neil, and raised our drinks, touching our glasses together, saying, 'To Alex' at the same time.

My friends went through the routine of talking about football, looking at women and drinking. Watching Saturday play out, a sense of boredom wrapped around me like a suffocating blanket. I didn't feel involved. I laughed at the jokes and agreed which girls were fit but it felt like I was watching myself from above. I tried to get involved but didn't feel like I wanted to be there.

The feeling didn't sit comfortably with me. These were my mates. We were out because one of them had become a father. I'd grown up with all of them.

'Your round,' Sam said, as he showed me an empty pint glass and snapped me out of the haze.

'Same again?' I asked everyone.

'Of course,' they responded.

I made my way slowly to the bar and focused on the staff. A barmaid smiled at me but moved down the bar to serve someone else. I stood and waited, watching drinks being poured, bottles being opened, and presented in front of the customers.

A hand softly touched my back.

I turned to my left to see who had placed it there.

Kate stood next to me. 'Hi,' she said, a nervous smile breaking out across her face.

'Hi.'

'How are you?'

'I'm good,' I said. 'What are you doing in here?'

She looked mock offended. 'What do you mean? Am I too old to be in here?'

'No, it's just I've never seen you in here before.'

'I can still mix it with the young ones.'

I laughed.

She continued, 'I'm out with the girls.' She turned and pointed to a group of three other women who were sitting on one of the big leather couches, laughing. A barman asked for my order. I gave it to him and turned to Kate. 'Do you want me to get yours as well?'

'No, it's OK. I'll wait.'

The barman turned and began preparing my round.

'Are you walking home later?' Kate asked.

'Yeah.'

Silence. I watched lager being poured into a tilted glass.

'Can we walk together?' she said. 'I'll bring the chips.'

'You do owe me.'

She laughed as the barman placed drinks in front of me. I handed him my money, picked up the drinks, and turned to move away from the bar. Kate moved into the space I left, brushing against me as she did.

'I'll see you later then.'

'Just let me know when you're leaving.'

I returned to my group and handed out drinks. I took out my mobile and quickly typed a message.

How's things, mate?

I flicked through my phonebook and found Sean's number, then pressed send.

'I meant to tell you,' Jordan said as I put my phone away. 'I'm going to do that management training programme. The one my boss wanted me to do at work.'

'Nice one,' I enthused. 'What made you change your mind?'

'Don't know really,' Jordan said, sipping his drink. 'It was getting closer to the deadline for signing up for it and I just thought, fuck it, why not? What you said about being trained to a management level and all that, it made sense.'

'Nice one,' I repeated. 'I'm pleased for you.'

My mobile vibrated in my pocket as Sean's response came through. I opened it. It read: *On a date. Will call tomorrow.*

As I put my phone away, I glanced at the time on the scratched screen. It was just gone ten. I checked my phone regularly for the next hour, wishing away the time. I excused myself at one point and went to the toilet, running cold water into my hands and splashed it onto my face, desperately trying to snap myself out of the low mood.

Kate stopped me as I walked back through the busy pub. 'What time are you leaving?' she asked.

I shrugged. 'Don't mind. You?'

She looked at her watch. 'About eleven.'

'Sounds good. I'll meet you outside.'

She went back to her friends and I rejoined mine.

I TOOK A hot chip from the white polystyrene tray and blew on it as Kate and I walked.

'It's been a while since we've seen each other,' she said.

'I wasn't sure if you wanted to talk to me after, you know, what happened.'

She ignored the reference to our night together and asked how I'd been.

'Honestly? I'm bored out of my mind. My mum and dad are away. I've got no job, and I've spent most of the last week sat in my house. Even tonight, I wasn't enjoying myself that much. I don't know what's the matter with me.'

'Oh,' Kate said. 'I didn't realise.'

'Why would you? You said yourself we've not seen each other for a while.'

We continued in silence, finishing the chips between us. Quietly, she said, 'I miss our chats.'

'Me too,' I answered, barely audible.

Another silence.

We stopped at a crossroads.

'How was your graduation?'

'Really good. Well, I say that. The ceremony was boring, but a load of us stayed the night in Leeds and had a massive night out. It was brilliant. Me and my mates ended up in a drunken circle singing 'Don't Look Back in Anger' at the top of our voices.' A memory of me and Sean leaning into each other, lager bottles held high above our heads, shouting the lyrics loudly entered my mind.

'That's my favourite song,' Kate said.

'What? 'Don't Look Back in Anger'?'

She nodded.

'Really. I wouldn't have had you down for an Oasis fan.'

'And why not?'

'Don't know. Just wouldn't.'

'I was at Knebworth I'll have you know.'

'Knebworth? Really? That's amazing. What was it like?'

'It was brilliant,' she said loudly. 'We got there really early, so fortunately we weren't stuck at the back. We were about a third of the way down. I went with a massive crowd from uni.'

'What was the gig like? I would've loved to have been there. I was only thirteen.'

'For us, it was great. We'd finished university a couple of years before, in ninety-four, then 'Definitely Maybe' came out and we were all listening to it. It was funny because we left uni and went to different parts of the country for jobs but every time we got together for a party or something that was the album playing. When they played Knebworth, it was just natural to get together and go.'

We were walking slightly quicker than normal, fuelled by the alcohol inside us. Kate edged nearer to the kerb. Her foot missed its step and gave way onto the road. My arm flew out and grabbed her waist, pulling her towards me. 'Careful,' I said.

'Thanks.' She lifted the strap of her hand bag back up her arm and placed it over her shoulder. She moved away from me, regained her momentum and continued to walk like a teenager trying to convince her parents she wasn't drunk. 'It was great being in my twenties in the mid-nineties. We had everything a generation should have.'

'Like what?'

'Great music, great political change, hope.'

'I'd never describe politics as great.'

'You wouldn't. Your mid-twenties will be spent with Labour trying to convince people they're not fucking up all the good stuff they did in the first place.'

'Such as?' I asked.

'Minimum wage, European Working Time directive. The average life in this country is better now than it was when Tony Blair took over. He was a hero in 1997.'

'My Granddad says he's an American puppet. A girl at uni called him George Bush's rent boy.'

'She sounds nice,' she said. 'What do you think?'

'Not really sure. I wouldn't like to do that job. I assume he had more information than we've ever heard about. And he's got to sleep at night knowing all the dead soldiers are because of his decisions. This is a bit heavy for me. I'm a bit drunk for war talk.'

I paused, then said, 'So what's wrong with music now? It's great at the moment. The Strokes and The Libertines are amazing.'

'I've not heard much of The Strokes. I like Coldplay.'

'The Strokes are brilliant. *Is This It,* their first album, is my all-time favourite. I'll lend it to you.'

'I don't think music's rubbish now. I just don't think it's as good as the nineties.'

We were nearing home. The night's cool air started to get to me and I rubbed my hands along my arms to warm up. We turned into our cul-de-sac and we both instantly fell into silence.

'Sshh,' she said. 'We don't want to wake anyone.'

I laughed and whispered, 'How quiet is it? Doesn't it feel like some of the people who live down here are just waiting to die?'

Kate hit my bare arm. 'That's a horrible thing to say.'

I laughed quietly. We walked down the pavement, side by side. We approached my house, and I turned to open the gate. 'Do you want to come in and I'll get you that Strokes album?'

She followed me through the gate.

I reached inside my pocket and found my keys. I opened the door and looked at the mess I'd left. Looking down into the kitchen, over the ironing board in the middle of the hallway, I remembered the dirty plates piled on the kitchen work surface. I walked around the ironing board, moving quickly down the hallway to turn off the alarm at the box in the cupboard under the stairs.

'Sorry about the mess,' I said as Kate stepped inside, her eyes taking in the scene.

I passed her and raced up the stairs, hoping my embarrassment at the state of the house hadn't registered on my face. In my bedroom, I found The Strokes album case lying next to my stereo, checked inside the case to make sure the CD was there then snapped shut the cover and bounded back down the stairs.

Kate stood at the bottom. The light from the bulb above her highlighted her face and I could tell by her eyes she was drunk. She smiled as I handed her the CD and said, 'Thanks.'

I stood on the bottom step, facing her. We were silent, looking at each other. 'I hope you like it. I love it. It's my uni album. That was all we listened to for the first year.'

'I promise to give it a good listen.'

Nervously, I stepped down the last step. 'I'm really sorry about the mess.'

'Tom, you've been inside me. I don't think an ironing board and some dirty plates are going to shock me.'

She laughed out loud and covered her mouth with her hand. 'I'm sorry. I'm not sure where that came from.' Her face gave away her genuine surprise.

'I didn't realise we were allowed to make jokes about what happened,' I said, trying to cover my own shock at what she'd said.

'Neither did I,' she said. 'I really don't know why I said that.'

Unsure how to respond, I tried a joke. 'It's a shame because I had loads of jokes about it. They'd seem a bit forced now.'

She laughed again and then we just stood facing each other. I cannot say exactly how long it was, but the silence seemed to stretch for months. We smiled nervously at each other and then avoided eye contact.

'I better be…' She didn't finish the sentence but held the CD up and pointed it towards the door.

'Yeah, no, er, you better go.' I reached around her, brushed her jacket with my arm, and opened the door.

She turned awkwardly, her face moving close to mine.

My heart rate increased.

For a small moment we stopped and looked directly at each other.

She broke eye contact and moved through the open door.

'Goodbye,' I said, the word sticking in my throat. Slowly, I closed the door on her.

I know that if this scene had played out in film I would've collapsed against the door and let out a long sigh, maybe even asked 'what just happened?' out loud. I didn't do that. Instead, I got a bottle of lager from the fridge. My head replayed the whole of the last few minutes over and over. I tried to think back to exactly how she'd said 'you've been inside me' picturing if it was a joke, or a slip of the tongue or an invitation to something more. I strained to remember, but my memory, clouded by the night's drinking and the confusion of what had just occurred blurred every detail.

I took a drink from the bottle.

Before I could take a second drink, there was a knock on the front door.

Chapter Eight

I woke up from a deep sleep alone, thirsty, and confused at where the noise was coming from. My phone vibrated along my bedside table. Sitting up too quickly, spinning, and planting my feet on the floor, I picked up the phone and pressed answer.

'Hello.'

There was a long pause before the response. 'All right, son?' my dad asked. 'Out last night, were you?'

I scanned the box room, seeing a pile of my own clothes. 'Yeah. Wet Neil's baby's head.'

'Good night was it?'

'Something like that.' Another pause. 'How's your holiday?'

'Good. Apart from your brother never being off the bloody phone to that girlfriend of his.'

I stood up slowly and stretched my back.

'I need a favour,' my dad said. 'I need you to cut a couple of people's lawns for me.'

'Who's?'

'Mrs Wallace and Jacqui King's.'

'Who's Jacqui King?'

'Next door but one to your granddad. Red door.'

'The fat one?'

'Yeah. The fat one. Do it tomorrow, if possible. Take the van and cut the grass, front and back, on both houses and make sure you do the edges properly.'

I picked my clothes up off the floor and dumped them on the bed. I was disorientated and struggling to keep up with my dad's request.

'Will I get paid?'

An echo of laughter came down the phone. 'If you do a good job.'

'Text me the details.'

'I've just told you them,' my dad said.

'I've just got up,' I snapped.

We exchanged boring details about how the house was and what the weather was like in Turkey, then ended the call.

I went to the bathroom and had a piss. The information ran through my head. Jacqui King, next door but one to my Granddad. Mrs Wallace, next door to Kate. I flushed and turned to the sink, splashing refreshing cold water on my face. I still felt drunk and realised I didn't know what time it was.

I went back to the boxroom and checked my phone. Half-past nine. I thought about climbing back into bed, crawling under the duvet, and hiding from the world, but I was painfully hungry. I stepped into a pair of shorts and pulled a T-shirt over my head.

I went downstairs into the kitchen, put two pieces of bread in the toaster and waited.

That's when I saw it. In the middle of the table, a pen casually lying next to it. The note scribbled on the back of a torn envelope.

I froze and stared at it.

Carefully, like a detective inspecting fresh evidence, I picked up the envelope between my thumb and forefinger and slowly raised it to eye level.

It read:

Hi,

I know you must be confused about last night after I said nothing could happen between us.

I'm confused too. I've never done that before.

I'll call you when I can.

K x

I read it and re-read it, flashbacks of the previous night appearing my mind. Kate standing at the door as I opened it. Her moving into the hallway and kissing me. Me letting it happen. The two of us going upstairs and having urgent drunken sex in the box room's single bed. No thought of right or wrong, no moral code stopping us.

Tiredness gripped us and we fell asleep without speaking.

When my dad's phone call had woken me, I realised I was alone but couldn't place the moment Kate had left.

Kate's note was right. I was confused.

The last time at Kate's had felt crazy and stupid. This felt different. Right wasn't the correct word. Maybe natural, or comfortable.

Toast sprung from the toaster, making me jump.

I went back to my bedroom, walking up the stairs trying to figure out what the kiss she'd written on the note meant. I looked out of the window. Stuart's car wasn't there. It was still early and he'd be in Newcastle for a few more hours. Instinct told me to go and see Kate but her curtains were closed.

I picked up my phone and started to type out a message. I only got as far as, *Hi.* I changed it to, *Hey,* and sent it to her.

There was no immediate response. I tried to go about my normal routine: eating breakfast, showering, etc., but my mind was filled with Kate.

AND, AS YOU'VE probably guessed, this is how our affair began.

The simple truth is it started with a phone call from Kate the following Tuesday. It was a rushed, uncomfortable conversation where we arranged to meet the following lunchtime.

I met her around the corner from her office, the engine running in my car. She got in and I drove for a few minutes, finding a quiet side road, bumping up the curb to park.

I assumed we'd sit in the car and she would again tell me she regretted what happened. I would drop her at her office and we'd part with another secret.

Instead, we decided to keep seeing each other. It was a straightforward question from me to her. 'Do you want to stop or carry on?'

She said she wanted to carry on and we spent the rest of her dinner hour leaning across the handbrake and gear stick kissing, before she stopped and a took a tin foil wrapped tuna and salad sandwich out of her handbag and ate it, washing it down with a bottle of water.

I dropped her back around the corner from work and went home.

That night I made an excuse not to play five-a-side with Stuart.

Chapter Nine

'There you go,' I said as I handed my dad a cold beer from the fridge.

He sat in his chair, the closest one to the television, and asked if I'd had any luck with the job hunt.

'I sent out a lot of applications this week. I'm just waiting to hear back.'

It was Saturday night. My parents had been back in the country for three hours. My brother had already disappeared out, mumbling something about seeing Laura. Foil takeaway cartons were spread out around our feet, half full of Chinese meals and rice.

'I could do with some help work wise,' Dad said.

'Oh right,' I said. 'Doing what?'

'Just the usual. I've got a few fencing jobs on and a couple of drives to flag. But I've got all my gardens to catch-up on because I've been away. You did a good job on those gardens I asked you to do.' I wondered when he had been to inspect them since landing. 'Do you want some work?'

'Yeah. Please.'

MONDAY MORNING, I got up at seven and dressed in old jeans and a T-shirt. Toast eaten, tea drunk, and in the van by half seven. My dad drove in silence. As we moved into a queue of traffic to turn onto a main road, I felt good for being part of the great commute. From my raised position in the van, I looked down on a woman doing her make-up in a stationary car, one eye on the mirror, one eye on the traffic. Another driver was drinking from a thermal flask.

'What did you do while we were away?' my dad asked while changing the radio station.

'Not a lot,' I said. The words 'started an affair with Kate across the road' didn't seem appropriate for the early morning drive. 'Filled out some applications, job hunted. Went out to wet Alex's head. Looked into travelling some more.'

Dad nodded and moved the van forward.

'That reminds me,' he said. 'Your mum and I were talking about paying you. Do you want us to keep some of it as savings for your trip? Or do you want it paying into a savings account?'

'Not really thought about it. Maybe saving it would be a good idea. How will you pay? Cash?'

'Can do.'

'Just give me all of it. I'll have to go to the bank to pay it in, so I'll put some in my normal account and the rest in savings.'

'Will do,' he said, pulling the van onto the main road and into another queue for traffic lights.

The rest of the day was spent working. I cut grass, trimmed hedges, lifted flags, carried broken fence panels, and replaced them with new. For lunch we sat on a wall and ate sandwiches my mum had prepared and drank tea made by the woman whose house we were working on.

'How was Chris while you were away?'

Dad took a big bite of his sandwich and shook his head, making a show of chewing his food in a way that indicated he had something to say. 'I can't work that kid out. He's on holiday, swimming pool, sunshine, the bloody lot. Kids his age knocking about. We told him he didn't have to be in until one o'clock every night. You know, showing him a bit of trust. And for the first week he spent most of his time sulking about, with his head in his mobile texting Laura. Honestly. I had to drag him out of bed and get him doing something other than sleeping.'

'He's just enjoying having a girlfriend.'

'Doesn't look like he's enjoying it.'

I laughed and took the last bite of my sandwich. I unwrapped a chocolate Penguin bar and started to eat, washing it down with a sip of tea.

'He picked up a bit in the second week. He hung out with a couple of brothers from Swansea. He came in drunk a couple of nights too.'

'How was he?'

'One day he was a bit sick.'

'What did you do?'

'Told him if he wanted to drink like a man, he'd have to suck it up like a man. I made him get up about eight o'clock and took him on a boat trip.'

'What do you think of Laura?' I asked.

'Don't really know. She's all dark eyes and dark clothes. Apart from that, I'm not sure. I've only met her twice. Your brother grunted an introduction and took her upstairs.'

'You think he's having scx with her?'

Dad threw the remainder of his tea onto the flower bed and said, 'If he is, I wish he'd fucking cheer up about it.'

LATER IN THE week, my mobile rang. I stopped cutting the edge of the lawn and put the edging sheers down on the grass I'd just mowed.

'Hello,' I said.

'Is that Tom?' a voice boomed down the phone.

'Yeah.'

'Hi, Tom. It's Georgina from Phoenix Recruitment. How are you?'

'Good thanks.'

'Good, good. I'm calling with great news. We've got some work for you if you're still interested. It's just for a couple of weeks. Starting on Monday, based in Manchester.' Her voice never dropped from the high singing tone she spoke with.

'I've found something, thanks.'

A deflated 'oh' came down the phone, then the singing sales voice returned. 'Well, that's brilliant. Do you mind me asking what?'

'Landscaping.'

'And was that through another agency?'

'No. Through my dad.'

'OK. Is it permanent?'

'More than two weeks.'

She was getting the point that I wasn't interested. 'OK. Well, keep us in mind if you need anything. We're always available to sort out something for you. Bye, Tom.'

She ended the call, and I went back to edging the grass.

A FEW DAYS later I stood outside another gardening job, brushing up grass cuttings. My phone rang. 'Hello,' I said, answering quietly and turning away from anyone who could hear me.

'It's me.'

'Hi,' my eyes scanned for my dad. I saw him pushing the petrol-powered lawnmower down the driveway towards the back garden. 'You OK?'

'Yeah. The office has just emptied, so I thought I'd call you. I can't talk for long. What are you doing next Tuesday night?'

'Nothing. Why?'

'I've just arranged to go shopping with a friend of mine. Amy, the pregnant one. We're going to the Trafford Centre to eat and do some shopping. Can we meet up after?'

'Me and you?'

'Yeah. I want to see you.'

My body tensed and again my eyes scanned the area around me. Clear. 'Where?'

'The Trafford Centre. Can you get there for about half-past nine? Text me where you are and I'll meet you. I really want to.' There was a noise in the background and Kate said urgently. 'Got to go.'

The phone clicked as she put it down and the sound disappeared.

I MET JORDAN for a couple of pints after work on Friday. For the first time in my life feeling like I'd earned them. I stood at the bar in my work jeans, covered in grass stains and dried cement, and quickly knocked back the first pint. My arms ached, my back was stiff, and I felt like I'd grafted.

'What you up to tomorrow night?' I asked Jordan.

'I've got a date.'

'A date?'

'Yeah. Not a fancy restaurant and all that shit. This girl from work was dropping a few hints about taking her out, so we're going to get pissed in town. Maybe grab some food and go back to hers.'

'Got her own place?'

'Yeah. She's twenty-four.'

'What's she called?'

'Charlotte.'

'Another?' I said, showing him my empty pint glass.

'Go on then.'

I turned to the bar and waited for a member of the bar staff to see me. A young one did and came over. He looked uncomfortable, dressed in the shirt and tie uniform, his spotty face giving away his youth. I nearly asked him for ID.

He took the order, placing the heavy headed pints in front of me a couple of minutes later. I took my wages out of my pockets, a dangerous amount of money in a pub, and made myself promise I'd go to the bank first thing in the morning and split it between my savings and current account.

We finished our drinks and went our separate ways, Jordan promising to give me the details of his date. I left the pub, tucked my hands into my pockets, and headed for home. At the shops near my house, I went into the chippy and waited to be served, my eyes scanning the large menus on the wall behind the counter. I ordered and flicked through the *Manchester Evening News* while I waited for the food.

'There you go,' the man behind the counter said as he handed me a white carrier bag, my chips, pie, and gravy on a tray inside tightly wrapped in white chip shop paper.

I dug deep into my pockets for my keys and opened the front door, put my food down on the kitchen table, and went into the living room to see who was home.

Chris sat on the couch, arms wrapped around Laura, his skinny pale girlfriend. Her dark-haired head rested on his shoulder; eyes fixed on the music video on the television. They were obviously stoned.

'Evening,' I said.

No reaction.

'Where are Mum and Dad?'

Again, nothing.

'Been having a little smoke, have we?'

This got their attention. Chris tried to look innocent, but when he caught Laura's eyes, the pair of them started laughing.

'Where are Mum and Dad?' I repeated.

'Out.'

'Well, do yourselves a favour and make sure they don't see you like this.'

I went back to the kitchen, plated up my tea, and put it on a tray. When I went back into the living room Chris and Laura were standing up off the couch.

'What you up to?'

'Going out.' Was the giggly response I got as they shifted slowly into the hallway.

THE NEXT MORNING, I stood in the kitchen waiting for toast to pop out of the toaster. The kettle had just boiled, and I poured water on top of a teabag in my mug. Chris walked into the room.

'Morning,' I said. 'You want a brew?'

'No,' he said. 'Mum and Dad out?'

'Mum's gone to Tesco and Dad's seeing a job.'

He leant up towards a cupboard, taking down a cereal bowl.

'How long have you been smoking weed then?' I asked casually.

'What?'

'Weed. How long have you been smoking it?'

'What's it got to do with you?' he snapped. His voice wavered a bit, but I could tell he was trying to sound hard and unfazed.

I gave him another chance. Keeping my voice even, I asked again, 'How long have you been smoking it?'

'What the fuck's it got to do with you?' he said, angrier now.

I grabbed his T-shirt and spun him around, pushing him into the back door. He tried to fight back, but I held him locked in position.

'What you doing? Get off me,' he shouted. 'You're a knobhead.'

'Listen to me,' I said. 'I'm not Mum or Dad. I don't have to treat you nicely. I'll put you through the fucking wall if you speak to me like that again. Understand?'

He nodded, and I felt the fight release from his body like a slow puncture. I held him for another second while I said, 'Now listen to me, because I'm not having a go at you for smoking it. OK? I just want to ask you a couple of questions.' I released my grip slightly, so he knew I was letting him go, but before I did, I added, 'All right? Can you play nice?'

'Yeah.'

I took my hands off him and went back to making my cup of tea. Chris readjusted his T-shirt and went back to his cereal.

'How long have you been smoking it then?' I said, spreading a knife across the top of the butter.

'About two months.'

'Where are you getting it from?'

'Laura's brother gets it for us.'

'I don't want to sound preachy, but is that all you're doing? Smoking weed? Nothing else?'

He shook his head and said, 'No. You going to tell Mum and Dad?'

I laughed at him. 'Why would I do that?'

He shrugged, unsure of what to say.

I continued to make my tea, then said, 'For God's sake don't smoke it in school. The last thing Mum and Dad need is you getting expelled for taking drugs. They won't see it as a bit of weed. They'll overreact and see it as you using a Bunsen burner to cook your heroin.'

Chris let out a small laugh, and I pictured my mum crying in the headmaster's office and my dad shouting like a crazy man about his son letting him down.

'So, before you go getting all teenager on me,' I said, looking directly at him, 'I'm not bothered. I just want you to be careful that's all.'

My relationship with Chris had always been a bit funny up until this point. I put it down to the six-year age difference. When he was born, the gap wasn't such a problem, although sharing my mum and dad did take some getting used to. They tried to involve me in his needs, passing nappies to help change him, carrying bottles, or just keeping an eye on him – a role I took very seriously during his first few weeks of screaming and feeding.

As we got older, the gap became more prominent and by the time I started secondary school, Chris was a fully formed annoying little shit. Suddenly I was grown up and off to explore the adventure of big school and he couldn't understand why I wasn't interested in playing Lego with him or kicking a ball about in the back garden.

When he followed my route to secondary school, I was at college. I'd forgotten about the nervous feelings of that first day, arriving at the school drowning in a blazer among a land of giant older kids, unsure of the order of things. My life was about learning to drive, getting into pubs and clubs underage, Melissa and the lads.

As brothers, we sort of passed in the hallway of our house, me going out as he was coming in.

The only things we ever really bonded over were football and the guitar. I had an old acoustic my parents had bought me for my tenth birthday that I practiced on for hours, learning chords and trying to recreate my favourite songs. I wasn't amazing at it. Chris asked me to teach him, so I did, noticing how easily he took to the instrument.

I left for Leeds as he was becoming a teenager. Returning home for weekends or holidays, I noticed the obvious difference in his build. His body shot up and grew solid. He'd retreated behind a fringe and lived in his bedroom, playing the electric guitar my mum and dad had bought him. Annoyingly, the sounds coming from his bedroom were better than anything I'd been capable of.

Being home after uni was probably the first time we were close enough in age to understand each other's perspectives. He was fifteen, and I was young enough to remember what that was like.

I poured milk into my cup of tea and stirred it in.

'How do you know so much about it?' he asked, referring to smoking weed.

'I'm six years older than you. Assume for now that everything you're doing, I've already done. But assume I was worse.'

His eyes widened with intrigue. 'Like what?'

'Secret,' I said, smiling.

I DROVE FOR ages looking for the perfect space; past parked cars and empty bays. I tried three different car parks, finally finding a space in the shadow of a hedge in the dark corner of an overflow car park, away from the gaze of the huge spotlights and other Tuesday night shoppers.

I quickly typed out a message and sent it. Although it was the end of August, I kept the engine running and turned the heater on, keeping a steady flow of warm air into the car.

I waited.

Dark started to cover the day; the colours of summer being slowly wiped from the sky.

Twenty minutes later a figure walked purposely out of the dark. The large dome of the shopping centre lit up behind her. Carrying a couple of shopping bags, she jogged the last few metres to my car and opened the passenger door, throwing the bags in the back.

Kate leant across and kissed me. We grabbed at clothes, desperate to touch one another.

'Hi,' she said when we finally paused for air.

'Hi. Good night?'

We studied each other's faces in the dark, our hands touching.

'It was OK. I spent the last hour checking my watch, wondering when was an acceptable time to leave and come here.'

'Where's Amy now?'

'On her way home. I made an excuse about going to the toilet, waited ten minutes, and then came here.'

We kissed again; her fingers slipped between mine.

'I've wanted to see you all week,' she said. 'I've glanced out of my bedroom window a few times, in the hope of seeing you.'

'That's a bit stalker like, isn't it?'

Her lips were about two inches from mine. 'Piss off,' she said, before placing them on my mouth.

We had sex in the car that night, both of us conscious we were in a car park. Then, we talked for about fifteen minutes before she said, 'I better go.' I drove her nearer to her car; she collected her bags from the back seat and quickly walked away, head down.

Chapter Ten

I stepped past Kate into her hallway, as she quickly closed the door behind me. Without speaking, we both walked into the dining room. She pulled me to her, and we fell. Her back landed against the wall. My hands moved over her body as she ran her fingers through my hair, holding me against her, kissing me urgently.

The doorbell sounded loudly through the house, dragging us from the moment. Shocked by the interruption, I asked her, 'Who is it?'

'How the hell should I know?'

Kate smoothed out the creases in her clothes as I used my fingers to manipulate my hair back into place. 'At least we know it's not Stuart.'

She looked confused.

'He'd use his key,' I clarified.

'Let's hope so.'

She checked herself in the mirror on the wall and walked back down the hallway.

I circled the dining table, checking my lips for traces of her lipstick in my reflection.

It was the voice of a charity collector at the door, selling good deeds with sad stories. I stood out of view, listening to the conversation. Kate politely declined, stating she already had a direct debit set up for another charity close to her heart. By the time she returned, I'd walked another lap of the room and closed the curtains. The darkened room surprised her.

'I didn't want a neighbour to see us from the back,' I offered, pointing towards the now covered window.

'Good point,' she said.

We were shaken up by the doorbell's lingering echo and a nervous energy had infected the room.

Slowly, we moved back to each other, hoping to recapture the intensity of the seconds before we were interrupted.

Two steps from each other my mobile phone rang.

'For fuck's sake,' I said as I pulled the phone out of my pocket and checked the name and number flashing on the screen. 'It's my mate, Jordan. I'll just send it to voicemail.'

'No. It's OK, take it. I think the moment's gone.' Kate was smiling, but I could tell she was as disappointed as I was. She walked into the kitchen as I pressed the answer button. 'Hello.'

'He's signed.'

'Serious?'

'Yeah. Done deal. Twenty-seven million or something.'

It was Tuesday, 31 August, 2004, transfer deadline day. Jordan was talking about Wayne Rooney signing for Manchester United.

We'd been following the story for the last couple of days, exchanging phone calls and texts with updates.

'Good news, mate. Thanks for letting me know.'

'Where are you?'

'Why?' I asked defensively.

'You're rushing off. Thought you'd want to talk about the biggest transfer news of the last few years.'

I thought on my feet, looking through to the kitchen at Kate who was sat at the table reading a newspaper. 'I'm just in from work, mate. I'm stood in my room naked. Just about to get in the shower.'

Kate looked up and smiled, shaking her head. I mouthed the words, 'I'm sorry.'

'Well, thanks for that image, mate,' Jordan said loudly. 'Just what I want in my mind. Your little penis.'

'Shut up.'

'I'll leave you to it. I'm off to Charlotte's.' Jordan had been doing a lot of that since taking her to town the previous week.

'Bye.' I put the phone down, looked at Kate, and apologised again.

'It's fine,' she said. 'It's not easy to get time together with all this sneaking around is it?'

'No,' I said. 'It's not.'

THE NEXT MORNING, I sat in the van reading about Wayne Rooney's transfer on the back page of a newspaper. My dad drove us to a fencing supplier to pick up some panels, embarrassingly singing along to Girls Aloud's 'Love Machine' at the top of his voice.

I felt my phone vibrate against my leg.

'I'm just a love machine,' my dad shouted, tapping his palm on the steering wheel.

'Hello,' I answered and leant across to turn down the radio.

'Hey,' Dad exclaimed. 'I was enjoying that.'

'I'm on the phone,' I said. 'Hello,' I repeated.

'It's me,' Melissa said. 'Can you hear me?'

'Yeah. Sorry, my dad was living it up to Girls Aloud.'

Melissa laughed. 'He's so cool.'

'Don't tell him that.'

The van slowed down and turned into a small gravel car park.

'What you up to tomorrow night?'

'Nothing, why?' The van started going backwards into the space between two other rusting vans with names of landscaping firms painted on the side.

'My cousin, Jane, is getting married in three weeks. I need a dress. I want a male opinion.'

'And?'

'OK, I want your male opinion.'

'Where?'

'The Trafford Centre.' An image of my last visit there flashed through my mind.

The door slammed as Dad got out of the van. 'So, what you're saying is you want me to walk all over the Trafford Centre while you go in a hundred different shops trying on a million different dresses, only to go back and buy the first one you tried on.'

'Yeah. It'll be fun.'

'Why me?'

'Because I know if something looks rubbish, you'll tell me.'

We made arrangements to meet the following night. I turned the radio back-up to find Britney Spears had replaced Girls Aloud. I switched it off and read the rest of the paper.

The van door opened again and my dad got back in. 'The panels are ready,' he said, pointing to a heavy blue corrugated metal door that had been pulled to one side, leaving half of the building open. Inside stood rows of concrete fence posts and piles of wooden panels.

My dad started the van again and manoeuvred it over to the opening. We jumped out and went inside, where a staff member was waiting with an order sheet.

'Over here,' he said, walking across to our order.

Dad checked the goods, signed for them, and we began loading the van.

'Your brother starts back at school on Monday,' he said as we heaved a post in the air, finding a comfortable carrying position.

'That's gone quick.'

'Barely seen him all summer.'

'He's in love,' I joked.

'He's in lust, it's different.' We placed the post on the van, then walked back to get the next one. 'You think he's OK, your brother?'

'Yeah,' I replied, wondering where this was going.

'Good. I worry about him sometimes. He's gone quiet recently. Very *in* himself.'

'Seems OK to me,' I said, trying to sound convincing and non-committal at the same time.

'Just keep an eye on him will you. He'll talk to you before he talks to me. I embarrass him, I think.'

'That'll be the renditions of 'Love Machine'. You embarrass me with that too.'

'Piss off.'

PETER EVANS' FACE broke into a disarming smile as he realised it was me stood on his doorstep.

'Hello, Tom,' Melissa's dad said. He stepped backwards and showed me inside. 'How've you been?'

'Good thanks,' I replied, moving into the hallway.

'Go through, go through,' he said almost pushing me towards the kitchen. 'Carol is in there.'

As I walked through to the kitchen, I heard him shout, 'Mel,' up the stairs. I found Melissa's mum at the kitchen table, an empty plate in front of her, along with a half-drunk glass of white wine.

'Hello, love,' she said. 'We're just finishing dinner.'

Peter sat back down and poured himself another glass of wine. 'You want a drink?' he asked.

'No thanks, I'm good.' I stood in the kitchen, unsure whether to sit down or not. 'Melissa not ready?'

'She's just coming.'

'You sure you don't want a drink?' Carol said. 'A juice or something?'

I shook my head. 'No thanks.'

'What are you up to these days?' Peter asked, sipping his wine.

'Just working for my dad and trying to get some money together for travelling.'

'Oh yes. Melissa mentioned you were going away. Where was it again?'

I repeated my planned route. 'Thailand, Vietnam, Cambodia, Australia, New Zealand.'

'Amazing. Have you booked anything?'

Another shake of the head. 'I'm working on it.'

'Good for you,' Peter said.

Carol stood up and started clearing the plates away. 'How are your mum and dad?'

'Good thanks. It's all working and soap operas. You know how it is.'

Peter and Carol laughed, almost in unison.

'Feels like ages since we've seen you,' Carol said.

'Yeah. It's been a while,' I said.

I heard the thud of Melissa's footsteps running down the stairs. She burst into the kitchen wearing jeans and a simple blue T-shirt. In her hand she had a grey zip-up hooded top she'd bought from the gym she'd joined. Smiling, she pushed her arms through the sleeves.

'Hi,' she said, grabbing her handbag off the back of the chair. 'You ready?'

'If you are,' I said.

She zipped up the loose-fitting top and said, 'Let's go.'

I smiled at Peter and Carol. 'Nice to see you.'

'Bye, Tom. See you soon.'

MY SHOPPING EXPERIENCE with Melissa as just friends felt no different to the ones we'd had as a couple, apart from the fact joke insults didn't end with a kiss. We walked the length of the Trafford Centre, stopping at every window with a dress in it. I'd point at a dress modelled by a mannequin and ask, 'What about that one?'

Melissa would consider it for half a second before replying, 'No. It's not what I'm looking for.' The first time she said it I naively asked what she was looking for. Her response, 'I'll know when I see it.'

Several times we did the rounds of every wall inside a shop, but nothing grabbed her.

In one shop, Melissa thrust her handbag into my arms and pulled three or four dresses from rails, held them in front of her, studied herself in a full-length mirror. She discarded two, then searched for a fitting room. I followed her as she disappeared behind a curtain and placed myself in a comfy leather chair.

The sound of curtain rings sliding across the metal pole prompted me to look up, and I saw Melissa transformed. The hooded gym top, T-shirt and jeans had been replaced with an elegant dark blue dress that showed off her newly toned body perfectly. It wasn't too short but stopped before her knees, revealing tanned, lean legs.

'What do you think?' she said.

I nodded. 'It's nice. Very nice.'

She stood on the tiptoes of her bare feet. 'try to image it with heels.' She relaxed back down to her normal size and turned to face herself in the fitting room mirror. She smoothed the dress down and tried to get a view of herself from all angles.

I noticed her face change slightly. 'What's wrong?'

'I'm not sure about it.'

'Why not? It's really nice.'

'I'm not sure I like the colour. I was thinking of something lighter.'

'I like it,' I said.

'I like it too. It's just the colour. It's not what I had in mind.'

'No harm in changing your mind,' I said. 'If the dress is right.'

She went back up on her toes and did a full turn, her head almost fixed in position to look in the mirror. 'I'll put it in the maybe pile.'

'What if someone buys it?'

'I'll ask them to put it away for me.' She reached to the back of the dress and started to unzip it, pulling the curtain shut with the other hand.

'You can do that?'

'Yeah,' she said from behind the curtain. 'They'll put it away for a couple of hours and if I don't come back, they'll put it on the rail again.'

'Well, you learn something new,' I said.

I stood in the men's section looking at jeans I had no intention of buying. Melissa, back in jeans and hooded top, carried the dress to the counter and passed it to the woman behind the till.

A male shop assistant approached me and asked, 'Can I help you?'

'No thanks. Just looking.'

'We've got some more jeans over there,' he persisted, pointing to another section of the store.

'Thanks,' I said.

He stood about two feet from me, not moving.

'Are you ready?' Melissa said, touching me on the arm.

'Sorry, mate,' I said, making a show of her arrival. 'The good lady awaits.'

We left the shop quickly.

'The good lady awaits?' she quoted, taking the piss.

'I needed a get out,' I protested. 'He was just going to stand looking at me until I bought something.'

'Maybe he fancied you.'

We separated to walk around a family who were spread out across the whole walkway with their pushchairs and shopping bags.

'Can't blame him.'

'You think a lot of yourself,' she said, touching my arm.

We walked with purpose through the crowd of evening shoppers, stepping left and right when needed to avoid crashing into on-comers.

'If you're walking this quickly to avoid all the dress shops, you'll be very disappointed. I know where they all are.'

'Do you not think I've learnt over the years that stopping you from shopping is a skill I don't possess?'

She laughed and linked my arm, which didn't feel uncomfortable. We walked for another few steps, past a bright pink HMV sign before Melissa put her other arm lightly on my shoulder and said, 'Not so fast.' She manoeuvred my body sideways into another women's clothes shop.

'Careful,' I said to her, my feet going the opposite way to where my body headed. I laughed for about half a second before I realised I'd nearly bumped into a man coming out of the shop.

'All right, mate. Calm down. No need to get physical,' he said. I heard him say it but didn't see him speak the words. I was looking to his left at his wife. Kate.

There are no words to describe how uncomfortable the following moments were. A swarm of thoughts infested my mind. I looked from Kate to Stuart and back again. Seeing them so out of context disorientated me, and once the thoughts in my mind started to spin, I almost felt dizzy. Stuart and Kate my neighbours. Stuart, Kate's husband. Kate, Stuart's wife. Kate, who I was having an affair with. We were all stood in the Trafford Centre, blocking the entrance of a shop. I quickly looked at Kate and tried to gauge her reaction to the situation. Her face gave away no hint of her feelings, although she later told me that her heart was beating like a hammer against the inside of her chest.

I realised I hadn't said anything which in itself would look like strange behaviour to Stuart and Melissa. 'Hi,' I managed slowly. Then too quickly, 'I didn't see you there, mate.' I placed my hand on Stuart's shoulder.

'You OK?'

'Yeah.' I nodded. My thoughts started to reduce in speed and focus returned. 'You just doing a bit of shopping?'

He held up a couple of bags.

'Sorry,' I said, remembering Melissa. 'Melissa, this is Stuart and his wife, Kate. They live across the road.' Finishing the introduction, I said, 'Stuart, Kate this is Melissa my' –I paused, the correct description escaping me. I settled on – 'friend.'

'Hi,' Melissa said, smiling at both of them. 'Nice to meet you.'

Kate said to Melissa, 'Are you dragging him round the shops?'

'Yeah. I'm looking for a dress for my cousin's wedding.'

'Found anything?'

'One potential. Just making sure it's the right one.'

Stuart gave me a knowing look. 'We'll leave you to it, then. Can't have you wasting precious shopping time standing here chatting.'

'Ignore him,' Kate said. 'He loves shopping.'

Anxious to end the conversation, I said, 'OK, see you later,' but at the same time Stuart spoke, saying, 'You watching England on Saturday?'

'Maybe, you?'

'Maybe. I'm busy at the moment so might have to work all day Saturday. Might watch it at home.'

Kate interjected. 'Good luck with the dress.' Then to Stuart. 'Let's leave these two to it.' She moved past us and joined the steady stream of shoppers on the main concourse.

'She seems nice,' Melissa said.

'She is.'

Despite more browsing, Melissa found nothing that was as nice as the blue dress, so we walked the length of the shopping centre to go back and buy that one. As we were leaving the shop, she suggested getting some food, offering to pay as a thank you for my help.

The waitress in the American diner we chose dropped menus in front of us, took our drinks orders, and went away in under twenty seconds. We studied the food options in silence then placed our menus down.

I looked around; waiters and waitresses dressed in polo shirts and baseball caps weaved in and out of tables carrying trays above their heads, flashing friendly smiles for tips. The barman was flipping bottles and pouring cocktails.

'This has been fun,' Melissa said.

'Yeah, it has.'

Our waitress reappeared and laid down drinks. She pulled a pad from her back pocket, scribbled down our order before racing off again, collecting empty plates from another table and going through swing doors to the kitchen.

'Will you come to this wedding with me?' Melissa asked. Before I could answer, she launched into an explanation about why she'd asked. 'My invite says to Melissa and guest, which was intended to be for Andy, but given that we're not together anymore' – her eyes dropped from mine – 'well, that makes things difficult. Emma's bringing Mark, and Mum and Dad will have each other. You know my family really well.' Her words were spilling out and I could tell she'd rehearsed the argument a few times.

'Is that a good idea?'

'Yeah. Of course, it is.' She smiled. 'It'll be fun. I really don't want to go on my own.'

'We'll just spend the day fielding questions from your family about whether we are back together or not.'

She sipped Coke through a straw, making me wait for her answer. 'No, we won't. It'll be fine. We'll know we're there as friends.'

I tried to think, but my mind kept going back to the same question. What will Kate say?

KATE RANG EARLY the next morning.

'What are you doing tomorrow afternoon?'

'Nothing.'

'Do you know where Hayes Road is?'

'Yeah.'

'Good. Meet me there at half-past one. Number thirty-six.'

And then she was gone.

ON SATURDAY, I slept late. I hadn't contacted Kate all day on Friday despite intrigue encouraging me. I tried to act normal around the house. As I watched *Soccer AM* with my brother, my insides churned with excitement and anxiety.

At about half twelve, I had a sandwich and then dressed. Leaving the house, I looked down the road to Kate's house. Only Stuart's car was parked on the driveway.

The address was just over a mile away, so I decided to walk. It was a nice day; blue sky and a warm breeze. I nodded a hello to a neighbour washing his car. I'd known him for years but didn't know his name.

'All right?' he asked.

'Yeah. You?'

'Very good.'

'Nice day for it,' I said, acknowledging his car.

'Yep.'

On I walked. As I got closer to Hayes Road, my excitement turned to something else. Worry. At no point since the phone call with Kate the previous morning had I thought this might be a setup. But walking, alone with my thoughts focused on my destination, questions punched my mind like a boxer's fist against a speed ball. Did Stuart know? Was I being set up and walking into an ambush? Why had Kate not been in touch since she rang me?

I tried to be rational. Stuart's car was at his house and I hadn't seen it pass me on the road. But he could've taken a different route or gone in Kate's car.

I felt sick.

Approaching a row of shops, I went into a newsagent's and bought a bottle of water. I drank it outside, watching two men in work clothes carrying a fridge into an empty shop. The place used to be a barber shop where my dad got his hair cut, but it looked like it was being transformed into yet another takeaway. The remaining red letters of the barber shop's name were being scratched off the window by a third man.

Hayes Road was a long suburban street. Tall, narrow Victorian houses stood to attention in rows along each side of the road. All had basement windows poking out from below concrete front gardens. I decided to do a loop of the road, taking in the detail of the house number I was supposed to meet Kate in. I walked on the other side of the road, past a dad struggling to get a new baby seat into the back of a car.

The house I wanted was in the middle of the street. Kate's car was parked outside. I noticed the bedroom curtains were closed. There was no sign of movement downstairs. I continued walking until I came to a small side road. I stopped and took out my mobile. Realising I would look stupid just turning around and walking back I crossed the road and kept moving forward. I dialled Kate's number and she answered after three rings.

'Hi,' she said, her voice casual.

'I'm nearly here.'

'I've left the front door open. Come straight in.'

I crossed over and turned back, my head down slightly to avoid eye contact with any neighbours looking out into the street. At Kate's car, I quickly turned up the small path that lead to the front door and pushed it open gently. I closed it quietly behind me and took in my surroundings. There were two doors off the hallway, the front one closed and the back one open. The back one seemed to lead to the dining room. There was a set of stairs directly in front of me.

Photos lined the hallway. I scanned the faces but didn't recognise any. The majority of them were of a smiling couple in different scenarios: on a beach, at a restaurant, on their wedding day. More wedding photos led me further into the house. Parents stood formally in wedding suits looking proud. Kate's face stood out in one. Dressed in a bridesmaid's outfit, she and three others stood next to the bride, holding flowers, and laughing naturally at something unseen in the photograph.

The house was quiet and I realised my thoughts of being ambushed were paranoid. Stuart would surely have confronted me as I entered the house. I heard the closing of a cupboard in another room.

'Hello,' I said, trying to keep my voice level.

The dining room connected the hallway and the kitchen. I moved slowly through into the dining room as Kate entered it from the kitchen at the other end. She smiled and I relaxed.

'Hi.'

'Hi.'

'Where are we?'

'My friend Amy's house. She's gone to the Lake District for the weekend and asked me if I'd feed the cat for them.'

'Oh. I see. I thought you might be luring me to my death.'

She laughed and her eyes lit up. 'Don't be stupid.'

THAT AFTERNOON WE lay in Amy's bed, looking up at the ceiling. Our clothes were discarded across the floor or hanging over the ironing board Amy had forgotten to put away before leaving the previous night.

Kate leant across and laid her head on my chest. We enjoyed the silence for a while.

'Was that Melissa your ex-girlfriend we saw on Thursday?' she asked eventually.

'Yeah,' I said.

'She's pretty.'

'Yeah, she is.'

'I think she still fancies you.'

'How can you tell that from meeting us in that awkward situation for two minutes?'

Kate moved from my shoulder and we leant on our arms, facing each other.

'Easily.'

'So, do you think she noticed that me and you are having an affair? Do you think she could tell you were going to ring me the next morning and get to meet you at your friend's house for sex?'

'Of course not. I could tell by the way she was touching you as she pushed you into the shop. And how her face showed a flicker of hurt when you just called her your friend.'

I laughed and leant back on the pillow, finding the same spot on the ceiling to focus on.

'What are you laughing at?'

'Nothing.'

'Tell me. What's funny?'

'She asked me to go to the wedding with her.'

'Which wedding?'

'The one we were dress shopping for. Her cousin's. After we bumped into you, we went for some food and she asked me to go to the wedding. I was unsure about it. She was adamant it would just be as friends.'

Kate started to tease. 'But you think you're so irresistible she'll fall for you all over again.'

'No,' I said. 'We slept together a while ago. Which you know because you saw what her boyfriend did to my face. When I told her I didn't want to get back with her after that happened, she put the phone down on me. I guess I sort of worried that she wasn't over us.' I sighed. 'This is ridiculous. Talking to you about this.' I paused, looking for words to describe our situation. 'When we're here. The whole thing is stupid. I've told her I just want to be mates. She's a big girl. She can handle it.'

'Are you going to the wedding?'

'I said I would.'

'Why don't you want to get back with her?'

'Lots of reasons.'

'Such as?'

I turned to face her. 'You.'

We spent the next hour talking and laughing, forgetting the world existed. There was no mention of Stuart or Melissa, no thought of whose bed we were in and how inappropriate it was.

Later, as we dressed, I said, 'This has been nice. Seeing you properly, I mean.'

She stepped back into the dress she'd been wearing, covering her black underwear. 'I know. It's much better than the Trafford Centre car park and snatched lunchtime phone calls.'

'Where does Stuart think you are?' The mention of him broke the magic of the past couple of hours. I felt like a dick-head for ruining it. 'Sorry,' I said in a low voice.

'He's working. I told him I might go shopping in Manchester.' I pulled the T-shirt over my head and scanned the floor for my socks.

'I think you should leave first,' Kate said. 'I'll sort this room out.'

Chapter Eleven

I told my dad a lie.

On the way home from work, he had asked me what I was doing that night and I told him I was going into town with a girl from uni.

When we got home, I showered, changed, and threw the tea my mum had made down my neck like someone was going to take it off me. Grabbing my keys, I got in the car and drove out of the suburbs, down the motorway, up the A6 to Buxton, a town normally forty minutes from home. It took me over an hour in rush hour traffic.

I pulled into the entrance of the Bear's Claw pub and noticed she was already there. I parked on the other side of the car park, locked the car, and walked into the pub.

It was quiet inside. I looked around at the interior of dark, low wooden beams and small round tables. High stools with thick red velvet tops were lined in front of the bar. A couple of them were occupied with old men drinking bitter. One read the local newspaper, the other spoke to the barman, a lad in his early twenties with hair down over his ears, like the front man of a band. There was a table of two middle-aged couples ordering food from a young blonde waitress.

Kate was sitting in the corner behind a thin white pillar reading a book.

She looked up and gave a small wave when she saw me. I walked over and, confident of not being caught, gave her a kiss.

'Fancy meeting you here,' I said.

'Fancy.'

We kissed again for a few seconds longer.

'You want a drink?'

'No thanks,' she replied, pointing to a small glass of red wine on the table next to her mobile phone. 'I didn't know how long you'd be.' She placed the book down next to it.

'I'll just get mine.'

I returned with a pint and sat down on a wooden chair, pulling it further round the table to be closer to her.

She leant forward slightly and touched my knee with her hand.

'So.'

'So.'

Our hands moved together, and we just sat for a second, enjoying the moment.

'How long have you been here?' I asked.

'About ten minutes.'

'Traffic was busy, wasn't it?'

'Yeah.'

She squeezed my hand. I squeezed back, and we giggled like school kids who had got away with not doing homework.

'I can't believe we're here.'

'I know. It's weird.'

I took a drink from my pint. She sipped her wine.

'What are you reading?'

She held up Nick Hornby's *About a Boy*.

'Any good?'

'So far. Only read about a hundred pages.'

'I've seen the film.'

'You like it?'

'It was OK. Passed a couple of hours.'

'But it was no *Gladiator*?'

'No, it was not. A girl I lived with at uni made me go see it with her one afternoon when it first came out. She loved the book and was desperate to see it but hated the idea of being in the cinema on her own, so she dragged me along.'

'Why would she not go to the cinema on her own?'

'No idea. Just funny about it. Said she felt like people were staring at her. Would you go on your own?'

'Yes. You?'

'Definitely. It's only like watching a film in your house on your own. Once the lights are off, you're only staring at the screen. You're not supposed to talk to people anyway when the film's on.'

'Exactly. I think people think if you're going to the cinema on your own you must be some kind of social outcast.'

'It's the guys with the holes in the bottom of the popcorn boxes giving everyone a bad name.'

Kate laughed, covering her mouth with her hand to keep the wine in. As her laughter faded, she said, 'What was your set up like a uni? How many people did you live with?'

'I was in halls in the first year. That's where I met my main set of mates. Sean, Matt, John, and me all lived next door to each other. It's weird that we all got on so well. But I guess it's just one of those things. We all used to go out together, play football, just hang out in each other's rooms. The doors were always open. Then in the second year we got a house, but there were six of us. Matt met this girl in first year, Michelle. They started going out together and when it came for looking for somewhere to live, we found this massive Victorian town house thing with six bedrooms. We all loved it but couldn't afford it between four of us so Matt asked Michelle and her mate, Beth – the girl I went to see *About a Boy* with – if they wanted the other rooms.'

'So, there were four lads and two girls?'

'Yeah. It was like a sitcom at times. I used to feel sorry for Matt because Michelle was his girlfriend and we were his mates and he used to be a bit stuck in the middle. She'd be like 'come and hang out with me', and we'd be like, 'let's go to the pub'. And he'd be torn.'

'Who did he choose?'

'He tried his best to keep the balance. But she gave him sex, which none of us were prepared to offer. She's great. They're still together. They've moved to London so she can do teacher training down there. Her family is from Reading or somewhere.'

'Are you missing uni?'

I thought about it for a while. 'Yeah, I am. I miss my mates a lot. We speak on the phone and there is always email banter going around, but I'm finding it a bit difficult not being there if I'm honest.'

'How so?'

'I don't know. I spent three years with them. They were like my family I suppose. I love my mates here, in Manchester, but the ones I met at uni, I don't know.' I paused. 'I'm not describing it very well. It's just they get me more, I think. I've changed a bit in the last three years. They were part of that.'

'I understand.' She rubbed her hand over mine softly.

'What about you?'

'Me? I stayed in Manchester for university. Halls for the first year like you. Then moved in with two girls off my course. We had this horrible little terraced house in Fallowfield. It was always freezing, even in the summer. But it was close to bus routes to town, so it made our nights out easy.'

'Do you still see any of your uni friends?'

'Amy is one of them. The pregnant one.'

We avoided any further description of Amy and the fact we'd spent an afternoon together at her house.

'What about the other girl?'

'Lauren. Not so much. She moved to Tenerife about six years ago. She got married and divorced quite quickly. She spent a few years just doing crappy jobs and not being sure what to do with herself. Then she met a guy one Christmas Eve in a pub near her parents' house in Chester. He did maintenance on apartment blocks in Tenerife. They hit it off and within three months, she was living there. She loves it. Speaks the language which helps. Made a real effort. She runs a small cleaning company now. Offices, apartments, that sort of thing.'

'Sounds good. What was uni like for you?'

'Normal, really. Late nights, bad food, hockey on Wednesdays.'

'You played hockey?'

'Yeah. Just in the second team. I had to stop at the end of my second year.'

'Did your mum make you stop so you could do all your homework?'

'No,' she said. 'I injured my knee.'

More seriously, I asked, 'What happened?'

'I tore the ligaments during a game,' she said with a philosophical shrug. 'It was near the end of the year. I had an operation and spent most of the summer on crutches.'

'That's terrible. What did you do?'

'Read a lot. Watched a lot of videos.'

'Do you have a scar?'

Kate nodded. 'Want to see?'

I looked under the table as she moved her grey skirt upwards, revealing her left knee. She pointed to a small scar, about an inch and a half long. I reached out and ran my finger along it.

We jumped as her phone vibrated on the table. Instinctively, I pulled my hand from her knee, as if the caller could see us.

'It's my sister,' she said, speaking directly to my internal fear it was Stuart.

Conscious that the phone's volume was drawing more attention in the quiet pub, I said, 'Answer it.'

'Hello,' Kate said into the phone. The conversation was short. Kate listened, asked a couple of questions and then ended it by saying, 'I'm just in the middle of something. I'll have a think and call you back.'

She placed the phone back on the table and said, 'I'm sorry about that. My mum is sixty next year and my sister wanted to talk about arranging a family reunion.'

'Older or younger sister?'

'Older. Joanne.'

'Are you close?'

She weighed the question in her mind. 'Yeah. We weren't when we were younger, but we are now. We used to fight like cat and dog.'

'With hockey sticks?'

Kate laughed. 'No. She wasn't into sport. Joanne always wanted to be a pop star. Rachel, my younger sister, and I used to mess up her dance routines.'

'Did you not experience middle child syndrome?'

'No. My parents were pretty good. They shared out their time between all of us. Family holidays were always in a villa somewhere with a pool, so it was just the five of us. No friends invited or anything.'

'That must have been fun.'

'It was,' she said. 'Happy families.'

Our drinks were empty. I stood up. 'What would you like?'

'I'll have a soft drink. Fresh orange, please.'

I walked to the bar. The long-haired barman stopped his conversation immediately and took my order. 'Two orange juices, mate, please.'

I turned back and looked at Kate who had picked up her book again. I noticed a small crease ran along her forehead as she concentrated on the words.

'Two orange juices,' the barman said. I handed him a fiver and he tapped buttons on the till before it pinged open. He slid the change out and gave it to me. I watched his eyes, trying to see if he was judging the scenario he was looking at in the corner. He just turned back to the regular at the bar.

I carried the drinks back to the table and placed them next to our empty glasses. 'Am I boring you so much you couldn't wait to get back to your book?'

'Not at all. I take a book everywhere with me. I feel a bit on show just sat around waiting. Especially somewhere like this.'

I don't know, even now, if she meant somewhere like this as in having an affair or somewhere like this as in a small local pub with hardly any customers. I never asked her to clarify. We both knew what we were doing; it was always there in the back of our minds, a cloud on the horizon, waiting to rain. The truth was this: I was enjoying myself, tucked away in the corner of that small pub out in the middle of nowhere, talking to her, spending time with her. It was easy to pretend we were a new couple going through the exciting early moments of a new relationship, getting to know each other and starting to fit into each other's lives. I look back on that night in Buxton, and the Saturday we spent at Amy's house as the times where the tectonic plates of our affair shifted. Those hours spent talking about our lives, our histories, how they shaped us, made the whole thing about more than just sex. Sat there on small wooden chairs, drinking fresh orange juice somehow made it all feel more like a real date. It was easy to forget she had a husband, and that he was someone I knew, someone I liked. I didn't care why she was here, why she'd made the decision she had done, at that very moment in time I was just glad she had.

'How are you finding working for your dad?' Kate asked.

'Strangely enough, I'm enjoying myself.'

'Why strangely?'

'I made a bit of a vow to myself that I wouldn't work for him. I was determined to stand alone. Get a job and stand on my own two feet and all that. I always thought it was a bit easy to just go and work for him.'

'Really? I wouldn't say that. If you work hard, what does it matter where the job comes from? People get jobs because of family and friends all the time.'

I tried to find the right words. 'I'm the first person in my family to go to uni. I think my dad was probably expecting me to come back and get a good job straight away. Now I worry he's thinking that I spent three years of my life pissing it up the wall in Leeds and I've come back and gone, "Can I have a job please, Daddy?"'

I took a long gulp of orange juice.

'Didn't he offer you a job?'

'Yeah. But I can't help but wonder whether he did it to get me off my arse and out of the house.' I shook my head. 'Yet despite all that, I really love it. The days are quite varied, it's not just sat down all day tapping numbers into a computer like that temp job I had. And given what I've just said about my dad, we're actually getting on pretty well. He's quite funny when he wants to be. Although he does have an unhealthy obsession with Girls Aloud.'

Kate laughed. 'Really?'

'Yeah. Not in a pervy way either. He loves their music.' I described him singing in the van, blasting out the words at the top of his voice.

She laughed again, a softer version of the crease in her forehead appeared. 'What are you working on at the moment?'

'We started a job yesterday which we'll be on for the next couple of weeks. This old couple retired about a year ago and have spent an absolute fortune on doing up their house. Now they want the garden redesigning. We're bricking the driveway, adding in flower beds, decking, a pond. Everything. My dad has gone round and had a look at it and then came up with all the ideas. They liked them and just told him to get on with it. This is the first time I get to see a project from start to finish.'

'I saw your brother yesterday, hanging around outside the park when I was driving home from work.'

'Was he wrapped around a skinny dark-haired girl?'

'Yeah.'

'That's Laura, his girlfriend.'

'Is she nice?'

'I'm not sure. We hardly see her. He spends most of his time at her house. Mum has tried to get him to invite her round for Sunday dinner and all that, but he's just not having it. Last time I saw her, the pair of them were stoned out of their minds on the couch in the living room.'

'Honestly?' She laughed. 'What did you say?'

'Nothing. Not much I can say. We've all done it. I had a bit of a word with him the next day, just checking where he was getting it from, and told him to make sure it didn't affect his schoolwork. Tried to be a good big brother.'

'Do you still smoke it?'

'Not really. I did a bit when I was younger. Nothing major though.'

'I've not smoked it for years,' she said.

'How long?'

'God, I can't remember the last time. Maybe Knebworth actually.' Her voice trailed off and I realised a figure was standing over us.

'Can I just take these off you, folks?' the barman said as he picked up the empty pint and wine glass I'd not taken back to the bar.

'Sure,' Kate said.

'Everything all right for you?' he asked.

'Fine, mate, thanks,' I answered, very aware of Kate's hand resting on mine on top of the table.

'If you need anything else let me know.' He turned and walked back to the bar.

After a moment of silence, I asked, 'Did you like smoking it?'

'Loved it. I couldn't smoke it every day like some people did, but when I smoked it now and then, I used to really enjoy it. But then' – she put on a serious voice and wagged her finger at me – 'I grew up, got a career, a mortgage, and realised the error of my misspent youth.'

She excused herself to use the toilet, and I watched her walk across the pub. I noticed the back of her work shirt was hanging over her skirt.

Sat alone I felt very on show. I picked up the book and studied the back of it, remembering the characters from the film as I read the detail. I placed it down and turned to look around the pub. I wondered what our story would look like to the other customers. Did we look like a couple of office workers out for a quiet drink? An early date in a new relationship? Was the ten-year age gap obvious? Did the barman notice Kate's wedding ring? Or my lack of one?

Kate returned and finished the last bit of orange juice in her glass. 'I think I should be heading back.'

'Good idea,' I said, rising from my chair.

She stood and put on her light grey suit jacket, placed the book inside her handbag and her arm through its handles. We walked purposely to the door.

'Thanks now,' the barman said. I gave him a half-nodded thanks back.

Outside, the temperature had dropped a few degrees. I walked Kate to her car, told her I needed to stop for petrol so wouldn't follow her home.

'OK,' she said. 'Probably best.'

I stepped forward and quickly kissed her on the mouth. Pulling away, I looked at her and said, 'I had a nice time tonight.'

'Me too,' she said.

She took her keys out of her bag and pressed a button. There was a short click as the doors unlocked. She opened the door and got in, touching me with her free hand as she did. I closed the door for her and she started the engine.

As I got into my car, she'd reversed out of the space and was on her way home.

Chapter Twelve

'Careful,' my dad shouted. 'Watch the bloody car.'

I stopped dead, struggling to hold the fence panel I was carrying. My muscles burnt as I tried to manoeuvre the panel away from the BMW without scratching the passenger door. Dad rushed over and took it from me, moving it to the other side of the driveway, leaning it against the house. The car belonged to the neighbour of the house we were working on.

'What the hell are you doing?' he snapped. 'I told you if you couldn't manage it to get me to help you.'

I felt about eight years old, being shouted at for leaving my Lego all over the floor when my auntie Linda and uncle John were coming for Sunday dinner. I lowered my eyes to the floor and said, 'I thought I could manage it.'

'Well, you know what thought did,' Dad said.

I methodically checked along the blue paintwork of the BMW's door for any signs of damage, relieved to find there weren't any.

Together, we picked the panel up and moved it into the garage at the bottom of the driveway where we were storing the materials for the job.

'You've been away with the bloody fairies all day. What's the matter with you?'

'Nothing,' I said.

He took a tenner out of his wallet and said, 'Go to the shops and get us some lunch.'

'Mum made us sandwiches.'

'And I'm sure they're lovely, but I wouldn't mind fish and chips. If you want your sandwiches, no problem.'

I took the money and walked towards the road. 'Oh, and, Tom,' my dad shouted.

I turned back, and he said, 'Don't tell your mother.'

Obviously, I was lying about nothing being wrong.

I took out my phone and re-read, for the hundredth time, a message from Kate.

Really, really sorry. Not going to make it. Stuart has changed his plans xxx

I'd received it the previous night when I was getting ready to go and meet her. Stuart was supposed to be going out for a few drinks with the lads and we had arranged to meet up in another pub well away from home. I'd found the message waiting for me as I stepped out of the shower, half an hour before I was due to leave.

Walking to the chip shop, I dialled her number. She answered straight away but said, 'I'll call you back in five minutes,' before the line went dead.

I carried on walking, my phone in my hand, waiting for it to start ringing.

I stepped inside the chip shop and joined the long queue of Friday lunchtime customers. My phone began to ring and I quickly pressed the answer button, not taking any notice of who had called. I got a shock when Melissa's cheery 'hello' came down the line.

'Hi,' I said, wishing I'd checked the caller's name and not answered. 'What's up?'

'Nothing. Just checking everything is still OK for tomorrow.'

'Tomorrow?' I questioned.

'The wedding. Don't tell me you've forgotten.'

'No, no. I haven't. Sorry. Just didn't realise what day it was. Yeah. Everything is fine for tomorrow.'

'Are you OK?' she asked. 'You sound quiet.'

'I'm just in the chippy,' I improvised. 'There are a few people in here. I'm sure they don't want to hear my life story. What's the plan for tomorrow?'

'Well, I've just finished work and I'm going to Steph's salon. She's going to do my hair and nails. I'm going home to check I've got everything ready for tomorrow. Then Jane wants me and Emma to go to her house, because she and the bridesmaids are having a few drinks and she wants us to meet them.'

'What about tomorrow?'

'Dad wants to leave from ours at eleven. Can you be round for then?'

'Yeah.'

'Dad is taking Mark, Emma's boyfriend, out for a couple of drinks tonight while we're at Jane's. Do you want to go so you can meet him before tomorrow?'

While she talked, all I could think about was that Kate might be trying to phone me at this exact point.

'Hello,' Melissa said. 'Are you still there?'

'Yeah, sorry.'

'Well, do you want to?'

'To what?'

'Meet my dad and Mark for a drink tonight?'

I moved forward in the queue as another person got served. 'I can't. I'm meeting Jordan and Charlotte for a drink. I've not met her before.'

'Where?'

'The Boathouse.'

'That's where my dad's going.'

I was at the front of the queue.

'Oh. I've got to go, I'm being served.'

WALKING BACK TO the job, my phone alerted me to a voicemail. I pressed the number sequence to allow me to listen to a new message and held the phone tight to my ear as Kate's recorded voice said, 'Hi. Sorry about last night. Stuart's friend cancelled on short notice so he just dropped it on me that he was staying in instead. I wish I could've phoned you to explain but obviously it was difficult as Stuart was around all night. Anyway, we can arrange something soon. I'll call you when I can. Speak to you soon. Bye.'

THAT EVENING, I stood at the bar in the Boathouse with Jordan, who had his arms around his new girlfriend, Charlotte. Early evening Friday drinkers were spread out all around us. Sam, Jordan's brother, was chatting to a group of people from his office.

'We went to see baby Alex last night,' Jordan said.

'How is he?'

'Very cute,' Charlotte said.

'Which is strange because he looks like Neil,' Jordan added.

'I've not seen them for ages,' I said.

I drank from my pint.

Jordan said, 'I've been on that management course all week.'

'How's it going?'

'Honestly? It's pretty interesting. I've had some good reviews in a few of the exercises we've had to do. And we've had lunch provided all week.'

My phone rang, Melissa's name flashing on screen.

'Excuse me,' I said turning away from the noise of the pub. 'Hi,' I said into the phone.

'Why were you being shitty with me before?'

Taken back by the force of her words I responded defensively.

'Yes, you were.'

'Hold on,' I said. I quickened my step and made my way out to the car park, 'I wasn't being shitty with you,' I repeated.

'It felt like that. If you don't want to come to the wedding just say and I'll tell Jane you can't make it. But I don't want you coming to feel like you're doing me a favour because I'd rather go on my own.'

'Where's this coming from?' I said, trying to keep my voice calm.

'I've barely spoken to you since I asked you to come. And now, the day before, I ring you to arrange the details and you're off with me. If you're not interested in coming then just say and I'll go on my own.'

Her words sunk in. I realised I'd been a bit short with her earlier. It wasn't her fault I was waiting on Kate to call me. If I seriously thought we could carry on a normal friendship then I should do her the decency of at least acting like it.

'You're right,' I said. 'I'm sorry.'

The silence on the other end of the line made me think she wasn't expecting to hear those words. I continued, 'Look, I've been a bit off the last couple of weeks. I've not been myself. But I'm looking forward to tomorrow. We'll have loads of fun. I promise. I know it's a big deal for you and I won't fuck it up. OK?'

'You'd better not,' she said.

'What time is your dad bringing Mark out?'

'About half-past eight.'

I looked at my watch. It was quarter to seven.

'OK. I'll wait and have a drink with them.'

'Thanks,' she said.

THE NEXT MORNING Kate and I stood in the street, hiding in plain sight.

Kate had been on her way to the local shops, passing my house as I was leaving for the wedding. I was dressed in the dark suit I'd worn to my graduation, holding the jacket in my hand.

'You look nice,' she said as I walked to the end of my driveway.

'Thanks,' I said, making a show of checking myself over.

Stood about two feet apart we looked like two friendly neighbours sharing a few words on a pleasant Saturday morning. But I was very aware of the truth. My eyes darted around me, glancing at the front bedrooms of the houses behind Kate. The family at number nine passed us slowly in their car. We acknowledged them with a wave, keeping up the pretence.

'You looking forward to it?' she asked.

'Yes. It'll be nice to see everyone. Melissa's family, I mean. It should be a good laugh.'

Quietly, she said, 'I'm sorry about the other night.'

My senses heightened, aware that we were stood in our street, surrounded by houses filled with families, friends, and neighbours. I took a small step backwards. 'It's OK. I understand.'

'I wanted to see you but I couldn't just leave.'

'It's fine. I know this situation isn't easy.'

I wanted to kiss her, to hold her, to just be with her for a few uninterrupted minutes. We stood in silence, contemplating our next move.

'I should be getting off,' I said, motioning to my car.

'Yeah,' she said. 'Have a nice time. I need to get milk.'

MELISSA SMILED AT me, the tears in her eyes slowly starting to trickle down her cheek. I smiled back and went to wipe them away with my palm. She stopped me and said, 'Don't. You'll smudge my make-up.'

People were on their feet applauding all around us as the bride and groom kissed. When they finished, they turned to face their guests, both of their faces wearing smiles of people living in the happiness of the moment.

Melissa reached into her small handbag and took out a compact mirror and white tissue. Gently, she dabbed the tears away.

The church organist started playing music as the newlyweds walked down the aisle hand in hand. Family and friends waved hellos and wished congratulations. Flashes flashed from cameras, capturing every step of the walk. As they passed our row, the bride excitedly mouthed the words 'I'm married.' to Melissa, who blew her a kiss.

We filed out of the pews and stood in line to give our congratulations to the happy couple. I shook the groom's hand as Melissa pulled Jane towards her for a big swaying hug.

'Tom,' Jane said when she saw me, dragging me into a tight, welcoming hug. 'Thanks for coming.'

'Congratulations,' I managed to mumble into her shoulder.

Melissa's family were outside the church exchanging hugs, kisses, and handshakes with extended family members. I recognised grandparents, uncles, and cousins. I stood back with Mark, Melissa's sister's boyfriend, buttoning and unbuttoning my suit jacket, trying to make it comfortable. I adjusted my tie twice, using a car window as a mirror.

'Is this the first time you've met the whole family?' I asked Mark.

'All at once, yeah. I've met the grandparents once.' He paused. 'This must be a bit weird for you. Being the ex and all.'

I nodded. 'It is a bit.'

'They seem like good people,' he said. 'The family.'

'They are,' I answered. Melissa came over holding out a camera and said, 'Will you take a picture of me and Emma?'

Emma and Melissa stood together in a pose. I held the camera up and took the photograph, capturing them.

Melissa reached out and took the camera from me and handed it to her sister. 'Take one of me and Tom.' She moved next to me and slipped her arm around my back. I did the same to her and we smiled. Taking the camera back from her sister, she pressed a button and our image appeared on the small view screen. I leant into her to get a better look. We were stood looking comfortable in each other's arms, Melissa beautiful in the dress she'd bought on our shopping trip, me looking smart in my suit. The pose reminded me of hundreds of photos we'd had taken when were together; at parties, on holiday, on New Year's Eve. Smiling, arms wrapped around each other. Happy.

Half a second later she pulled the image away from my eye. 'Now Emma and Mark,' waving her sister and her boyfriend together.

'ARE YOU HAVING fun?' Melissa asked as we sipped Champagne in the bar of the spa hotel where the reception was taking place.

'Yeah,' I said.

Pockets of people had spread themselves around the room, dissecting the ceremony and catching up with family they'd not seen since the last wedding or birthday that had gathered them all together.

'Do you promise?'

'Yeah,' I said. 'Why do you keep asking?'

'No reason,' she said turning away slightly, her eyes taking in the room. She looked like she was contemplating saying something, but then decided against it.

The master of ceremonies tested his microphone and requested we all move through an open archway into the dining room. We carried our Champagne glasses through, following the rest of the guests. Ten round tables covered with crisp white tablecloths were set up throughout the room, matching the wedding's colour scheme. Name cards and wedding favours were placed in front of each place setting. The top table stretched out across the back of the room, awaiting the bride and groom's arrival.

When the guests were all seated the master of ceremonies returned, standing framed within the archway. He lifted the microphone to his lips and said, 'Ladies and gentleman, please be upstanding to welcome the newly married Mr and Mrs Sinclair.'

We rose to our feet and applauded as the smiling newlyweds made their way through the path between the round tables.

Although I'd not seen Melissa's grandparents since we'd split up, the meal wasn't as awkward as I'd been expecting. I'd worried that the subject of our relationship, or more specifically the ending of it, would be brought up early on in conversation and create an atmosphere. Instead, people politely asked how I was, how my parents were, and what my plans were for life in general.

The repetitive clinking of a heavy stainless-steel knife on a Champagne glass continued as the noise in the room decreased. The master of ceremonies continued the tapping until he had everyone's attention. 'Ladies and gentlemen, it's now time for the speeches. First we shall hear from the father of the bride.'

Another round of applause filled the room before Melissa's uncle accepted the microphone and gave a nervous smile to the crowd. He gave his speech, his eyes fixed firmly on a piece of A4 paper containing notes in his hand. As to be expected his speech was filled with heartfelt love for his daughter and a couple of funny stories from when she was younger.

The father of the bride was replaced by the groom, who smiled at his bride, told her how beautiful she looked, thanked family and friends who had travelled a distance, made a half joke about his stag do and handed the microphone back to the master of ceremonies who said, 'Now the moment you've all been waiting for. The Best Man.'

There was a loud cheer from a table filled with the groom's mates as the best man stood. He was built like a former Saturday rugby player, his stomach sticking out over his waist, his shirt starting to un-tuck slightly from his suit trousers.

He took the microphone and as silence fell said, 'Giving this best man's speech reminds me a little bit of losing my virginity.' There was a low intake of breath throughout the room. 'I've spent the build-up to it nervous, excited, and sweating uncontrollably. I will spend the act itself trying to make it last as long as possible, while secretly wishing it was over so I could tell people I'd finally done it. And I'm going to spend the rest of my life wishing I'd practiced it more because I know people will be asking if I was any good.'

Melissa's dad nearly spilt his drink as laughter erupted throughout the room and you could see the best man's shoulders relax.

We listened to stories about the groom's past, embarrassing photos from the stag do were passed around the room and the best man finished with a nice story about the night his friend met his new wife. The guests gave him a standing ovation and he stood for a few seconds longer, milking the applause.

Later, I stood next to him at the bar. 'Nice speech,' I said, as we both waited for our drinks.

'Cheers,' he said. 'I was shitting bricks before it. I barely ate anything.'

'It was great.'

His drink arrived. He paid, tipped his drink towards me and disappeared back into the guests.

The barmaid handed me my pint. I paid but stayed leaning on the bar watching the bride and groom slow dancing, her head leaning on his shoulder to a romantic song I didn't recognise. Family and friends pointed cameras at the couple, taking photos and videoing every move. I could see Melissa at the front of the ring of people, camera held in front of her face.

'She always thought that would be you two you know.'

Surprised, I turned to my right where Emma stood. Melissa's sister smiled as we both turned back to the dance. 'Really?' I said, just for something to say. I knew Emma was right but I didn't want to admit it.

'Come on, Tom, don't piss about. You know how she feels about you.'

I turned back to face her. 'What do you want me to say, Emma?'

The barmaid interrupted us to take Emma's order. I sipped my pint and stared towards the dance floor's happy scene.

'I think she thought that when you broke up with her you would go to Leeds, have your fun, come home, and you two would just get back together, get married, and everything would be OK.'

I knew what she was saying was true but stayed silent for a few seconds before saying, 'We're just friends.'

'I know you think that. But does Mel?'

'She should.' I took another drink from my pint, uncomfortable.

'Tom, she's my sister. I love her. I can see the way she looks at you. If you want to get back with her, get back with her. If not, don't give her false hope.'

I looked Emma directly in the eyes. 'Emma, Melissa's important to me. We are friends. I'm not trying to give her any impression that we are going to get back together.'

'Good. Because I don't want to have to kick your ass.'

We shared a smile but Emma's eyes told me her message was serious.

Emma carried her drinks back to the table and I stood watching smiling couples join the newlyweds on the dance floor as the next song began. Thinking about what Emma had said I realised that when I split up with Melissa, I too had thought it was a temporary situation. I figured I'd go away, sleep with a few women guilt free, then come back to Manchester and pick up where we had left off. That feeling had changed the morning after we'd last slept together. I woke up realising I'd changed. Being away from home had given me a taste of something more, something different. The thought of going back to where I was when I was eighteen filled me with dread.

I think part of my willingness to keep up my friendship with Melissa was because I worried she'd spent three years waiting for me to come back to her. I felt like I owed her something.

Melissa appeared in front of me and grabbed my hand. 'You're coming to dance.'

I didn't resist. She led me across the room. Passing our table, I handed my pint to her dad, who laughed.

On the dance floor the song changed to Paul Weller's 'You Do Something To Me'. We held each other close and moved slowly to the music.

Melissa looked at me, 'It means a lot to me that you've come today.'

'It wasn't a chore,' I said. 'I've had fun.'

We danced in silence for a few seconds, looking at each other.

I broke the spell and said, 'I know we've had a bit of a weird few months. What with what happened with Andy and everything. But it means a lot to me that we can still be friends.'

'I'm glad we can still be friends too,' Melissa said.

We stood on the dance floor, holding each other, neither of us talking until the end of the song.

'HOW WAS THE wedding?' Kate asked, the next afternoon.

I laid on my bed looking out of the window at her house, phone clamped against my ear.

'It was fine.'

'Fine?'

'OK, fun. What do you want me to say?'

'Tell me about it.'

'Why?' I asked, slightly irritated.

'Because I want to know how your day was.'

'The bride looked beautiful. Her dad cried during his speech. The speeches were funny. It was a wedding. I drank too much and today I'm a bit hung-over. What's to tell?'

The whole situation was strange, me lying on the bed, knowing she was just across the road. We were so close to each other, yet so far away. I moved to the window end of my bed in the hope of catching a glimpse of her, to feel some physical connection while we talked. The practical part of me was looking out for Stuart's car returning from the supermarket, so I would know when to end our conversation. 'Why are you being so awkward?'

'I'm not being awkward.'

'You are.'

'Why do you want to hear about the day I spent with Melissa?'

'I don't want to hear about the day you spent with her. I want to hear about your day.'

'You want to know if something happened between us, don't you?' I tried to keep my voice light.

'No,' she said, full of tension.

'You can relax. Nothing did.'

'I said I wasn't asking for that reason.'

I sat bolt upright on the bed, 'Stuart's back.' I watched his car drive slowly down the road, stopping to let another car pass.

'You should go,' I said.

His car moved forward again.

'Will I see you this week?' she asked.

Stuart swung his car into the driveway.

'Maybe,' I answered. 'But I'm going away this weekend.'

The car door opened. Stuart got out, then leant back in, re-emerging with a bag of shopping.

'Oh,' Kate said.

He slammed the door and pressed the button on his keys to lock it.

'You need to go,' I said, ending the call as Stuart inserted his key in the front door.

Chapter Thirteen

I slept late on Friday and awoke to an empty house.

I got up and ate breakfast, showered, shaved, and dressed. In my bedroom, I pulled a holdall down from the back of my wardrobe and dropped it on the bed. As I picked things to take out of drawers or off hangers, I ticked them off a mental list. Reaching into the wardrobe, I took out a shirt and held it up. I realised it was the shirt I'd worn to Buxton and my mind flashed back to Kate and I sitting in the Bear's Claw. I folded it and placed it in the bag on top of a couple of T-shirts and my shoes. I stuffed some spare socks in and zipped it closed.

Just as I was thinking about her, my phone beeped and a message from Kate appeared on the screen.

Have a nice time x

My eyes scanned my CD collection and I grabbed a handful of albums for the drive.

Packed and ready, I killed time checking and replying to emails. John had sent an email from Australia copying in Sean, Matt, and me. It was titled: *Sorry I can't be there, but I'm busy…*

I clicked open and a picture of John in a bar with a fit looking tanned girl whose arms were wrapped around him appeared on screen.

I closed the email to find Matt had replied with three sentences of abuse for John, the email ending with the words *miss you* and a kiss.

I left at about quarter past eleven, opening the car and throwing my holdall into the back seat, and putting the albums I wanted to listen to on the passenger seat. I opened one case and placed the CD in the player, pressed play, switched on the engine, and started driving.

It didn't take me long to get out of the suburbs. As the roads started getting longer, my speed increased. I pulled onto the M6, the car pointing south, moved easily into the outside lane and put my foot down. Hindsight may have altered my view of that moment, but I felt as if the pressures of home had been left behind, shrinking in my rear-view mirror. The long road stretched out in front of me and I just headed down it.

After about an hour, I stopped at a motorway service station. I ordered a Burger King, sitting at a small table in the corner while I ate. I sipped Coke through a plastic straw and watched the world rush by. A businessman in a sharp suit stood in the queue for coffee and spoke rapidly into his mobile, his voice rising with annoyance at the person on the other end. A crying baby at the next table distracted me. I turned as his tired looking mum picked him up and tried, almost pleaded, to calm him down. The noise increased and the mother caught my eye. I smiled and bit into my burger. She half smiled back, but her face portrayed a look of stress and embarrassment. A couple about my age sat across a table for two, jokingly feeding each other cold looking fries.

The sucking sound of my straw against the cardboard at the bottom of my cup signalled my drink had finished. I stood, the chair legs scraping across the floor. The baby had stopped crying and was now staring at me, wide-eyed. I waved and his mum allowed herself a full smile.

I walked back through the noise of the service station, out of the automatic doors and into the car park, the light zoom of motorway traffic the only background noise.

I continued to drive. Although I had a prearranged destination, there was an overwhelming sense of freedom in driving alone, a bag of clothes in the back, music playing loudly, knowing I could go anywhere and do anything, answering to no one.

THE FIRST TIME we went to Sean's house for the weekend, John, Matt, and I were all amazed. It was a bank holiday weekend in May, towards the end of our first year, and he'd invited us down for a weekend of barbeques, drinking, and planning our inter-rail trip around Europe. The three of us drove down together, following the directions Sean had written for us to Bath's outskirts. We thought we'd got lost when we took a turning down a narrow lane, flanked either side by large perfectly cut hedges. The surface changed and the tyres crunched small pebbles below the car. The road opened up into a square in front of us revealing a beautiful house. For want of a better description it was massive. Detached, surrounded by lawns on either side and at the back. A Land Rover and a BMW were parked next to each other in front of the house.

'This can't be it,' John said.

'It's fucking huge,' Matt stated.

As he said it the front door opened and a girl who I recognised from a photo in Sean's dorm room to be his twin sister, stood there smiling. She waved at us and we instinctively waved back, like three dumb struck kids.

'Fuck me,' John said. 'I knew he was well off but this is taking the piss.'

When we first met at uni, Sean was known as the posh one of us. There was something in the way he spoke, something in his tone (he called his granddad Grandfather once and I remember thinking I'd never heard anyone do that in real life before). He didn't flaunt it; in fact, it was the opposite. He talked about his school days like the rest of us, once mentioning the school was private and that he'd boarded for a couple of years but didn't push the detail or make out like he was better than us for it. He would answer questions about it, giving details of the procedures and rules, how everyone stayed at school on Saturday morning to do sport or how eating together in the dining hall was always preceded by the head teacher saying grace. On an overnight train through France, he told us of his time there, the frustration of being stuck inside the same building night after night, bored, bound by the rules of the place, enforced by the ageing teachers. He lived for the now at uni, the moment of freedom and enjoyment that had presented itself to him. I think part of that was a release of the pressures of growing up in a place where you and your peers are expected to do well, expected to succeed.

I think the shock of the size of the house was strange for me personally because I was used to living in an area where everybody's house looked the same. People I knew lived in semi-detached houses and if their dads (like my own) ran a business it was doing work for other people; gardening, plastering, joinery. If not, they sold cars or worked for IT companies. Seeing where Sean grew up made me question what life was like living in a house that people in my area aspired to live in or would buy with lottery winnings.

After spending the night there, I realised families, rich or otherwise, were the same. Sean argued with his sister the way I fought with my brother. His dad arrived home from work tired, poured himself a drink and sat motionless in front of the television. His mum fussed around, determined her guests would be looked after, but didn't realise that the details she revealed about her son to his closest friends would be used later as ammunition for taking the piss out of him. (She told us that Sean being away at uni was similar to when he boarded, only he didn't stomp and shout when he was home, screaming he was never going back.)

I drove along the narrow lane on this day, pulling up outside the house. Sean's car was parked outside. I got out, grabbed my bag, and walked to the front door.

Sean opened it, smiled and said, 'We're going back out again.'

'Where to?'

'We need to pick up Matt from the train station.'

I drove out of the narrow lane and slowly turned into the main road. 'What's the plan for tonight?'

'Few quiet ones tonight, just in the local. My sister will be coming, I think. She's looking forward to seeing you guys. Tomorrow, depending on the weather my plan was to head to the park, take a ball. Turn left,'

I knocked my indicator downwards and pulled the wheel left, the car easing around the corner.

He continued, 'Then head back here, put the barbeque on, have a few drinks, bit of music, some dancing. Your basic birthday party really.'

'Where are your mum and dad?'

'The house in France. They decided it would be better to get out of the way, let everybody stay over here.'

Matt was waiting for us in the car park of the train station, smartly dressed in his work suit, laptop bag over one shoulder, sports bag over the other. We parked next to him and he got in, 'Afternoon wankers,' he said, slamming the door shut.

'Is that closed?' I asked sarcastically.

He opened the door again and slammed it a second time. The thud vibrated through the car. 'Yeah,' he said, smiling. 'So, how are we boys? Ready for a weekend of recreating those first few months in Leeds?'

'Oh yes,' Sean replied.

We drove back to Sean's house and Matt got changed out of his work clothes. He walked back into the kitchen as Sean opened the fridge, took out three bottles of Budweiser, clicked the tops off with a bottle opener that was mounted on the wall and handed us the cold bottles. We tapped the necks together and said, 'Cheers.'

We opened the wooden French doors that led from the kitchen and stepped out on to the stone patio. A small table and chairs had been placed next a brick barbeque. The three of us sat down and took in the view. The sun was just starting to drop in the sky, creating an orange glow across the horizon. The lawn at the back of the house ran down a small slope to a wooded area at the bottom of the garden. I knew from previous visits that beyond the trees was a small brook that ran along the fence at the back of Sean's land.

Taking a long drink of beer, I felt my body completely relax.

'How's London?' Sean asked Matt.

'Expensive,' he replied. 'Rent is ridiculous.'

'Are you gentlemen hungry?' Sean asked.

'I could eat,' I said as Matt nodded.

'Well then, let's eat.'

SEAN'S LOCAL WAS just that. Five minutes' walk from his house, a white building with the name The Lion's Inn arched over the entrance in gold lettering. It was where Sean's whole village seemed to drink. Wooden tables placed outside next to the river were full of Friday evening drinkers enjoying real ale and glasses of white wine. We entered and Sean nodded a familiar hello to the barman.

'Hello Sean,' he said. 'What can I get you?'

'Three pints of lager,' said Sean. 'And a couple of menus.'

The barman produced a glass from underneath the bar, tilted it below the pump and started pouring a local lager I'd never heard of. 'There's a half an hour wait on food I'm afraid. Kitchen is busy.'

That was understandable due to the amount of people huddled around tables inside, creating a nice buzz of atmosphere. Our eyes scanned the room for an empty table but couldn't see one so after Sean paid for our drinks we went back outside. A middle-aged couple dressed in walking gear were just leaving so we slid onto the benches they were vacating.

It was a peaceful scene. The bright outside lights of the pub automatically clicked on, illuminating the river as the evening light slowly faded from the sky. We ordered food and ate slowly, sipping our drinks and catching up, filling each other in on the details of our lives. Matt told us about his flat and Michelle's stresses of her teacher training course. The long hours and lack of sleep were getting to her, and Matt was getting the brunt of it.

'I get the pressure she's under, I really do,' he said. 'But for fuck's sake, everything in life is not shit. You know what I mean?'

Sean and I stayed silent. Matt continued, his accent getting more Scottish the more animated he became, which made me laugh because I'd forgotten he did that. 'We live in London. People keep telling me it's one of the world's great fucking cities. Last weekend I suggested she not do uni work for the afternoon and we could go act like tourists for a bit. You know? Take her mind off it all. Get our photos taken with one of them men in the stupid hats outside Buckingham Palace. She went mental at me. Shouting about how important her work is. How she can't just fuck off to London for a day.'

'What did you say?'

'Well, I didn't help matters because I said we weren't fucking off to London because we lived there already and I only said to go out for the afternoon. We had a right proper row. Blazing. Then the tears came.'

'Yours, obviously,' I said.

'Piss off. She starts telling me she's sorry, that she knows I'm only trying to help. She's drowning under the weight of the work.'

'You sorted it now?'

'Oh aye. Sorted it that night. I went for a run for a couple of hours in the afternoon, then came back, got two bottles of wine and a Chinese. We got pissed in the flat and she chilled out a bit.'

'Sounds like you need a weekend off.'

Matt tipped his glass towards Sean. 'Can't hurt like.'

We passed through the usual conversations about families, work, and sport, plus we reminisced about our time living together in Leeds, when sitting around in front of pubs was a daily occurrence, not just a once in a while thing.

'I'm just glad we've met at your house,' I said to Sean.

'And why's that?'

'We all get our own bedroom. I don't have to share with your snoring.'

'Piss off,' he said.

'You remember that time in Barcelona when we met those girls from Liverpool?' Matt said. 'They had that apartment and you,' pointing at Sean, 'and John took the two girls in the main bedroom? You both shagged them and then you fell asleep naked and kept everyone else awake with your snoring?'

'Don't know what you're talking about?' Sean said, laughing at the memory.

'I remember,' I said. 'You,' referring to Matt, 'fell asleep on the couch and I ended up sharing a room with the annoying mate.'

'Oh yeah. She had a bit of a thing for you.'

Sean turned his body to face me and said seriously, 'Now, Tom, I know you've always denied it but did you or did you not shag that girl?'

'I did not shag her,' I replied, my face straight.

'Bullshit,' Matt said. 'I'll never believe you about that.'

I drank from my beer and focused on the light flickering across the river. 'Truth?' I said.

'Truth,' Sean said.

'Blow job.'

'I fucking knew it,' Matt said.

The three of us started to laugh. Although the joke wasn't funny the laughter caught hold of us and we couldn't stop. Sean was struggling to swallow his drink and Matt and I had tears rolling down our faces. We both looked at Sean and another explosion of laughter erupted from us.

'Is this a private party?' a voice said. We all regained control and looked up to see Sean's twin, Helen, standing over us.

'Hello,' we said. Matt and I stood up and gave her a hug and kiss.

'Does a lady have to get her own drinks around here?'

'Course not,' I said. 'Anyone else?'

Matt and Sean raised nearly empty glasses.

As I walked away from the table, I heard Sean ask Helen where her friend Sarah was.

I MET SARAH on Saturday afternoon.

She walked in unannounced through the back door at about half-past twelve. I glanced up from reading the sports section of a newspaper as the door opened and a smiling blonde girl stepped into the kitchen, holding a small gift wrapped present. 'Morning all,' she said.

The room reacted to her presence. Sean's local friends, who had been drifting into the house since late morning, all rose from their seats and moved across to where she stood, greeting her with hugs and kisses. Questions were fired at her: 'when did you get back?', 'how was it?' She tried to answer, to look the friend in the eye, but the next question, or next hug quickly came at her. As she was released from a hug with Helen's friend Grace, Helen walked into the kitchen.

'Hey.'

There was a very girly moment of the two of them skipping across the kitchen and meeting in the middle, hugging and rocking side to side, each ending up on one foot. They moved apart and Helen said, 'You look amazing.'

'Why, thank you.' Sarah spun around, her long blonde hair lifting from her shoulders. 'Happy birthday,' she said, handing over the present that now had creased wrapping paper.

'Thanks.' Helen took her hand and said, 'Matt, Tom, this is Sarah. My best friend in the whole world.'

'Hi,' Sarah said, giving a small wave.

'Hi,' I said back.

'Do you want a cup of tea?' Helen asked Sarah as she let go of her hand and walked around the breakfast bar.

As Helen refilled the kettle Sarah became the focus of the room again and the questions continued. Everyone wanted details of the last two years of her life. How she travelled, where she liked, where she didn't, how the jet lag was affecting her since she'd been home.

'Guys, slow down. I've been away for two years. Do you want a day-by-day account? Max,' she said, turning to Sean's friend from school. 'What have you been doing for the last two years of your life?'

'Getting drunk mostly,' Max said with a shrug, before eating a mouthful of a sausage sandwich.

Everyone laughed.

AN HOUR LATER we set up camp in the park, laying out blankets, placing bags of supermarket bought food and drink on them. Sean produced a football and kicked it towards me.

I controlled it and did a couple of keep-ups before kicking it to Matt.

Sean took off his hooded jumper, placing it on the ground across from a small tree stump, making a goal. He stood between them and Matt fired a shot at him. Sean dived dramatically but missed the ball and it flew in the bushes behind.

'I'll go,' Matt said, before disappearing to find the ball.

Sarah stood next to me as I waited for Matt to return. 'Are you going to let the girls play?'

'Are you any good?'

'Good enough. I have three older brothers.'

'Then yes.'

She ran her fingers through her hair, tying it into a ponytail, giving me a clear view of her pretty face. She had the deep-set tan of someone who had lived in sunnier climates for a prolonged period of time, not a red British burnt tan. 'What's the game?'

'According to Matt, kick as hard as you can into that bush and lose the ball.'

'My favourite.'

Matt emerged from the bushes, stopping to unhook a twig from his T-shirt.

He kicked the ball towards me and I passed it to Sarah. She took a shot at goal, not connecting with the ball properly and it rolled slowly towards Sean. 'That was embarrassing,' she said.

'No comment,' I responded.

A few others joined in and the game grew, another goal appeared, made out of a picnic basket and a T-shirt. We played for about half an hour, stopping occasionally to grab food or drink from the shopping we'd brought with us.

I did a nice trick to take on Sean at one point, squaring the ball into Sarah's path for her to roll it into an empty net, scoring her first goal. She ran to me and put her hand up to high five me. 'Told you I could play,' she said proudly.

Later, we sat on the grass, the sun warming us and refreshed ourselves with bottles of lager.

'I can't get over how warm it is,' I said, sipping the alcohol.

'Weather is always better down south my friend,' Sean said. 'I'm always telling you that.'

Helen sat down next to me. 'Have you sorted all that stuff out with Melissa?'

'Yeah. Ages ago. We're friends now.'

'Friends or friends with benefits?'

'We've not had sex if that's what you're asking.'

This would have been a great moment to share the story of Kate.

Away from Manchester, away from her and the pressures of sneaking around, the secrets, and the snatched phone calls. Sat on the grass with my friends who would potentially never meet her, the sun shining, them genuinely interested in how I was doing.

I could have talked for hours about how my life had become a series of prearranged secret meetings for sex or hiding out in pubs miles away from home trying to get to know a woman who I was breaking every moral code with.

But I didn't.

LATER, WE STOOD in Sean and Helen's garden, drinking and talking. Everyone from the park had come back to the house, plus a few other guests arrived, including Helen's boyfriend Phil who'd driven up from Brighton. I was introduced to a couple of people, but didn't catch their names properly. They started talking to Helen, wishing her a happy birthday and getting details of the day. I excused myself and went inside to find a toilet.

The downstairs toilet was locked and I decided to wait. A couple of minutes later the door opened and Sarah walked out.

'Hi again,' she said, smiling.

'Hi.'

There was a pause while we changed places. I placed my hand on the door handle she was holding, brushing very slightly against her hand in the process. We looked at each other for half a second too long and then she turned away, saying, 'I better leave you to.'

'Thanks,' I said.

She turned to walk away and I said, 'I'd like to talk to you about travelling, if that's OK?' The words left my mouth like a runner false starting.

She spun back round, 'Sure.'

Despite her acceptance, I felt the need to explain why. 'I'm looking to go and wouldn't mind getting some advice.'

'No problem. I'll go to the fridge and get us a couple of beers and you do,' she paused, 'well, whatever it was you were going to do in there. I don't need details. Meet you outside?'

When I returned to the party, I walked outside and looked around. People stood in little groups, lit by two large wall lamps that shone out across the patio and over half of the lawn. As the light faded towards the edge of the grass, down towards the wooded area, I could see the small red burning ends of cigarettes. My eyes tried to focus through the dark, hoping to spot Sarah.

'Tom,' she shouted from behind me, attracting my attention to a group of people by the brick barbeque. Sean was playing cook, apron hanging loosely from his neck as he studied the colour of the charcoal piled underneath the grill.

I walked over. Sarah handed me an open bottle of lager and Sean offered me a burger.

'When they're cooked, yeah.'

'I see,' Sean said, flicking a long metal fork into the air. His eyes told me, as they had done hundreds of times before, that he was on the edge of drunk. He went back to studying the food.

Sarah asked if I knew everyone, indicating the other three people in the group.

I shook my head.

'This is Daniel and his girlfriend Lauren, who have come over from Dublin. This is my sister, Katherine.'

She put her hand behind Katherine's back gave her a little squeeze. Katherine laughed and said, 'Hello.'

'Everyone, this is Tom.'

I gave a slightly embarrassed wave as Sean said, 'Tom is my best friend in the north of England.'

Ignoring him, Daniel offered his hand for me to shake. 'Nice to meet you.'

'And you,' I said. 'What were you guys talking about before I interrupted?'

'George Bush,' Sean shouted, making a stabbing motion with his fork.

'Sarah was just asking us what she'd missed while she's been away. I was just telling her we went on the anti-war march in London last February,' said Lauren.

I nodded, unsure of the correct response.

'While I was away all anyone seemed to talk about was George Bush and Tony Blair,' Sarah said.

'Well, between them they've changed the world we live in,' Katherine said. 'Their decisions have affected a generation of people. Blair would be better quitting as Prime Minister now.

'A generation,' Sarah said. 'Is that not a bit strong?'

'No. Kids, and they are kids some of them, are going to fight in wars they would never have had to fight if it wasn't for those two'

'I think Blair's in a tough position,' Sean said.

'This should be fun,' replied Helen, turning to look at Sean expectantly.

'The attitude that Blair caused the war is insane. He didn't crash the planes into the towers.'

'I know he didn't but he had choices after that.'

'What do you think?' Sarah asked me.

I looked at Katherine and then Sean who said, slightly sarcastically 'It is fine, mate, speak your mind. We're all friends.'

'I'm not getting involved,' I said neutrally. 'This is a bit heavy for me.'

'Come on, mate,' Sean encouraged. 'Don't worry. Katherine's bark is worse than her bite.'

'Shut up, Sean.'

'Another friend of mine feels a bit sorry for Blair,' I offered, quickly taking a drink from my bottle and thinking of Kate.

There was a short silence while people digested my words.

'Sorry for him?' Katherine asked, trying the words out for herself, seeing if they could be interpreted another way if she spoke them more slowly.

'Yeah,' I said, nodding for emphasis, eager to end the debate.

'Why sorry for him?'

Aware all eyes were on me; I gave my explanation. 'They just think it's a shame Blair is going to spend the rest of his days in power trying to convince people that one decision to go to war should not overshadow all the hard work and good work he did in the first place.' I was aware that my words were basically Kate's words. Words she'd said to me on a walk home from the pub, the night we slept together in my single bed while my family were on holiday.

Katherine snapped me back to reality. 'The man, and I use that term loosely, led us into an illegal war. A war that's killing thousands of innocent Iraqi civilians.' Her voice raised a level. 'Not to mention the British troops who have to fight in this war.'

'I think it's naïve to join the army if you expect not to fight,' Sean said. I glanced at him and the smile on his face confirmed he was just winding Katherine up.

I raised my hands in an attempt to show Katherine I wasn't an enemy.

Katherine continued, 'What good things is this friend talking about?'

Something in the way she stressed the word 'friend', like it was dirty made me instantly protective of Kate and my choice to be with her. Who the hell did this girl think she was talking about Kate like that? My Kate. I suppressed my anger, instead quoting Kate word for word.

'Minimum wage, European Working Time directive. The average man's life is better now than before he took over. Don't forget that in 1997 Tony Blair was a hero.'

'Go on, Tommy boy.' Sean laughed. 'He's got you there Katherine.'

Katherine ignored him and said to me, 'You make some good points. But unfortunately, I think that despite all that good work, Tony Blair will only be remembered for taking this country to war and killing innocent people.'

'Maybe you're right.' I conceded in an attempt to get back on common ground and away from a discussion that had brought thoughts of Kate crashing to the front of my mind. 'I also think this is getting a bit heavy and it only started because Sean was trying to wind you up.'

Laughter spread around the group.

Within a few minutes the conversation around the barbeque turned to discussions of the correct colour of charcoal.

Sarah took my hand and asked, 'So, do you want to talk about travelling?'

Before I could answer she pulled me out of the harsh light on the patio and walked across the grass, down through a small wood chipped path that led through the trees, away from the noise of the party. Light from houses on the other side of the brook helped us find our way to the edge of the deep bank that was covered with overgrown grass. A continuous flow of dark silver water moved along the bottom of the brook.

I looked up at the clear sky, seeing stars scattered across it, as if someone had just tossed them there randomly.

'Sorry about her,' Sarah said. 'She can be a bit high and mighty.'

'It's OK,' I said. 'Hope I didn't piss her off.'

'She'll get over it.'

We listened to the sounds of the party and the slow trickle of the brook.

'It's nice to have some peace and quiet,' Sarah said, drinking from her bottle. 'So, what do you want to know?'

'I'm not sure really. There is one thing I'd really like to know but you might not want to answer.'

'Try me.'

'How did you afford to go away for two years?'

She considered the question. 'Honestly?'

'I'd prefer you not to lie.'

'My dad is rich.' She took another sip of her drink. 'But he's also, somewhat annoyingly, got a strong work ethic. He told me he would match every pound I saved for travelling through earnings. So, I worked two jobs. One in an office as a receptionist and then I was a waitress a few nights a week and at the weekend. I did that for a just over year. I also sold everything I owned of value. My car, my laptop. Things like that. I bought a ticket, a rucksack, and a decent camera and just went away.'

'You sold your car?'

'Yep. I didn't need it in Thailand.'

The answer was so obvious. I'd been keeping everything I needed to live a normal existence at home. My car gave me freedom in the suburbs of Manchester but its worth in money could help provide me with the means of travel. My brain started calculating at a hundred miles an hour. 'No car tax, no insurance, petrol.'

'Exactly.'

'That's genius.'

'I wouldn't go that far.'

We laughed at how childishly enthusiastic I'd become.

'Where did you go?'

'I started in India,' she said, before taking me through her whole trip, including Thailand, Vietnam, Cambodia, Christmas on a beach in Malaysia. Singapore, driving across Australia, sky diving in New Zealand, Fiji, South America, LA, San Francisco, Chicago, New York, and places I'd never heard of that she assured me I needed to go to. She told me about friends she'd met, nights out, amazing sights, feeling homesick, knowing that it was temporary, that she had to push against the force pulling her back towards home because of the fear of regretting leaving before she'd experienced as much as possible. Occasionally I interrupted to ask questions or for advice about where to stay or how to get from place to place. I asked how she found travelling alone. She assured me that lone travellers just meet people. She explained how loads of people in hostels were in the same position. I remembered all the single travellers we'd met in Europe who seemed at ease being out in the world alone. The rhythm of her voice as she spoke almost sang the stories, her words dancing. Her eyes lit up when she remembered the amazing exotic places that had recently been her life.

The temperature dropped during the hour or so we sat there. I pulled my knees in closer to my body, not wanting to move. I was mesmerised. This beautiful, tanned, travelled girl had lived the life I wanted. Her words spoke to my need to get away. The situations she described were experiences I craved. She made it sound so easy, so real.

'So, there you have it. That's my last two years. Any questions?'

'What was your favourite place?'

'New Zealand and New York.'

'So anywhere new then.'

'That's the point, isn't it?'

Yes, it was.

'What's the one thing you recommend I take?'

'There's two. A good camera and a bottle of Febreze.'

'Really?'

'Yep. To freshen up everything after a few days without a washing machine.'

'I wish we'd thought of that when we went around Europe with Sean. He stank half the time. Why did you come back?'

'My cousin is getting married in December. The time felt right.'

For the first time we both fell silent. I drank from my bottle. Neither of us filled the silence. I looked at the water in the brook and the clear crisp sky. I looked at her, knowing the whole day had led to this moment. From the flirting in the park, the little looks and smiles, the last hour of conversation. All of it had been part of the build-up to this very point. We shared a half smile; our nervousness revealed.

Sarah leant towards me, placing her lips softly on mine. We kissed for a few seconds. Instead of relaxing and enjoying the moment I was stabbed with feelings of guilt. I pulled my lips away and looked to the ground.

'Is everything all right?' she asked.

'I like you,' I said.

'And yet we're not kissing anymore.'

'I'm sort of seeing someone,' I offered.

'Sort of?'

'It's complicated.'

'It's always complicated. That's what makes it fun.'

Silence.

She broke it. 'This girl, I assume it's a girl.'

'It's a girl.'

'Do you love her?'

There was the question. The question I'd suppressed deep inside me. The question I'd avoided asking myself, for fear of what the answer might mean. What the impact would be if I dared contemplate what Kate meant to me.

My eyes were fixed on a dark patch of grass. I spoke, the words sticking in my throat. 'Yeah, I think so.'

'You think so?'

'I love her,' I said, my words more confident.

'Does she feel the same?'

I forced my head up, trying to compose myself and looked at her. 'I don't know,' I said. 'She's, well, it's difficult. She's involved with someone else.'

'Oh. I see what you mean by complicated.'

I spoke quickly to avoid any more questions, knowing I'd be likely to tell the full story. 'I'm really sorry. This is a bit of a revelation for me. This is not how I imagined this moment going.'

'Me neither.'

We smiled. 'I like you; I really do. But I need to be honest. I feel guilty. I don't think this is a good idea.'

'That's a shame,' she said.

We went back to the party and gathered around the barbeque again. It was now in full use, overcooked burgers and sausages resting on metal rungs over the grill. People stood with plates, waiting for Sean to serve them.

I went into the house. The clock on the kitchen wall read 9.50 p.m. I took two bottles of lager from the fridge and opened them both.

Katherine, Sarah's sister stood at the breakfast bar with a bottle of tequila.

'Hello, Tony Blair,' she said.

'Hi.'

'Truce drink?' she asked, holding the bottle up.

'Go on then.'

She lined up two shot glasses and we threw the tequila down our necks.

'Another?'

'Can't hurt.'

We repeated the ritual.

The alcohol didn't feel like it had any effect.

'Excuse me,' I said. 'I need to make a phone call.'

Two bottles of lager in hand I walked back outside, drinking from one continuously as I manoeuvred my way back along the track to where Sarah and I had been sitting. I tried to make sense of what I'd admitted to her. Halfway down the second bottle, I took out my phone and dialled Kate's number.

It rang, and she answered quickly. 'Hello,' she said, sounding tense.

'What are we?' I said immediately.

'What?'

'What am I to you?'

'Tom, where are you?'

'It doesn't matter where I am. I want to know the answer. What are we?'

'I can't do this now. You're drunk. We'll talk in the week.'

'When can I see you? I need to see you. Can I see you next weekend?' She hung up before I'd finished my sentence.

I WOKE UP very hung-over. Sean took Matt and me for breakfast at a small café in the village and as we waited for our food, he asked me who the girl I was in love with was. He explained that Sarah had told Helen what had happened the previous night. I sat there with two of my best friends in the whole world and knew I could finally share my secret.

But I didn't.

I lied and told them I'd met a girl called Rebecca and I hadn't mentioned her because she was seeing someone else and we'd agreed to keep it quiet. Neither of them noticed Rebecca was the name of our waitress.

Chapter Fourteen

Sat silently side by side, we stared out from Kate's car into the dark night, tension beating like a pulse between us.

I caved first. 'I'm sorry I phoned you when I was drunk. I shouldn't have done that.'

'No. You shouldn't.' Her voice simmered with anger.

'I know. It's just I wanted to—'

'I was in a restaurant toilet, on a night out with Stuart. For our wedding anniversary.' She cut me off and pronounced the words slowly, carefully. 'It was lucky I'd gone to the toilet otherwise that phone call would've been while I was sat at the fucking table.'

'I know it was wrong, but I had to know how you felt about me.'

'Why? Why was it so urgent to know?'

'Because I love you.'

The words escaped loudly from me, surprising us both. In the two days since returning from Sean's party, I'd rehearsed this conversation hundreds of times. At no point had I intended to reveal my feelings with such a clumsy delivery.

After seconds of silence, Kate told me to stop. She told me I couldn't say that.

'Stop what? Telling you I love you? But it's true.' Saying the words hadn't freed us from tension as I'd expected. 'I think you should know the truth.'

I turned to face her. She looked down at the steering wheel. I watched the swelling of a tear form; hang for a second before falling onto her jeans below. She pulled in a deep breath and looked at me. There was a hardness to her face I'd not seen before.

'You want to know what we are, Tom? We are an affair. I'm a thirty-one-year-old married woman who is fucking a kid ten years younger than her because she's unhappy with her marriage. Nothing more. Is that what you want to know? We are a cliché.'

Her words hung in the air.

'You don't mean that.'

'And I can't see you this weekend. My husband is taking me to New York for our wedding anniversary.'

CLICHÉ. THAT WAS the word that kept coming back to me as I thought about the conversation in the following minutes, hours, days. The word that pounded against the inside of me as I tried to make sense of everything that had been said.

Was I a cliché? Following the same pattern as everybody else in my generation? College, university, travel. Returning home thinking I knew something about the world. Thinking I'd been the first to discover it, like Christopher fucking Columbus, only treading the same worn path so many before me had walked. Was I destined to meet somebody, marry, have kids, and end up sitting in my favourite chair watching soap operas my wife liked and I hated?

Cliché. Cliché. Fucking Cliché.

I was angry and confused. Kate's description of our situation didn't feel true. During our time together, it never felt like she thought we were just fucking, that we were just an unhappy wife and a younger man willing to cross the moral boundaries of her marriage with her. It felt like there was a connection between us, that we were building something real. In the moments after sex, when the thrill of the 'affair' had gone and we were left talking, learning about each other, sharing the pieces of each other you only share with someone who you want to become an important part of your world, it didn't feel like we were there to escape the unhappiness of her marriage. Those moments had felt real to me.

I was frustrated too. If this had been a normal relationship, one involving just the two of us, if she wasn't married, I could've gone to see her or call her and at least know I would have got some form of explanation, some form of closure. Instead, I lay on my bed, her just across the road, knowing there was no way in the world I could walk over to her house to try to talk.

Only now, with the benefit of hindsight, I can see the whole situation from Kate's perspective. When we were together, I never gave much thought to what it must have felt like for her going back to Stuart afterwards. How kissing him, asking how his day had been, moving through the motions of marriage must have, at times, felt like a sham. How did she feel when she caught a glimpse of her wedding ring when typing an email or answering her mobile phone, knowing she'd broken the vows she made on the day Stuart gave it to her?

I wondered how the guilt manifested itself in her. Did she eat less due to the constant butterflies in her stomach or tell Stuart she loved him more on the days we were together? There must have been moments when they were together, lay in bed on a Saturday morning or driving to a parent's house for Sunday dinner, when I suddenly appeared in her mind, shattering the illusion.

My phone call during her wedding anniversary dinner must have been one of those times. By phoning at that exact moment, the worlds of her marriage and her affair came close to crashing into each other. The pressure of sitting back at the table, sipping her wine, eating her food, on that night of all nights, without acting differently to before she'd gone to the toilet would have been enough to break anyone.

With hindsight, it's easy for me to be more understanding. At the time, I felt as if my entire world had been crushed.

Chapter Fifteen

I remember that Friday I spoke to Jordan about the two of us having a night out 'to town, like the old days.' I remember meeting at about six and getting the tram into Manchester. I remember walking into a pub full of after-work drinkers, men with ties relaxed around their necks, flirting with women who smiled back politely and sipped cold white wine. I remember thinking that after two or three more of them she'd be all over him. I remember talking the usual talk. I remember moving on to different pubs and noticing the after-work crowd thinning out, being replaced by groups of teenage girls talking too fast and laughing too loudly, being watched by teenage lads dressed in creased shirts wearing too much hair gel, standing around trying to look cool from behind pint glasses that seemed too big for them. I remember drinking and Jordan talking about Charlotte more and more. I remember I told him he was in love. I remember he told me to fuck off. I remember we walked from bar to bar, them and us getting louder. I remember we ordered shots and toasted ourselves. I remember paying money to get into a shit Australian themed bar with shit Australian bar staff wearing shit Australia T-shirts. I remember our shit Australian accents and student girls dancing and I remember fists in the air to the sound of bad music. I remember realising I'd not been in there since I was underage, and I remember thinking that now I wasn't with Kate I should call Sarah. I remember realising that ship had sailed and that it was a bad idea to call someone less than a week after turning them down because you confessed love for another woman and that a good idea was to dance to the bad music on my own while Jordan went for a piss. I remem...

Chapter Sixteen

I woke up in a room I didn't recognise next to a girl I didn't know.

We were crammed together in a single bed; the girl facing me making a light snoring sound, blonde hair spread across her face. Her warm, clammy body was pressed against mine. My mouth was dry and I could feel a crusty film on my lips. I had no idea how we had ended up there.

My eyes flickered rapidly, trying to bring the room into focus. We were in a tiny dorm room of university student halls. There was a large poster of Johnny Depp from the film *Chocolat* on the wall overlooking the bed, a small desk with a mix of textbooks and fiction books in small piles next to a computer screen and keyboard. The computer chair in front of the desk had my clothes hanging over the back of it. A half-finished glass of wine sat on the bedside table next to an open, empty condom wrapper. The single bed we were in was pushed up against a wall covered in photographs that had been Blu-Tacked into a large collage. I guessed she was a first year.

I moved, desperately trying not to wake the girl, carefully pushing myself up. I slowly placed my hand over her sleeping body. My legs followed, and I managed to manoeuvre my way out of the bed. Unsteady on my feet, I picked up my shoes. As I lifted my clothes from the back of the chair, coins fell from my pocket and crashed to the floor, followed by my keys and mobile phone. I picked them up quickly, making more noise. I headed for the bathroom and locked the door behind me.

Where was I? What time was it? Answers to the questions wouldn't form in my mind. The only thing I could say for sure was that I was still drunk.

I ran the cold tap into my cupped hands and twice poured the water into my mouth. I dressed in the previous night's stale clothes and listened for sounds coming from the bedroom. I couldn't hear any movement, so as quietly as possible I unlocked the bathroom door, turned to the dorm's front door, opening it quickly and shut it behind me. I didn't look back as I half jogged down the empty corridor, bracing myself for the girl's voice behind me. It never came.

Stepping out of the halls' main doors fresh air hit me. I walked across the car park and followed traffic noise to a main road. My surroundings became familiar. I was still in central Manchester, off Oxford Road.

The city was waking up. I got onto Oxford Road and made my way towards St Peter's Square to get a tram home. I thought about getting one of the buses that passed me but decided to keep walking and try to remember the events of the previous night, hoping the surroundings of the city would spark memories of the missing time. The same questions repeated. How had I got here? Where was

Jordan? Who was the girl? I was glad I was still in town and not creeping out of a damp student house onto a dodgy terraced street the middle of the backend of Manchester where no one would choose to live if not for the cheap rent.

I passed a couple of closed takeaway kebab and pizza places and the Manchester Aquatics Centre. I looked down the street towards the centre of town. The tall brick tower clock rose from the Palace Theatre on the other side of the railway bridge that stretched across the road. The time wasn't quite in focus but it appeared to be just before eight o'clock. A train slowly entered my eye line from behind the trees on the left-hand side of the road and crossed the bridge, disappearing from view again. Nothing came back me to.

A parade of buses drove towards me. A chunky blue double-decker pulled into a bus stop and Saturday workers filed off, each dressed in different uniforms. I walked underneath the railway bridge and saw an independent coffee shop had an open sign outside, advertising fresh coffee and breakfast goods, scribbled on a chalk board. I put my hand in my pocket and counted my money and went in, ordering a strong coffee and a bottle of water.

Outside on the pavement I snapped open the water and drained the cool liquid into my dry mouth, three-quarters of the bottle disappearing. I swallowed then drank the rest. The drink was a relief to my tired body. I dropped the empty bottle in a bin and sipped my coffee. Hunger bullied me but I felt too sick to eat.

Five minutes later I walked into St Peter's Square; the Dutch Pancake House on my right, the circular central library the backdrop to my view, its four stone pillars stood to attention at the front. I crossed the road and watched a dirty white tram pass in front of the Midland Hotel, then stop at the station. The doors slid open and people poured off onto the platform. I stood on the opposite side watching them quickly move in different directions, towards different lives. A tram arrived. I got on and found a seat in a quiet section. I rested my head against the window and the tiredness I'd been fighting off kicked in. I shut my eyes and slipped into a state of semi consciousness as the tram travelled at speed, rocking from side to side. I woke with a start as the driver's voice announced we were at the stop before mine. I walked with unsteady legs towards to the doors. When the tram was stationary, the doors automatically opened and I stepped off. My mobile phone rang, surprisingly showing Jordan's number on the screen. 'Hello,' I said, with a croaky voice. 'Was she worth it, you dirty fucker?'

'Worth what?'

'Leaving me in town.'

I walked out of the station and said, 'I'm going to be honest with you, mate. I have no idea what happened last night. I remember being in the shit Australian place and you going for a piss and then I woke up this morning in a student dorm in the middle of town. If I left you in town, I'm very very sorry.'

Jordan laughed. 'You have no idea what happened?'

'No. I remember you going for a piss and me dancing on my own and that's about it.'

He laughed again. 'When I came back to the bar you were dancing with some blonde who, if I'm honest, mate, wasn't very fit at all.'

'I didn't get much chance to check this morning.'

'Why?'

'I woke up having no clue where I was, grabbed my clothes and got the fuck out of there.'

'You didn't?'

'I did.'

A burst of laughter came down the phone. 'You're a terrible person.'

'You don't mean that.'

'No, I don't. You're a fucking hero. Can you get married soon so I can put this in my best man speech?'

'Just tell me what happened last night.'

'I came back to the bar and you were dancing with the blonde girl,' Jordan explained. 'You stopped when I came back and we, me and you, had a drink. She wouldn't leave you alone though and started kissing you and basically trying to shag you right there at the bar.'

Images of recollection flickered in my brain.

Jordan continued, 'Charlotte rang me to see if was staying at hers not long after and I said I was going. The girl said you were staying at hers and you just shrugged.'

'So, I just left you to get back on your own?'

'Well no. You gave me a tenner for a taxi and then carried on dancing.'

'Mate, I'm so sorry.'

'I thought it was fucking hilarious,' Jordan said. 'And what was I going to do, stand in the way of you getting laid?' He paused. 'You were in a well enough state to shag her, right?'

'The empty condom wrapper on the bedside table would suggest yes.'

'Well, that's a victory for safe sex.'

I laughed and said, 'What are you doing up so early?'

'Woke up and wondered if you were OK. You were drinking at quite the rate of knots last night. I asked you a couple of times if you were OK.'

Panic ran through me, wondering what I'd revealed. 'What did I say?'

'Just that you fancied getting drunk and didn't need an excuse.'

My heartbeat slowed. 'Are you booking it then?'

Confused, I said, 'Booking what?'

'Your trip. We passed that travel place last night, the one on Deansgate. You stood in front of the window and pointed at it and said, and I'm quoting "I'm coming back here tomorrow and I'm going to book a trip that takes me away from this fucking shit". I'm assuming you meant shit-hole.'

I was certain I didn't mean shit-hole. The shit I was referring to would have been everything to do with Kate. 'So, are you going to book it?'

'Yes, mate. I am.'

I OPENED THE front door to be greeted by my dad; his voice was firm, anger bubbling under the surface saying, 'Where the hell have you been?'

'Manchester,' I said.

'You've been out all night.'

'I know.'

'Your mother hasn't slept properly, waiting for you to come home.'

I stood in the hallway and realised that I didn't need to have this argument. I could ignore the words being said to me, calmly walk upstairs and change, go back to Manchester and put in place my plan for freedom.

Instead, I said, 'I don't understand why.'

'What do you mean you don't understand? She's your mum, and you didn't come home. Of course, she's going to bloody worry,' he said.

'Did she worry about me for the three years I didn't live here?'

'What?' he snapped.

'I didn't live here for three years and went out most nights and I bet Mum slept just fine. So, I don't understand why she worries all night when I'm here.'

'She just does.'

'I didn't fucking ask her to,' I said as I walked to the stairs.

I'm aware the above exchange makes me sound like an arrogant, cocky, spoilt little shit. I'll admit I could've handled it better. Maybe apologised for not ringing earlier in the morning, but at that moment as I stood in front of my dad, tired, hung-over, wearing last night's clothes, my breath smelling of alcohol and coffee, all my frustrations about living back at home with my parents seemed to magnify. I felt trapped by their rules and expectations about how I should behave, their constant questions about where I was going or what time I would be in, or being told not to forget I had work in the morning. Even the simple act of my mum doing my washing pissed me off. When I came back home, I'd done my own washing, as I had done adequately for three years. Yet now my mum would walk into my room, take what she thought needed washing and it would disappear into one of the several piles of clothes that formed in the utility room in the garage, only to resurface days later cleaned, ironed, and hanging in my wardrobe. For the few seconds when I was arguing with my dad that morning, the fact my mum did my washing felt like the worst thing any parent could ever do for a child.

The sound of my bedroom door slamming shut boomed through the house. I laid on my bed and let my body relax. I was angry the exchange with my dad had ruined the good mood I came home in. I wanted to announce that I was booking the trip of a lifetime as I walked in the door. Instead, I'd ended up in a shouting match.

AFTER A LONG hot shower and some food, I dressed in clean clothes, checked my online savings account, returned to the station, and boarded a tram back to Manchester. A nervous energy ran through my body as a bell pinged when I opened the door of the travel agency. There were a couple of people waiting to see the advisers, so I sat down and flicked through one of the brochures, imagining myself lay on one of the white beaches or swimming in a clear, turquoise sea.

Despite the build-up in my head to what a life changing moment this was, booking the trip didn't take that long or seem that difficult. My agent Daniel's matter of fact tone didn't lend much to the excitement of the event. He efficiently tapped the keys on his keyboard and quietly read through my options regarding flights and destinations, showed me the prices on his computer screen and simply offered me a list of dates that I could leave on. Twenty minutes later I handed over my credit card.

The bell pinged again as I left the agency, in my hand was a print off from Daniel's computer, detailing my itinerary.

My leaving date: 27th December 2004.

MY MUM AND dad were sat in the lounge watching television when I got back home. I mumbled half an apology to my dad for our earlier exchange and then asked them to turn off the TV.

'I've booked my trip,' I said.

'Oh right,' my mum said. 'When?'

'I leave the day after Boxing Day.'

'Can you afford it?' my dad asked, ever practical.

'Yeah, I'm going to sell my car and I've got some savings together now. Plus, I'll have whatever I earn between now and then. I might work in Australia too.'

'What are you going to do for a car?'

'I won't need one while I'm away. No point in it being sat there for a year or two.'

My mum asked, 'Is that how long you're going for?'

'Yeah.'

'Where are you going?'

'I'm flying to Thailand, then on to Vietnam and Cambodia, then Australia and New Zealand. Fiji maybe. I've not got a full plan. I'll just see where it all takes me.'

'What are you going to do for a car when you get back?' my dad asked.

'Why are you fixating on my bloody car? I'll get a different one. Or get the bus. Or walk. I'm not bothered about my car. I'm telling you I'm going away for a year or two and all you can talk about is that I'm selling my car. I don't want to be tied to a life where my car comes into my thoughts when I'm making a decision about travelling around the world.'

'I just want to make sure you've thought it through.'

'I've been thinking it through for years. I'm bored of thinking about it. I want to do it.'

My dad nodded. 'OK.'

Chris walked in and said, 'What's going on? Why does everyone look so serious?'

'I've booked my trip. I'm going after Christmas.'

'Is that it?'

'That's it.'

'I thought it was something important,' he said before looking at my mum and saying, 'I'm going out.'

I SPENT THE rest of my night in my room. I made a long list of the things I'd need to buy and studied the pages of my travelling book with fresh interest and excitement.

Each place felt closer, felt more real.

Chapter Seventeen

I snapped off a piece of tape between my teeth and stuck the sign to the inside of the back window of my car.

'You selling it?' a voice said.

Trying not to bang my head, I carefully manoeuvred myself out of the car. Stuart stood in the street, studying the information on the sign. It simply stated the price I wanted for the car, or the nearest offer, my name and telephone number.

'Yeah,' I said.

'How come?'

'I've booked my trip to go travelling, so I don't need it anymore. I'd rather have the cash for going away.'

'Makes sense,' Stuart said. 'When do you go?'

'I fly to Bangkok on the twenty-seventh of December.'

'Nice one. Where after that?'

I explained the brief outline of a route I'd planned and, although I knew the answer, asked, 'What have you been up to?'

'We got back from New York this morning. I booked it for our wedding anniversary. Little surprise for the wife.'

On the surface, I was in this conversation. My body language played along and showed interest. My head nodded in the right places, but inside my heart pounded rapidly.

We both turned to watch Kate walking down the road towards us. She gave us both a slim smile before opening her handbag and looked deep inside it for something. I knew this was to avoid eye contact with me.

Stuart said, 'Guess who's going travelling?'

Kate looked at me. 'Really?' she said. I heard her voice divert slightly from its usual delivery. She regained her composure before saying, 'Have you booked it?'

'Yeah,' I said, before spitefully adding, 'I've got nothing to keep me here.'

The hurt in her eyes appeared instantly. The only word she could manage in response was 'oh,' before physically turning her body towards Stuart and slipping her arm through his.

'You want to hear all the places he's going?' Stuart said.

'No, it's OK,' Kate said, not needing to hear the list we had talked about over and over again in the secret hours we'd spent together.

She said to Stuart, 'We need to get going.'

'Oh yeah. See you soon,' he said to me.

I stood fixed to the pavement and watched them walk away from me, arm in arm.

DRAMATICALLY, IT WOULD'VE been better if my mum had smoked. That way on Wednesday when my dad and I walked into the kitchen after work and found her sat at the table, she could have been taking a long thoughtful drag on a cigarette before holding it carefully between her fingers and studying it as it burnt slowly down towards the filter, smoke curling up towards the ceiling, her eyes showing an unnatural steel. Instead, we found her still in her work clothes, drinking tea, her hand shaking as she lifted the lipstick-stained mug to her smudged mouth.

'What's wrong?' my dad asked instinctively.

My mum turned towards him, her eyes dazed and said, 'I think you better sit down.'

My dad remained on his feet, leaning against the sink, arms folded across his chest.

My mum continued. 'I've just had a phone call from Chris's head of year.'

With all the recent dramas in my own life, I'd not taken a lot of interest in my brother. I noticed all the usual teenage stuff at home; his loud guitar playing blasting out of the amp in his room, the shouting matches with my mum, the slamming of doors. I was there when my dad ordered him to get to his room and my brother told him to 'fuck off' before leaving. I could feel the tension brewing as my dad had to restraint his temper from erupting uncontrollably. But I'd not noticed his issues.

'What did they say?' my dad asked.

'He's not been going into school,' my mum said.

'What?' my dad exploded. 'Where is he?'

'I don't know,' Mum said quietly.

'Have you phoned him?'

'Of course, I've phoned him,' my mum snapped.

'What did the school say?'

Mum started to explain. The head of year, Mrs Thompson, a small, almost round, history teacher who used to walk the corridors of the school clapping her hands saying, 'Right boys and girls, time's up, lessons to go to, learning to be done,' had called my mum at about half-past two. She told my mum that Chris had not been in school for the last two days. Further inspection of the school records had led them to realise Chris had only been attending lessons sporadically from the start of the school year. Could my mum, dad, and Chris all come into the school for a meeting the next day?

'How do we handle it?' Dad asked.

'I think we should let him explain what's been going on. There may be a reason for it. Bullying or something.'

My dad made a low grunting noise, indicating he didn't agree. Mum looked at him and shook her head.

I was very aware of just being stood in the middle of the kitchen, not doing anything. I felt like I was standing on the wrong side of the parenting door. It felt unnatural to be watching my parents discussing how to deal with the situation with Chris. I realised they'd probably had conversations about my actions like this. No rulebook, just following their own instincts and trying to work out what the best solution was.

The tension increased as the sound of Chris's key slid into the front door.

We all turned to watch him enter the hallway. He let his school bag slip from his shoulder, landing with a thud on the floor. He looked up and said, 'All right?' before moving to the stairs.

Mum took control. 'Chris, can you come here, please?'

'I just need to get changed,' he said.

'Now, please.'

He was on the stairs now. 'Can I just get changed?'

'Now,' my dad said, his voice hard.

Chris walked in to the kitchen and casually said, 'What's up?'

'We've had a phone call from Mrs Thompson. She says you've not been going to school.'

'What?' Chris said, doing his best to sound shocked. I studied his face, which betrayed his voice. The colour drained quickly from it, and his eyes darted from Mum to Dad, assessing how much they knew. It reminded me of coming in on a Friday night when I was younger and studying their faces to see if they could tell I was drunk or could smell cigarette smoke on my clothes.

A noise filled the room, growing louder. It took me a couple of seconds to realise it was my mobile phone. Everyone stared at me and I pulled it out of my pocket. Kate was calling me. I opened the back door and answered.

'It's me,' she said.

Quickly, I made my way towards the back of the garden, stopping next to the shed, well away from the house and anybody's earshot.

'Are you there?' she asked.

'Yeah,' I said.

'Why did you say that yesterday? That you had nothing to stay for?'

'What is worth staying for?' Kate remained silent, so I carried on, 'You? Us?'

More silence.

I heard my dad's voice shouting from the kitchen. I looked round to see my brother's face framed in the window, his eyes firmly fixed on the floor.

I turned my attention back to Kate. 'Because I told you I loved you and you said we were a cliché.'

Kate said, 'I didn't mean that.'

'Well, that's what you said. So, you don't get to have it both ways. You don't to say that you're only fucking me because you're unhappily married and then ring me up and ask why I don't feel I've got anything round here to stay for. I thought I meant more to you than that.'

She said, 'You do.' But I barely heard her because my brother was shouting back at my parents in the kitchen.

'I've got to go.'

'Tom, don't. Wait.'

Her plea was too late. I shut off the phone and jogged back down the garden. As I entered the kitchen my dad shouted, 'I'm going to take you to school tomorrow and march you to your form room, just to make sure you fucking go.'

Chris said, 'You can't do that. That's well embarrassing.'

'Not as embarrassing as having Mrs Thompson ring your mum and tell her you've been bunking off school.'

I watched Chris form an argument in his mind. He went to respond, but sense stopped him.

'And you're grounded,' my dad added.

'Until when?'

'Well, first, until you get it into that thick head of yours that you've done something wrong. And then, until I say so. Now get upstairs. I'm sick of looking at you. It makes me disappointed. And don't even think about picking up that guitar.'

Chris turned and ran upstairs, his feet pounding on every step. The noise stopped for half a second and then the thud of his bedroom door slamming vibrated through the house.

The rest of the night slipped back into the usual routine of a weeknight at home. Mum cooked while Dad had a shower. I took Chris's food up to his room. I knocked on the door but didn't wait for him to acknowledge it. I opened the door and found him lay on his bed staring straight up at the ceiling, his headphones in. He looked at me and pulled at the wire on his chest; the headphones falling from his ears.

'What?' I lifted the plate to indicate why I was there.

'I don't want any.'

'That'll show Mum and Dad. A hunger strike.'

'Fuck off.'

I walked out, taking the plate with me and left it on the kitchen worktop.

We ate in front of the television, watching the day's local news stories, the food on trays, balanced on our laps. My mum took the plates out, then returned to her chair and watched her soaps. Bored, I went to my room. The house was silent, which would have been nice if it wasn't for the dark clouds of tension hiding in every corner.

ON THURSDAY, I got up for work as normal and found my dad in the same place I'd found my mum the previous day, a mug of tea on the table. He wasn't dressed in his normal landscaping clothes. Instead, he wore his good jeans and a polo shirt.

'Are we not working this morning?' I asked, as I took bread out of the bread bin.

'After I've taken your brother to school.'

'Oh. I thought that was just a threat.'

He took a sip from the mug in front of him. 'It wasn't.'

'Why are you up so early? He doesn't start for an hour and a half.'

'I don't want him getting up early and sneaking out.'

'Is he definitely in his room?'

'Yep.'

'You checked?'

'Yep.'

MY DAD FOLLOWED his threat to and then spent our workday only talking when giving me instructions in a firm tone. We finished at half-past two and went home so he could shower and change before his meeting with Mrs Thompson.

At about half-past four, the three of them returned home. Chris went straight upstairs. My mum looked drained. I saw my dad rub her back and give her a kiss on the head in the kitchen. She collapsed into a chair in the living room and let out a long, deep sigh.

'What did they say?'

Another sigh. 'They haven't suspended him. Thank God. Mrs Thompson explained everything she told me on the phone yesterday. He's been missing lessons on and off since he went back in September. He's had a few days where he's been in for morning and afternoon registrations, but not to lessons. Monday and Tuesday were the first times he's not been in at all.'

'Why haven't they suspended him?'

'Mrs Thompson said there is a real change in him since the new school year. He's talking back more to the teachers, not doing homework, obviously not going to lessons every now and then. But up until last year, all the teachers spoke highly of him. Basically, she said that they know he's a good boy and they think his past record at the school earns him the chance to put all this right.'

'What happens now?'

'He's on a warning. His attendance is being monitored more closely.'

She rested her head back against the chair and closed her eyes for a few seconds. 'I think he has changed a lot recently.'

I wanted to tell my mum how it is. To explain that he's rebelling against her and my dad. Desperate to do something that makes him stand out from the crowd, not realising every school year that has been before him has tried all the same tricks and all the games to get one step ahead of the adult world that rules over them. We all rebel against our parents, don't we? It's natural. I still was. Travelling is a rebellion. To be able to come back and look your parents in the eye and say, 'I've seen more of the world than you'. It's only as you get older you realise you might have seen more of the world than them, but until you've lived with the responsibilities of life the way they have, it's your parents who know more about how the world works.

Chapter Eighteen

Friday night I sat in the Silver Moon sharing the story of Chris' truancy with my mates. There was a big group of us, including Melissa and Stephanie. Neil and Lisa were out as her mum was babysitting. After the initial update about the changes in Alex, and the 'oohs' and 'aahs' from the other girls at the table, they seemed happy to be out in semi adult conversation. We were sat on large couches around a knee-high table that was filling up rapidly with empty glasses.

After the continuing drama of the previous couple of days it was nice to be out talking, laughing, and joking, relaxing with a few drinks.

I glanced up a few times when people entered the pub, expecting to see Kate walk in, but she didn't. I'd not heard from her since our conversation in the garden. I was trying hard not to think about the fact that whatever we were before I'd confessed love for her was now over. The dynamic of our relationship had changed and it didn't seem possible to put it back to what it was before, like an elastic band that's been stretched too far.

Jordan tapped me on the arm and said, 'Drink?'

I nodded.

Charlotte stood and went with him to the bar.

Melissa caught my eye and smiled. She mouthed, 'Is your mum OK?' Meaning about the Chris situation.

'Yeah,' I said.

Neil leant over and said, 'Jordan said you're selling your car.'

'Yeah, mate. Why? Know anyone who wants it?'

'How much do you want?'

'Two grand.'

'My brother might be interested.'

'Cool. Get him to ring me.'

'I'll sort it tomorrow.'

Melissa asked, 'Why are you selling your car?'

I looked her in the eye as she sipped her drink. 'I've booked my trip so I need the money.'

Her eyes widened. She slowly put her drink on the table and said, 'You've booked it?'

'Yeah. I go on the twenty-seventh of December.'

'Why didn't you tell me?'

It felt like every eye around the table was looking in my direction, all waiting to hear my answer. 'I just didn't get around to it,' I said.

Melissa stood up quickly, barely flinching as she caught her leg on the table. She did a half run to the door, knocking into a woman entering the pub.

Stephanie raised herself from her chair and stood over me. 'What did you say that for?'

'Say what?'

'You're a dick-head.'

'What have I done?'

'Why didn't you tell her you were going?'

I failed to answer quickly enough, so Stephanie turned and headed out the door after Melissa.

I remained in my seat, confused at what had just happened.

'Are you guys still together?' Lisa asked.

'No,' I said forcefully.

'Then why is she so upset?'

'I don't know.'

Jordan and Charlotte appeared at the table, holding several drinks between their fingers. He looked at my face and said, 'What's up, mate?'

'Nothing,' I said, standing up.

Melissa was sitting on a bench, Stephanie's arm draped over her shoulders. Melissa was slouched forward, elbows on her knees, her head resting on her hands. I approached cautiously, stopping about seven feet from them, and said, 'Mel, do you want to talk about it?'

She looked up at me, tears in her eyes. 'Go away.'

'Come on, Mel. Don't be like that.'

Stephanie said, 'Tom, just fuck off.'

'Let me just speak to her.'

Stephanie stood up and moved towards me, pushing me backwards, not in an aggressive way but to get me out of Melissa's earshot.

Before Stephanie spoke, I said, 'Steph, listen to me. I just want to talk to her. I want to know what's going on.'

'You didn't tell her you were going away.' Again, her voice raised a level.

'I know. I know.' I held my hands up to try to calm her down. 'Look, I'm not trying to upset her more. I just want to talk to her.'

'I'll ask her.'

She turned away from me, leaving me stood in the street looking over at Melissa, feeling completely useless and thinking this whole situation was ridiculous. I saw Melissa nod, and Stephanie turned around to me and, with a grand gesture of her arms indicated I was allowed to move forward. Stephanie disappeared back into the pub.

I gently placed myself next to Melissa, who wiped the tears from her cheeks.

'Hi,' I said.

'Hi.'

There was a moment of silence as we both watched two middle-aged men sway towards the taxi rank further up the road.

'I don't know why I'm crying so much,' she said.

'Do you want to talk about it?'

'Can we go for a walk? I don't want to sit here being judged by everyone that walks past.'

We stood and walked to the main road, crossing to the middle, waiting on the white line as the black taxi carrying the middle-aged men u-turned from the taxi rank and went around us into the traffic. We moved to the pavement and quickly away from the lights and noise of the takeaway places, turning onto another road. Looking down it, we could see rows of street lights illuminating small areas of pavement and road. There were no other people, just five or six cars parked with two wheels on the pavement. In the immediate contrast of quiet, we could hear the rhythm of our own footsteps and breathing.

'Are we just going to keep walking in silence?' I asked.

'For now,' Melissa responded.

After two or three minutes, we turned left down onto another quiet road. In front of us on the other side of the road were two large black metal gates, closed and locked across the entrance to a park. Either side of the gates was a three-foot-high wall that ran in front of the beds of shrubs and trees that had been grown so close together they acted as another barrier from entering the park. Melissa walked towards the wall and sat down on it. I placed myself next to her.

'Can you let me say what I've got to say without interrupting me? This is going to be hard for me.'

'OK,' I responded.

'Here goes.' She took a deep breath and composed herself before saying, 'I can't believe I'm going to say this. When we spilt up after you started uni, it hit me really hard. I knew there was always a possibility it would happen, especially when you decided to go away and I decided to stay here and get a job. But when it did, I didn't know how to handle it. Every time you came home, I swore to myself I wouldn't see you. I didn't want to hang out with you because I knew I'd want to get back with you. But I couldn't help it. I missed you. I wanted to see you.'

She paused, collecting her words together before continuing. 'Part of me always thought that you'd do your three years at Leeds, come back, and we'd just get back together and start building a life together. Over time, I knew that wouldn't happen. Then you spent your first summer travelling around Europe with your new friends and I realised that you'd moved on. I found that really hard. I made a real effort to move on and try to get over you. I went out with people and whatever, but nothing seemed as good as what we had when we were together. Anyway, I started to find it easier. The benefits of time and all that.'

'Mel.'

'Let me carry on.'

'Sorry.'

'Then you came home in May and we spent that night together. And I woke up confused. I didn't know what I wanted. The next night when you called me, I was glad because I wanted to talk to you seriously about getting back together. About what that night meant to you. To us. And you told me you thought sleeping together was a mistake. I was devastated.'

'I was just being honest.'

'I know. Maybe I wasn't being honest with myself, but I just thought there was something between us that night. Something like the old days. Anyway, I thought I could handle being just friends. And for the past few months, I've tried it. And to be honest, I feel like you've not been that bothered.'

'That's not true.'

She barely heard me and just carried on. 'You've seemed distracted. Like your head is elsewhere.'

Kate flashed in my mind. Kate had been my distraction from the real world, from my home life, my brother, the hours spent doing gardens, not paying much attention to how straight the grass was, my body walking the lawn mower up and down but my mind thinking about the last conversation I'd had with Kate, or wondering when she'd next be able to get away for an hour. She'd distracted me from Melissa and the old days.

Melissa continued. 'This is hard for me to say but I want you to tell me the truth.'

I looked at dark ground and braced myself for the words to come.

'Do you want me to be part of your life in any way?'

I'm not sure what I was expecting her to say, but it wasn't that. 'What? Yes, course I do. Why would you ask that?'

'I feel like I've been trying to be your friend, making an effort to keep things some kind of normal between us and, well, like I said, I feel like you just can't be bothered. And then tonight, it felt like everyone else sat in that pub knew you were going travelling but me.' She was getting upset again. She pushed her words out faster and tensed her body, determined not to allow it to cry. 'Travelling. Not going away for a few days, or a couple of weeks with Jordan on a lads' holiday. Travelling for what, a year?'

'Something like that.'

'This is what I mean. What I'm trying to say. You're going away for a year and you don't even tell me about it. I have to find out from Neil in the pub.' She took a deep breath. Her left arm touched my right one and I could feel her shaking. Instinct told me to put my arm around her, but I knew it was an inappropriate gesture that she'd reject.

'I think of you as my best friend,' she said. 'I think, even now, you know me better than anyone else in the world. And I think you don't even give a shit about me enough to tell me you're going away for a year.' She didn't raise her voice for the last sentence. In fact, her voice trailed off as she said it, like she could barely bring herself to say the words aloud.

I stayed silent, partly out of shame, partly unsure if she was finished.

'So, I'm giving you the opportunity to be honest with me. Right now. Do you want me in your life?'

I was about to answer when her handbag started making a sound. She clicked the metal clasp open and pulled out her mobile phone. 'Hello,' she said as the ringing stopped. She listened and then said, 'No it's fine.' More listening. 'Babe, honestly go without me.' Silence. 'I'm OK. We're just sat on a wall near the park. I'll speak to you tomorrow.' She let out a small laugh. 'I love you too. Have fun.' She made a kiss sound and put the phone away in her bag.

'Was that Steph?' I asked as I slid my cold hands into my jeans pockets and pulled my arms tighter into my body.

'Yeah. They're going to town. She just wanted to check on me.'

'I didn't know you felt like that about me.'

'Which bit?'

'Well, all of it. But mainly the bit about not knowing if I want you in my life or not.'

'Well, do you?' she asked.

'Of course, I do.' I faced her, noticing for the first time the smudged make-up around her eyes where she'd been crying. 'I'm so sorry that you think that I want nothing to do with you. It's not true. I miss us too. And honestly, sometimes I find it hard to just hang out with you. Partly because I thought you wanted to get back together and I didn't want to give you the wrong idea, but also because it's weird hanging out with you but not being with you. In a relationship, I mean.'

She brought her eyes up from the floor and met mine. I continued, 'But it's true, I've been distracted. Not just from you. From the whole world. I've felt trapped. Like the suburbs are closing in around me and forcing me into a life I don't want. Living at home, working for my dad. I've felt like I wanted to cry some nights when I sit in the house and see my parents doing the same thing over and overnight after night. I've not had any money to break the cycle and it's been getting me down.'

Sat on that wall, letting my feelings pour from me honestly, I knew I had to be careful not to continue the confession and talk about Kate. That was a step too far in my friendship with Melissa. She couldn't hear about my affair. My genuine feelings for Kate would break Melissa's heart, and I didn't think our friendship would survive.

'It might sound stupid, but it's been really getting to me.'

'You don't think I don't feel like that?'

'Like what?'

'Trapped. The thought of working every day in the same office for the rest of my life. Living round here. Watching myself turn into my parents. Before when I said I imagined us building a life together when you came back from uni, I didn't imagine the life being around here.'

'Really?' I asked.

'God no. I imagined we'd travel together then get jobs in London or somewhere. Or go and live in Australia for a year and experience a world miles away from here.'

'I didn't know you felt like that.'

'You wouldn't. You've been distracted and ignoring me.' She said those words sarcastically, accompanied by a small smile. She leant against me, 'This is me,' she said. 'You can tell me anything. We don't have to be together to share in each other's lives you know. I care about you. You can talk to me. Just don't bloody ignore me.' She punched me on the arm lightly.

'I'm really sorry I made you feel like that.'

A drunken man appeared in our eye line, carrying an open pizza box, dangling a slice of pizza above his mouth, with cheese hanging down above the open hole. He swayed and took a bite of the food. As he walked away, we heard him slur 'I bloody love pizza' to himself.

Melissa and I laughed. She turned to face me and we leant into each other and gently kissed. It wasn't a passionate kiss, just the soft touching of lips. I could taste the salt from her tears. I slowly pulled my mouth away and said, 'We OK?'

She nodded. 'Will you walk me home?'

'Sure.'

'So,' she said, standing up and wiping the moss from the wall off the back of her jeans, 'tell me about this trip then.'

We walked back to her house with our arms slipped behind the small of each other's backs. I told her of my plans, my route, and the details I knew of what would be my life for the next year at least.

A low light shone from the single bulb on her porch as we stopped at the end of her driveway. We stood wrapped in each other as only people who've shared some intimacy can. My arms wrapped around her waist, her head leaning on me.

'I'm sorry I made you think I didn't want anything to do with you,' I said sincerely.

'It's OK.'

A pause.

'Friends?'

'Friends,' she agreed.

I let her go.

'Night, Tom.'

'Night.'

I watched her walk up the driveway and let herself onto the porch. In the light, she turned and waved. I waved back, put my hands in my pocket and began walking home.

I LOOKED DOWN at Alex asleep in the carry cot that Neil had pushed into my arms so that he and his brother, Dave, could look over my car. They inspected every inch, running their hands over the paint, looking serious.

'Do you want to take it for a test drive?' I asked Dave.

'Yeah,' he responded. 'That all right?'

'Sure. Take your brother with you, then you don't feel like I'm pressuring you.'

Dave was nineteen. He had a big build like his brother, but with more defined muscle. His hair was shaved close to the bone. He didn't look fully comfortable in the presence of others, his eyes never making contact with the person speaking to him.

I placed the carry cot on the pavement. Alex started waking, whiny noises coming from his small mouth. His tightly clenched fists pushed upward as he stretched his body out. 'All right, mate?' I said, smiling at him.

The crunching of gears was heard loudly from down the street. I stood up and saw young Paul's car coming towards us. I stepped off the pavement, putting my hand out and indicated for him to stop. He slammed on his brake and brought his car to a halt in next to me. I walked around the driver's side and he wound his window down.

'Hi, mate,' he said. 'What's up?'

'Do me a favour,' I said. 'Cut the racing down here out will you. There's kids live on this street. If one of them runs out and you hit them, you're fucked.'

He looked mortified and mumbled a response of, 'Yeah sure. No worries. Sorry, mate. Sorry.'

I added, 'Plus, I'm trying to sell this car and if you crash into it, I'm not going to have anything to sell.'

'Yeah, yeah. No worries.'

I walked away and he drove away carefully.

Alex started to cry, and Neil let out a frustrated grunt. He picked his son out of the carry cot and held him close. 'What's wrong?' Alex continued to cry, and Neil tried to calm him. 'Come on little man. No need for this.' The noise subsided and Alex leant on his dad's shoulder.

'That's better.'

'You want to go with your brother and I'll take Alex for a few minutes.'

'You sure?'

'No problem.' I held my hands out and Neil passed him to me. I held Alex high in the air and kept him there. His face lit up into a smile. I brought him down and lifted him again. As I did, I looked over his head and saw Kate driving towards me. She smiled as I lifted Alex again. I brought him down for a third time. Neil slammed my passenger door, wound down the window and said, 'Who was that?'

'Just a neighbour,' I said.

'She's pretty fit.'

'She's not bad,' I said, playing along.

THEY RETURNED WITH the car about ten minutes later. I was inside the house, my mum using the opportunity to play with and cuddle Alex. I jumped up as the doorbell rang.

'How much do you want for it?' Dave asked.

'Two grand.'

He tried to look as if he was swilling the number around his mind. He pulled a face, showing me he was checking if he was getting a good deal or not. Eventually he said, 'OK. When can I take it?'

'When the money is in my bank,' I said. Neil laughed.

Dave stuck out his hand and said, 'Deal. I'll get the cash together by Wednesday.'

I shook his hand and stepped outside, taking the keys Dave was holding in his other hand. I opened the door and peeled the tape off my for-sale sign. 'Guess I won't be needing this anymore.'

'Where's my son?' Neil asked.

'Inside. My mum's reminiscing about the days when my brother was nice.'

SUNDAY WAS A strangely relaxing day at home. My brother, after not being allowed out on Saturday night, got up early and offered to clean my dad's car. He spent an hour or so cleaning it outside and in, polishing the dashboard and steering wheel. The tension around his wagging school had started to subside. We sat down for the first time in months for a family lunch, which could almost be described as pleasant. My brother didn't actually apologise for what he'd done, but I could see how much my parents appreciated his efforts. In between the three courses my mum had prepared, we talked to each other, as opposed to rushing through the food so we could all go and get on with different things in different parts of the house.

THE RENEWED CALM showed itself to be more of a false dawn two days later when I walked into the lounge to find my mum sat on her settee, feet curled underneath her, crying. On the arm of the settee next to her was a bag of weed. People were on the television screen, but their voices were mute. She looked up at me as I entered the room, disappointment showing on her face.

'Look what I found in your brother's bag,' she said, picking up the bag of weed between her thumb and forefinger and holding it in front of her like a detective on a drama series would with crucial evidence. To my lack of response, she said, 'Do you know what it is?'

'Yes,' I answered. 'Do you?'

'Of course I do,' she said. 'I'm not a naïve as you think I am.'

'I didn't say you were,' I said defensively. 'I was just checking that's all.'

She looked me in the eye and said, 'Do you know where he got it?'

'It wasn't from me if that's what you're implying.'

'I wasn't implying that at all,' she responded.

There was a pause, neither of us sure how to continue. I said, 'Are you going to bring it up with him?'

'He's got drugs in the house. Of course I'm going to bring it up.'

I wanted to tell her it was just a bit of weed and it wasn't a big deal, but I knew that was not the response she was looking for. Instead, I carefully said, 'He's going to want to know what you were doing going through his bag.'

'I was looking for his PE kit to do his bloody washing. I wasn't snooping. I wouldn't do that. Although it looks like I should have been.' She paused, her eyes looking around the room, distracted. 'I don't understand that boy. He's determined to mess up his chances of doing well this year. First, he bunks off school, now this. If he's not careful, he's going to get bloody suspended and then he can forget any chance of college. Do you know the teachers at his school used to rave about him until this year? They couldn't say enough about his work. What a nice lad he was. Between me and you, I can't help but think Laura's a bad influence on him.'

'He's just a teenager,' I said, trying to reassure her. 'He's just experimenting, rebelling. Finding out what he likes and doesn't like.

We've all done it. I bet even you and Dad were a bit wild in your youth.'

'What's that supposed to mean?'

'You've just admitted you know what a bag of weed looks like.'

'I know you think we're boring,' she said, almost ignoring my previous comment. 'But we have responsibilities. We can't be out every night. I'd bloody like to be out every night. I'd love to be doing what you're doing, travelling the world. Enjoying myself. But life's not like that at our age. Maybe when we're retired and we've got rid of you two. You were never like this, causing us all this trouble.'

'Maybe I was just better at hiding it.'

Her eyes met mine. 'What are you saying?'

I was still in the middle of the room at this point, staring down at her. I sat down on the chair opposite her, leaning forward. 'Do you really want to know about the things I got up to when I was a teenager? Or at uni? Honestly? Because we can have this conversation Mum, but you might not like everything you hear.'

'Did you bunk off school?'

'There were a couple of occasions towards the end where me and Melissa spent the afternoon at her house instead of going to Maths or English or whatever. Never full days.'

'Have you smoked this stuff?' she said, lifting the bag towards me.

I thought about the answer I should give. There was the answer she wanted to hear, the answer that would reassure her that she hadn't, in her mind, turned two sons to drugs, and then there was the truth. I decided that at twenty-one I could have an honest conversation with my mum about this sort of thing. So, I answered. 'Yes.'

For a brief moment, disappointment flashed across her face. 'Do you still?'

'I haven't smoked it for a while. I'm not against it, though. Have you?'

I could tell my mum was weighing up the pros and cons of honesty at this point, as I had done a few seconds earlier. 'A couple of times when I was younger. I was a teenager in the sixties remember.'

I smiled and said, 'And here was I thinking you would sit in your room all day listening to 'Love Me Do' on vinyl.'

'I think I still have that somewhere.'

'Can I have it? It'll be worth a fortune now.'

She said, 'Have you done anything else I should know about?'

'In the spirit of honesty and truthfulness, I've taken ecstasy once at a party in my first year of uni. A few of us wanted to know what it was like. It was more just to say I'd done it.'

After a long pause, she nodded and said, 'I'm glad you feel you can be honest with me.'

'Me too.'

There was a silence before she said, 'I know you don't want to be here.'

'What do you mean?' I said, genuinely shocked at her words.

'Here. In this house. Living back with us. I can tell. I know it must be difficult, having lived away from us for so long, to come back and try to fit in. You're not a kid anymore. I understand that. Me and your dad just want the best for you. We work hard so you can have the things, and the chances we never had. So, is it too much for us to ask for you and your brother to try to be good people?

'University wasn't an option for us. But we wanted you to go to experience it and to give yourself a better chance in life. The same with this travelling thing you're doing. We want you to go. But we also worry about you.

'We don't want you missing out on job opportunities. And most of all, we want you to be safe.'

'I will.'

'And now all this with your brother. It's stressful having children of your ages.'

'He'll be OK. Things will calm down.'

'I hope so.'

My mum stretched out her arms and I gave her a hug. 'I love you.'

'Love you too, Mum.'

I LIE ON my bed in my box room on top of the single red duvet, staring at the ceiling, thinking.

Thinking about my parents and my brother.

Thinking that the angry and disappointed shouts of my dad I'd heard from downstairs aimed at my brother were shouts for normal teenage things. Things to test authority. Things every teenager in the country had done in some form. Underage drinking, wagging school, smoking, taking drugs, having sex. They were all just ways for kids to act like adults, to prove to everyone they were cool, that they were not tied to the rules set for them by the generation above. Things I'd admitted to my mum I'd done, to show her that my brother wasn't different from me or anyone else, that it was natural for kids of his age to act the way he was acting. To try to convince her that his choices were no different to mine and she thought I'd turned out OK.

I lie there thinking about her words, 'Is it too much to ask that you try to be good people?' Thinking about how they applied to me. Was I a good person? Did I live up to the expectations my parents had set for me?

The girl who I'd slept with in Manchester came into my mind. Waking up alone the next morning, hung-over and disorientated, she wouldn't have thought I was a good person for leaving without any exchange of words. To this day, all these years later, I cannot remember her name. She played no further part in my life.

I heard a door shut downstairs, followed by the quick slamming of feet as somebody raced up the stairs. Another thud of a bedroom door closing. I guessed Chris was now in his room, probably lying on his bed the way I was, fuming at the unfairness of it all. My dad was not one for sitting and talking through the issues of Chris's wrongdoing, explaining the reasons for his, and my mum's, disappointment. His instinctive reaction was anger. Anger at my brother's stupidity. He shouted because that got his message across.

He wasn't wrong for doing it, despite what Chris was probably thinking at that exact moment. Dad was never going to sit Chris down and explain the dangers of drug use, quote studies from professionals or articles from *The Guardian*. Drugs were bad, taking drugs was wrong, and having drugs in your school back was a big fucking no-no. These are the facts according to Dad. You did something wrong, now you're in trouble. You want to act like a man? Take your punishment like a man. Admit you were wrong and do something to make sure it doesn't happen again.

It was only speaking to my mum earlier that night that I began to see it from their point of view. There are so many things parents want for their children. A good education, stable job, good health, enjoyment of life, to be in a position to take opportunities that they never had. And each incident of teenage rebellion, each show of disregard for the rules of the home, was another moment where potentially the child could go off the path to the good life the parents wanted.

What did my parents mean by being a good person? To be kind and fair, to treat people with respect, to work hard. All the things they were taught by their parents.

How would I be judged in their eyes? With the evidence my parents had, at the same point in my life that Chris was at, I would say fairly well. But my parents didn't have all the facts. My mum had more information now, but they didn't know everything about my life. Should they? No, I don't think so. Kids need to try things and make mistakes. It is part of growing up, learning from the errors you make. But I wasn't naïve. Actions of the children are a reflection of the parents. A judgement for my actions was a judgement against them. That's why they were so angry and disappointed with Chris. In their eyes if it'd been a teacher who had found the weed in his bag, it wouldn't just have been Chris the teacher would have blamed. Somewhere inside them, even if it was not said aloud, they would wonder what my parents had done wrong.

That day I realised the arguments between parents and children boil down to the interpretations of right and wrong. My parents thought taking drugs was wrong so they got angry with my brother. Chris thought smoking weed was OK. So, they argued and fought and went around and around and back and forward, shouting and screaming and slamming doors and disagreeing with each other.

Kate. That situation couldn't be misread. What we had done was wrong. I'd entered a relationship, however loosely that term can define what we had, with a married woman. The wife of someone I knew and who would probably refer to me as a friend. If Stuart found out Kate and I had been sleeping with each other he had every right to feel I'd broke whatever bond we had formed. To him, I wasn't a random person who'd entered his marriage.

Was Kate worse than I was? Yes, she'd broken her vows and cheated on her husband. But I was happy to play my part; to sneak around, to deceive her husband, my family, and friends.

Anger grew inside me, fertilised by frustration. I was angry at her for calling us a cliché, angry at myself for not realising we were. Angry at my own stupidity for getting involved and for allowing myself to fall in love. Frustrated that for the first time in my life the end of a relationship wasn't on my terms. This didn't help my feelings. The way we ended, a phone call interrupted by my family shouting at each other, didn't seem worthy of the feelings I had for Kate.

It was as if I was grieving. The initial sudden shock of not being with Kate had worn off and I was left alone, with no understanding of the empty, hollow feelings that remained inside me.

I curled up on the bed and wished I could stay in that box room until it was time to go to the airport and fly off to another part of the world that didn't have Kate in it. I knew any distance between us wouldn't dilute my feelings for her.

You see this was where every argument of good and bad fell apart. The good person in me, shaped and formed by my parents or not, was capable of understanding that what Kate and I had done was wrong. We had broken rules and moral codes and done something terrible. The problem was none of that mattered to me. No words of anger or looks of disappointment could convince me that it wasn't worth it. If the secret of our affair was ever released into the world, not one judgement from a neighbour or punch from Stuart would change the way I felt. I loved Kate. I wasn't sure when it became true, or why it happened, but it had. And I was grateful that I was able to experience it. I didn't care why she started the affair. I'd just been glad to know her, to touch her, to be excited to talk to her. What I felt was real.

Tears rolled down my face and onto the faded red single duvet. I lay there thinking about Kate. Thinking about my feelings. Thinking about love.

CHRIS LAID ON his bed, staring at the spot on the wall where his guitar used to lean. The black Marshall amp it stood on was still there, useless.

I moved to the middle of his room with caution.

'I hope you're not here to say I told you so,' he said.

I shook my head slowly. 'No. I'm not. I don't think that will help you. I just wanted to see if you were OK.'

'I don't know why you bothered coming back here to live. You were well lucky living away, not having to listen to their bullshit.' He was being defiant, acting as he'd done nothing worthy of punishment. 'I fucking hate them.'

'No, you don't,' I said.

'I do. I can't wait to be old enough to go to uni and get the fuck out of here.'

He moved on the bed, sitting up. I sat down in the now free space where his feet had been. He had pulled his knees up towards his chin, wrapping his arms around his legs.

I spoke, trying to get the weight of my words across to him without shouting. 'Look, mate, you've done something wrong. OK? You're being punished for it. The sooner you accept that, the easier your life with Mum and Dad will be.'

He tried to force a word into the conversation, but I put my hand up and said, 'Let me finish.' His eyes dropped. 'I know you're only doing what your mates are doing, you're only doing what I've done in the past, but that doesn't mean Mum and Dad aren't going to get annoyed about it.'

'It's like they've never done anything wrong. I bet Dad didn't go to school every day when he was my age.'

'He didn't. He used to work for Granddad's mate on the milk floats some days. He'd get up before five o'clock some mornings, work, then go to school. There were some afternoons when he knew Nana wouldn't be home, he just thought 'fuck it' and went home to bed, or to hang out with his mates somewhere.'

'Really, he'd get up that early?' Chris asked. 'How do you know that?'

'He told me about it on a job a few weeks ago.'

'Oh. So why is he so annoyed with me? If he's not perfect himself.'

'Because that's not how it works, is it? Mum and Dad want more for you and me than they had for themselves. Every parent does. That's why they work so hard, why Dad is up and out to work before you even think about getting out of bed. That's how it's supposed to work. Each generation does better than the last. We'll work hard to let our kids have more than we had.' I paused and let the words register with him. Then I asked, 'Do you really want to go to uni?'

He thought about it for a second, as if it was so far off in his future that he couldn't honestly contemplate what it meant. 'I think so. You always came home with good stories. I remember you saying you were glad you didn't live around here all your life. Even if you ended up living here when you'd finished at least you could say you left for a bit.'

I nodded. 'It's true. What do you want to study?'

He shrugged, in the same movement, relaxing his grip around his legs and stretching them out. 'I'm not sure. Music maybe. I've been looking at a couple of courses about it at college. Sounds quite good.'

'That's cool,' I said, impressed that he had a vision of what his future might hold. 'Let me ask you something then, if that's what you want to do, to go to uni and study that, do you think it's a good idea to be wagging school now and taking weed to school with you? A decent college isn't going to let you in if you've been expelled from school for that kind of stuff, is it?'

He didn't answer me, but I could tell the words had pierced his mind.

'Look, Mum and Dad are angry because they don't want you to mess up any chances you've got to do something with your life. That's all. They just want you to be happy and have a nice life. It sounds soppy and a bit shit to hear, but it's true. So just ride the punishment out, make a bit more effort with school and if you're going to smoke weed and get pissed with your mates, just make sure you're a bit more careful about where and when you do it. OK?'

'Yeah.'

I stood up and walked towards the door.

From behind me Chris's voice said, 'How long do you think it'll be before I get my guitar back?'

I turned to look at him. 'Be nice to Mum and give it a couple of days. Then ask.'

I softly shut the door behind me. On the landing, I saw the top of my mum's head appear up the stairs. As she reached the last step, she looked at me and said, 'Everything OK love?'

'Yeah,' I said. 'Everything's fine.'

LATER THAT NIGHT, the house phone rang. I answered it in the hallway. A nervous teenage girl on the other end said, 'Is, er, Chris there please?'

'Who's calling?' I asked.

'Michelle.'

'Chris,' I shouted. 'Michelle's on the phone.'

Seconds later, my brother ran down the stairs. I covered the phone and said, 'What happened to Laura?'

Taking the phone from me, he said, 'Split up ages ago.'

Chapter Nineteen

Everything changed on Bonfire Night.

The early November night brought around a tradition on my parents' road. Since I can remember, Mr Keane, or John as he became as I grew up, would host a bonfire and fireworks display in his back garden. His house was at the top of the cul-de-sac, at the tip of the turning circle. The natural curve of the road at that end gave him and his neighbour, the Sullivans, more land than the rest of the houses on the street. John and his wife, Lorna, started hosting the annual night before I was born for their two children and the other young families on the street. Anthony and Carla grew up and moved out, but the tradition remained.

Three weeks before Bonfire Night, John would start informing neighbours in the street that he was planning another party. Days before, if he'd missed anyone, he'd go knocking on doors and invite the last remaining neighbours. I'd missed the last three because I was in Leeds.

The parties were simple. Lorna prepared food in the kitchen, piling up hot dogs and burgers on large round plates. Helpful neighbours, usually my mum and a couple of others, would then slice buns in two and spread the word around. People would queue and the helpers would serve the food, pointing people to ketchup bottles and salad on another table. The kids and parents stood wrapped in winter coats around the large patio, holding sparklers in gloved hands, eyes fixated on the flickering fire, intermittently watching the end of a firework burn and fizz before the small rockets shot into the air.

If the party was a school night it would die down early, people taking tired children in the post-excited low off to bed. On a weekend though, like this Friday night, the adults would take advantage of the wine or beers provided and spend a few hours just hanging out with their neighbours, people who they generally only let on to in passing as they drove out of their driveways or exchanged quick conversations as they passed tools they'd borrowed back across the fence.

I say adults because it wasn't only people with children who came. Couples and single people from the street attended every year too. They brought nieces and nephews or just came alone to experience the event.

That's how I ended up standing next to Kate, alone, in the dark garden.

I'd seen her arrive without Stuart. She was dressed for the occasion, her winter coat buttoned to the top, scarf wrapped tightly around her neck. Her black woollen hat was pulled down over her ears, revealing a small view of her hair between the end of the hat and her coat collar. She had black leather gloves on. I watched her accept a hug and kiss from Lorna and hand over a bottle of wine as a thank you present. They exchanged a few words, then Lorna disappeared and Kate walked into the garden, round to the patio where children awaited the start of the display. She smiled hellos to a couple of neighbours and followed swirling sparklers with her eyes.

I stood on the other side of the garden and watched her crouch down to a small child's level, listen carefully and watch the child point into the sky to recreate a firework exploding with his hand.

My attention was then pulled away as John moved to the middle of his garden and tried to get everyone's attention. A couple of other men stood by his side as he welcomed everyone, said he hoped they enjoyed themselves and requested everyone please keep off the grass while the fireworks were going on. Then he and the other men turned around and walked to their fireworks and lit them.

Rockets rushed into the sky, exploding colour. I watched for a few minutes, stood alone and sipped from a bottle of lager.

Kate appeared silently at my side. Neither of us looked at each other, instead keeping our focus on the display. Excited noises came from the patio where parents' and children's necks were angled to the sky, watching the parade of colour.

'I don't know what to say,' she said.

'There isn't anything to say,' I responded.

'It doesn't feel like that.'

I remained silent, my arms folded across me, defiant. It was an act.

'I owe you an explanation,' she said, still looking upwards. 'A real one. Not a shouting match on the phone.'

'What's to explain?'

'Us, me, everything.'

'What's to say?'

She sighed. Her body was so close I feel could feel the rising and falling of her shoulders. 'Honestly, Tom, I just can't live with the last thing that ever happened between us was you putting the phone down on me. I cannot live the rest of my life knowing that I could've told you everything, could've explained how I felt, why I said the things I said, and didn't get the chance. It hurts me to think that's how we ended.' She turned to me and said, 'Stuart is away tonight. I'll be home all night after this. If you want to talk, you know where I'll be. If not, we don't ever have to speak again.'

She walked away.

I stood motionless, watching fireworks dance in the sky.

I WALKED AWAY from the party with purpose, glancing around me to see if anyone was watching. I moved towards the right of the road, stepping onto the pavement before disappearing through the open gate of Kate's driveway. I walked quickly along the gap between the side of the low fence and her car towards the back door, keeping myself as close to the house as possible. I knocked sharply against the back door with my knuckles.

Kate opened the door slowly, and I entered silently. She had shed the coat, scarf, hat, and gloves. She wasn't wearing her boots, but her jeans were still tucked inside a pair of thick, multicoloured socks.

The kitchen was dark, lit only at the far end by the light coming from the living room that shone through its open door across the hallway. We sat down at the kitchen table facing each other, surrounded by the dark.

'I didn't think you would come,' she said.

I ignored her words and said, 'Before you explain anything, I think I need to say my piece.'

'OK,' she said, giving a small, understanding nod.

'I didn't ask for any of this. I'll admit I fancied you. I'll admit I thought about what it would be like to be with you. But it was a fantasy to me. A 'what if' I didn't think would ever happen. Even after what happened that night when Stuart was in Portugal and you were upset over the baby. I was happy to say we went over the line and never talk about it again. That was what we agreed.'

She went to say something, but I cut her off, physically raising my hand and holding it in front of her. 'Don't,' I said. 'Let me finish.' Her mouth shut without words leaving it.

I could feel myself shaking. I clenched my fist and dug my nails into my palm. 'But, having agreed that, the night this affair or whatever we are, this cliché.' I saw her flinch as if the word had stung her on the forehead. I continued, 'That night you knocked on my door You came to me. And then, days later, I gave you the choice. We can keep doing whatever it was we were doing or we could stop. We sat in my car and I asked you, outright, do you want to carry this on or not? You said yes. So, you'll understand why I'm confused. I wanted you. I know that was wrong, but I'm a twenty-one-year-old single lad. What the fuck am I supposed to do? You're married, but you seemed pretty fucking happy to go along with everything. And I might be stupid, or naïve, or whatever, but I was pretty sure I was more to you than some lad you could shag because you were unhappy at home.'

'You were,' she inserted quickly.

'Maybe I broke the spell. Maybe I went over the line by telling you I loved you.' I laughed softly and said, 'Fuck knows I didn't do it in the best way, calling you during an anniversary dinner.'

She laughed too, her eyes lighting up behind the small pools of tears that now filled them. I continued, 'But I couldn't carry on just pretending. That night, the night I called you, I met someone. A girl called Sarah; at my friend's party I'd gone to. She was amazing. Beautiful, funny, just been travelling. We sat by a brook and talked for ages and she kissed me. It was everything you'd want from a situation like that. I think if I'm honest we could've got together and had a proper relationship. But something stopped me. When she kissed me, I felt like I was betraying you.' I saw surprise appear in her eyes. 'That's why I called you. I'd just turned down a girl who was, on paper, perfect for me. For you. I wanted, no that's not the right word, I needed to know, had I done it because I was stupid or because you felt the same about me as I felt about you? That's why I told you I loved you. That's why I demanded an answer. Because I needed to know it was because you felt the same. And then you called us a cliché and basically my whole world fell apart.'

A vacuum of silence appeared in the room as she took in what I'd said.

'OK,' she said slowly. 'Is that everything?'

I thought for a second and said, 'Yeah.'

It was her turn to take a deep breath. She wiped her eyes with the long sleeve of her jumper. 'I was scared,' she said. 'The night I called us a cliché, I was scared that everything we'd done, everything we'd become, was suddenly becoming real. When you phoned me, I realised how easy it was to get caught. One phone call at the wrong time and Stuart would know. I stood in that restaurant toilet and it hit me how close we were to being found out. And then you told me you loved me. Everything had changed. I guess deep down I knew we were building to that. But I thought we'd just carry on as we were, grabbing time together until you went travelling, then we could both just get on with our lives. I thought our feelings would just go unmentioned. But when you told me how you felt it scared me. I was scared of my own feelings for you. When you said those words, that you loved me, I knew in that moment that I felt the same way. And that was the thing that scared me the most. Because in that moment I knew my marriage could easily be over. I was stuck between being scared of leaving and scared of staying.'

Neither of us spoke. Both of us were just relieved that the weight of the last few weeks lifted with each honest word spoken.

She continued. 'I knocked on your door that night, when all this really started, because I was unhappy. I think every affair starts because someone is unhappy in the relationship. Happy people don't have affairs.'

Since we had started our affair the subject of their marriage had never raised its head. We avoided talking about it for fear of it exposing the reality of our situation. Now she sat opposite me, looking straight into my eyes, and I knew she was about to let me into that part of her life. I wasn't sure if I wanted to know what she was about to say. I knew deep down she wasn't happy with Stuart. Even before we started sleeping together, I'd noticed throw away comments about him being away again, or out with the lads, or how their social lives didn't often involve each other. I knew their marriage wasn't always a happy place.

'When I left you in the middle of the night, after that first night together, I came home and sat at this kitchen table thinking for hours. I was honest with myself. That was the first time I admitted to myself how unhappy I was with Stuart and what our lives had become. It was very hard to do, because we seemed so normal. We had, have,' she corrected, 'good jobs, a nice house, good friends. But something was wrong. My family had noticed it. Sometimes we'd have Sunday dinner and my mum would pull me to one side in the kitchen and ask if everything was OK. I'd lie and say yes. Say Stuart was tired because of work, or we were just a bit stressed about something trivial and brush it off. But that was the problem. We were unhappy and I couldn't put my finger on why. I just was. I was sick of being second in line to Stuart's mates. He has a real need, even now after we've been married for five years, to prove he's still one of the boys.

Weekends away, football, always just 'nipping out for a pint with the lads'. And I never wanted to be the wife that stops that, even now I don't want him to not do something that makes him happy. But I wanted him to put some of that energy into me. And for a long time, way before me and you, he had stopped doing that.'

She paused but I didn't fill the silence.

'So that night we, me and you, slept together, I sat here and I felt stupid. The reasons I've just given didn't seem like enough to cheat. Stuart didn't hit me, he didn't cheat on me, to my knowledge. We had our issues and problems but what I'd done went beyond any unhappiness I blamed him for. I knew he was unhappy too, but it didn't excuse what I'd done with you. I knew it was wrong. I knew I was stupid. I sat up until it was nearly light. I was tired, physically and emotionally. I'd dried tears down my face. But I couldn't get up to go to bed. I couldn't sleep in the bed I shared with my husband. I slept right here,' she marked the spot with her finger by jabbing it onto the table, 'for about an hour so. When I woke, I made the decision that nothing would happen again between us. For two days I thought about how to tell you I didn't want to see you again. I decided to tell you when we met up on the Wednesday lunchtime when you picked me up from work.'

'What changed?' I asked, my voice cracking slightly after being intently silent for so long. My mouth was dry and a feeling of nervousness invaded me.

'You,' she said simply. 'Although I decided to not see you again, I couldn't stop thinking about you. The way you made me feel. The way you made me laugh. How easy it felt being around you. I'd not had that for a long time. And when you asked me if I wanted to carry on seeing you every instinct in my body told me to say no, but I couldn't help but say yes.' She shrugged, as if resigned to the fate of it all. 'If I'm brutally honest I think I thought I could have some fun. Some fun with a young lad who wasn't going to want anything. And I was attracted to that idea.'

Another pause.

Another silence.

As I write this, thinking back on that night, sat at her kitchen table, I've noticed something for the first time. During all the time we sat and explained our feelings, we never touched each other. At points as Kate talked, tears were rolling down her face, but not once did our hands reach out across the table and join together, as they had done so easily in the past. It's strange that I've only noticed it now, all these years later. I suppose at the time we must have been denying ourselves that psychical connection until everything that needed to be said had been.

'It was not an easy decision to say yes to you. For those first weeks especially, despite the excitement of being with you, it was the most horrible time of my life. I was cheating on my husband. A man I made promises to. Promises to love forever. That did not sit easily with me.'

'So why did we carry on?'

'I wanted it to stop. But then I'd go two days without talking to you and I'd miss you. Miss you to the point it hurt. I'd be like a teenager looking out of my bedroom window just to see if you were walking down the road, or if your car was there.' I almost smiled at my own memories of doing the same thing.

'And like I said before I figured that we'd just carry on until you went travelling and then we'd just get on with our lives.'

'Until I went and fucked it all up and told you I loved you?'

'Exactly,' she said.

She stood up, causing her chair to scrape loudly across the tiled floor. As she walked towards the sink, I looked at both windows in the room, making sure nobody could see us through the drawn blinds. Kate lifted a glass off the draining board and ran cold water into it. Leaning against the sink she drank it in one.

'So, what do we do now?' I asked.

'I don't know,' she said, putting the glass in the sink. 'What do you want?'

'I don't think that's fair to ask.'

'Why not?'

'Because my answer involves asking you to leave your husband.'

It seemed like hours until she spoke again, eventually saying, 'I think I need to hear it.'

'You sure?' I said.

She nodded.

What did I want? In a perfect world, I wanted her to leave her husband to be with me. I wanted to walk down the street with her, hand in hand. I wanted to be proud to be with her, not hide in the shadows. I wanted her to quit her job and come travelling around the world with me, enjoying the experiences we'd talked about me having over the last few months. I wanted to return to life as a couple, with a past to talk about and stories to share. I wanted to be with her for the rest of my life.

And I told her all this that night.

'That's a lot to want,' she said.

'I'm not asking you to leave,' I responded. 'If you ever leave Stuart, for me or just to not be with him, that has to be your decision. Because I don't ever want there to be a day where you blame or resent me for forcing you. If you say after tonight you want to make your marriage work, I'll understand. This thing of ours, whatever it was for you, can be over. I'll walk away. I don't have a choice in that. But I won't make it difficult for you.'

'I need to think about everything,' she said.

Chapter Twenty

The morning after, I woke to the sound of the front door shutting loudly. Seconds later, my bedroom door swung open, and my brother almost fell through it. Regaining his composure, he said, 'Can you drive Dad's van?'

I rolled over and tried to adjust to the scene, light pouring into the room from behind Chris.

'What time is it?' I said, my head still clamped to the pillow.

'Half ten,' he answered impatiently. 'Can you drive Dad's van?'

'Yes,' I responded, starting to sit up. 'What do you want?'

'I need a lift to band practice.'

'What?'

'I need a lift to band practice.'

'I heard you.' I sat up and tried to process the information he was firing at me. 'Start again,' I said. 'At the beginning. Are you in a band?'

'Not yet. A few lads in sixth form have got a band. They haven't got a lead guitarist, so they've asked me to jam today to see if I fit, or if I'm good enough. But I can't get there. Mum and Dad are out and I need you to take me.'

'Who was at the door?'

'The singer, Adam. He was just asking me to come down today.'
I could see the enthusiasm advertised on his face. He was almost
bouncing on the balls of his feet, like a boxer waiting for the ring
announcements. 'Can you take me?'

'Yeah,' I said. 'Of course, I can.'

'Right. They start at twelve. In Adam's garage.'

'OK, no problem.'

He left the room, without saying thank you, and seconds later I
heard the noise of his guitar plugging into the amp then the distinct
sound of feedback as he started playing riffs.

For those few minutes, as the pleasure and excitement shone
from Chris, I didn't think about Kate. I didn't think about what we'd
said the night before, or that she might be across the road, deciding
whether to end her marriage and run away with me.

Instead, I lay in bed, content with listening to my brother playing
his guitar, enjoying himself.

I DROPPED CHRIS off outside a large, detached house in Timperley.
Looking down the side of the house, past a BMW 5 series that was
parked on the driveway, I could see through an open garage door.
Four lads were setting up instruments, plugging in wires, and
checking sound levels. Chris sat full of nerves and worry.

'You OK?' I said.

'Yeah,' he said, almost inaudibly.

'try to relax,' I said. 'You know you can play.'

He climbed out of the van, pulled his guitar case off the middle passenger seat, and slammed the door.

LATER CHRIS CAME bursting through the front door, after one of the band members had driven him home, visibly buzzing.

'Everything OK?' I said from my position on the couch, watching football results ticking across the bottom of the screen.

'Yeah, it was brilliant.'

'What did you do?'

'I met everyone, then listened to a couple of their tunes. Then we played a couple of covers I knew. I think that was just to see if I could play. They said they liked my playing, then we worked on a song. I listened to it a couple of times, then just started playing a riff and it built from there. It was good. Jake, the rhythm guitarist, taught me the chords and they want me to work on the lead parts.'

'So, you're in?'

'I'm in,' he said.

Then, for what felt like the first time in months, he smiled.

DRESSED IN TWO long sleeve tops underneath a hooded jumper, a hat pulled down over my ears and gardening gloves to protect me from the cold November weather I stood at the bottom of a tree we were going to cut down, unravelling a rope. My dad set up the ladder. It was Wednesday, and I still hadn't heard from Kate.

'Your brother has got band practice tonight.'

'OK.'

'Your mum is a bit worried.'

'Mum is or you are?'

'We both are.'

'What are you worried about?'

'We think he should be concentrating on his schoolwork, not being distracted.'

I stopped what I was doing with the rope and looked at my dad. I understood his worry, that in the last year of school, when Chris should be focused on getting good GCSE results, he would spend day and night playing his guitar. I said, 'Practice is only Wednesday nights and Saturday.'

'I suggested we tell him he can't practice with the band unless his schoolwork is done and he's done some revision each week.'

'Seems fair. He should get a homework diary from school or something so you can keep an eye on what he's got.'

My dad nodded, showing his thanks and how impressed he was that I had valid points and opinions all in the one movement. We'd built this bond over the few months we'd worked together.

I'd been away from home, lived on my own, and survived. I didn't call home every two minutes for money or help. To my dad that was more important and beneficial than the degree I'd got.

Standing on your own two feet, surviving as an adult; he respected that. It entitled me to an opinion in the adult world, something I'd not been granted before I'd left.

I felt my phone vibrate in my pocket as a text came through. Quickly, I pulled my glove off and took the phone from my pocket. It was from Jordan. *Fancy a pint tonight after work?*

I typed a response and put the phone back, covering my hand again.

My dad asked, 'Everything OK?'

'Yeah.'

'You've been a bit distracted the last couple of days.'

'I'm fine,' I lied.

'OK.' He shrugged. 'Let's cut this bloody tree down then before it starts pissing down.'

Driving down our road the next night, I saw Stuart appear on the other side of the road, stepping out from under the light of a street lamp. He crossed the road with purpose. I froze in my seat, paralysed by fear. Fear he knew, fear of the showdown, fear of what my dad would say. As my dad brought the van to a stop outside our house, Stuart smiled and gave a small wave, moving to my dad's side of the van.

'Hi, Stuart,' my dad said, opening the door.

'All right? A couple of my fence panels are coming loose. This bloody shitty weather isn't helping. The posts are not the most stable. I was wondering if you could have a look.'

Relaxing, I slid out of my seat and gently closed the door, moving around the van towards the house.

'Sure,' my dad said. 'I'll nip over in the morning and have a look. I'll ring you when I'm done, let you know what it'll need.'

'Cheers,' Stuart said. I was at the front door when I heard him say, 'Tom's got my number.'

'WHAT'S THE NAME of this band, then?' my dad asked Chris as we waited for my mum to tell us tea was ready. We sat in the lounge, warm and dry following after-work showers, watching the *North-West News* on the tele.

'The Death Stars,' Chris said, looking up from a homework book.

'I'm thinking about starting a band called George Lucas's Lawyers,' I said.

Dad laughed.

Chris didn't. Instead, he said, 'I don't get it.'

'What's not to get?'

'Who's George Lucas?'

'Who's George Lucas?' both my dad and I repeated.

'Do you know what Death Stars are?' my dad asked.

'Yeah,' Chris answered, defensively. 'From *Star Wars*.'

'But you don't know who George Lucas is?'

'No.'

'Ask the lads in the band,' I said. 'They'll tell you.'

'Don't do that,' my dad said. 'They'll kick you out of the band.'

I laughed. Chris didn't. My mum shouted tea was ready.

'IT'S THE ROOT that's the problem. That's what's causing the cracks. Once the cracks start, you're knackered. Nothing holds together once the cracks start.'

Stood in Kate and Stuart's garden, my dad was talking about a tree root and a grey concrete fence post.

He could easily have been talking about their marriage.

THE PHONE CALL came later that afternoon.

'Hello,' I said.

'Can we meet? I'm ready to talk now.'

Chapter Twenty-One

It was pissing down.

I was in the park, waiting for Kate by the small building that housed several football changing rooms and showers for the local kids' team, who had two pitches on the other side of the building. I leant against the peeling red paint of the football changing rooms' main door, my body tucked under the small concrete roof that stuck out from the grey brick building, huddled into myself to keep dry. I stared into the dark, rain falling continuously in my view. Puddles of mud appeared in flower beds. Rain started to flow along a couple of the pathways as the water crashed to the ground in large drops.

A figure ran through the dark, a hand clamping a hood over their head, quickly manoeuvring across the puddles on tiptoes. As my eyes adjusted to its movements, it became clear that it was Kate. She gave a short leap over the last puddle, landing next to me.

Nervous, my stomach tightened beneath my layers of wet clothes.

Kate slid her hand underneath her hood and removed it, revealing her damp face. Water had settled on her nose. She smiled and my stomach relaxed.

'I want to come with you.'

We stood under the grey concrete roof, smiling, kissing, and holding each other. She looked into my eyes and said, 'I love you and I want to be with you.'

THE NIGHT AFTER meeting in the rain drenched park, we met in a warm, late booked hotel room, out near Manchester Airport. We arrived at separate times, her first. She checked in and text me the room details. I walked quickly through the reception area, holding myself back from running until I got to the stairs, which I took two at a time, before walking again to the room. I don't know the excuse Kate gave to Stuart about why she'd be away for the night at short notice. I never asked.

That night was the most amazing time I'd spent with Kate in all the months we sneaked around. We stretched out on the bed, dressed in identical white dressing gowns, eating room service burgers, and drinking red wine from the hotel bar directly out of the bottle, the roar of aeroplane engines taking off just outside the window. The only way I can describe it is to say we felt like a proper couple. If we wanted to kiss, we could do it without looking over our shoulders. We were relaxed, laughing more than normal in these meet up situations. We'd made our decision to be together, and those hours in the hotel felt like a celebration of it all. We had three different travel books open on the bed and Kate studied my pre planned route, adding things she wanted to see and experience, including Route 66. We talked about where we'd go, what we'd do, the memories we'd create that we'd share forever. There was no talk of after we got back and how we'd go about setting up a life together, no discussion of how we'd tell the people in our lives we were together. We just enjoyed being together for that night.

We would have been better to stay in that room forever. Or walked out of the hotel, across to the airport, and boarded a plane to anywhere, built ourselves a life away from everything and never looked back.

But life is never that easy. Simple dreams are never simple when the details of life become involved.

THE ROMANCE OF it all soon subsided as the practicalities of the situation became obvious.

Kate hadn't told Stuart about ending their marriage, or my involvement in it. She wasn't sure what to say or how to say it. How do you tell someone your marriage is over and that you're going to travel the world with a neighbour ten years younger than you? How do you explain to someone that you promised to love forever, through good times and bad, that you've been having an affair?

We didn't know how to explain to our families what had gone on under their noses for the past few months. I could already see the look of raw disappointment in my mum's eyes.

Even if we bit the proverbial bullet, revealed our secret to the suburban world we had deceived for so long, and coped with the fallout, we had other decisions to make. For instance, it was the middle of November and I was booked to fly to Thailand in six weeks. Kate's employer required her to give three months' notice, so we had to decide whether she'd fly out and join me, and if so where, or whether I would wait in England for another six weeks and we'd fly out together.

We tried to talk about all these things over the next few days during snatched lunchtime phone calls. We met up a couple of times, back at the football changing rooms, under the cover of darkness.

'Why don't you just hand your notice in and not tell him? Then I'll fly out to Thailand and whenever everything sorts itself out you can just fly out and meet me wherever I am.'

'How can I hand my notice in and Stuart not find out?'

'I don't know. I'm just saying it's an option.'

'It's not an option.'

There was a moment in the silence after she said that, where the seriousness of what we'd done, what she'd decided to do, became real. All the decisions about where to go, what countries to visit, how amazing being together in the open would be, faded away and we were left with the reality that her husband would become an ex-husband.

'I don't know what to do,' she said, leaning her head onto my chest. I pulled her into me and I hugged her, gripping her tightly. Her body began to shake as the tears poured out. The weight released from her and I held her up.

After a minute or so, I took hold of her shoulders and moved her away from me so I could look at her. Tears stained the skin underneath her eyes. 'Listen to me,' I said. 'We can do whatever you think is best. We can go right now, and tell Stuart what's been going on and what we are doing, or we can wait until you're absolutely ready. When you're ready, we can do whatever you want. We are in this together.'

She blinked, pools of tears appearing. She wiped the water away. 'I'm sorry,' she said. 'This is harder than I expected. I keep thinking of things that I'll need to sort out before I can go. I keep thinking about whether I'll have to leave enough money in my account to pay my half of the mortgage, and what I'll do with the finance on my car.'

This was the brutal truth of our love affair. The detail of Kate's life that, despite our love and our romantic dream of running away together, she was tied to. Mortgages, car deals, mobile phone contracts, life insurance plans – all the necessities of the suburban life that meant a quick escape was impossible.

And, of course, her marriage.

IN THE BACKGROUND of this drama, my life ticked on as normal. I worked with my dad, asked my brother how band practice was, had a couple of drinks with Jordan, who had decided, along with getting a promotion, to move into Charlotte's house. I drifted through these moments and struggled to not show any signs of the turmoil that churned my insides. I lived on edge, worrying that any second Kate would ring and say, 'I've told him' and the secret would be out and I would have to deal with the aftermath. Strangely, the thought of dealing with Stuart didn't worry me as much as it had done previously. Since finding out Kate's true feelings for me the hardest part was waiting for the moment of release. Stuart would be angry, he'd hate me, maybe even fight me, but at the end of it all I'd have what I wanted: Kate.

Nearly two weeks after Bonfire Night, and my full confession of what I wanted out of our relationship, Kate came up with a plan. She explained it, stood in the dark by the football changing rooms, our now regular meeting place.

'I'm not going to tell him about you,' she said. 'I'm going to tell him after you've left that I'm not happy and I want a divorce. When I go back to work after New Year, I'll quit my job and have a few months of dealing with whatever the fall out is with Stuart. In that time, I'll tell him I've decided to go travelling on my own. We can meet up then and no one will have to know we are together until we get home. We can put off the anger and stresses that are going to come from our families until we get back. We'll have had nine months or longer to be together, just the two of us. We can enjoy each other without any hassle from anyone else. We can come home and sort all the rest out later.'

Chapter Twenty-Two

We were drunk, which wasn't an excuse. But it was a contributing factor to us dropping our guard.

It happened on the first Friday in December. The suburbs had been transformed, with houses decorated in Christmas lights illuminating the dark. Cards had started to appear in our living room, signed by people our family only had contact with in the form of exchanging annual Christmas cards. On that day, Stuart was down south somewhere at his biggest client's Christmas do. Kate was out in Manchester on her company's own Christmas do. I went out with the lads locally.

After our nights out we met at Kate's house.

Just after two in the morning I cautiously sneaked down her driveway, my eyes scanning every house on our road to make sure no curtains twitched or nosey neighbours spotted me moving towards the front door I knew would be left slightly open.

She stood in heels and a short red dress, framed in the kitchen doorway.

'Hi. Good Christmas do?'

She ignored me, instead saying, 'Come here.'

We moved backwards into the dark kitchen. We came together, kissing hungrily as I wriggled out of my jacket. She started to urgently undo the buttons of my shirt, pushing it off my shoulders and letting it fall behind me. I dropped to one knee and ran my hands up the outside of her legs, under her dress. I grabbed the top of her sheer tights and in one rough motion pulled them and her black silk knickers down. She flicked off her shoes and stepped out of the tights as I softly kissed up the inside of her left thigh. As I reached the top, I stopped, teasing her, before feeling her body react as I kissed between her legs.

I stood up, undoing my jeans, and she lifted her dress. I hooked her leg up and moved into her. She stopped kissing me, her head moving over my shoulder. I could hear her breathing close to my ear, getting heavier.

I felt her body tense, her arms wrapping tightly round me.

'Stop,' she said.

'What?'

'Stop, stop.' There was panic in the delivery of the words.

Her focus had shifted to behind me over my shoulder. I don't know why, but I turned my head round and caught a glimpse of the light in Mrs Wallace's kitchen across the small fence. The old woman was standing by the door that led to her hallway, looking out towards Kate's house.

We quickly dropped down below the window level, out of sight.

'Shit, shit, shit,' Kate said, each word getting louder and more hysterical.

'Do you think she saw us?' I asked.

'I don't know,' she said. 'She looked straight at us.'

Sat side by side our heads leant back against the cupboards, making a dull thud.

In the silence, I realised my jeans were open and I tried to pull them up and close them without showing myself above the line of the kitchen window.

I looked at a devastated Kate, the stress of the situation etched on her face. She was concentrating on the section of tile between her bare legs, her head resting on her hands. 'I can't believe this is how it's all going to come out.' She lifted her head up and screamed, 'Fuck, fuck, fuck,' before throwing her head back hard against the cupboard.

Kate picked up her tights and started to untangle her knickers from them. Once apart, she threw the tights to one side and put her bare feet through the holes in the underwear, pulling them quickly up. She had to stretch out on the floor to get them over her knees and up to her waist without standing. Sat in the middle of the kitchen, she said, 'What do we do?'

'I don't know,' I said. 'I didn't see enough of her to know for sure if she caught us.'

'She was looking straight at us.'

'I know. But it's dark in here. Just because she looked this way doesn't mean she could see clearly in to here. Even if she saw us having sex, she'll just assume I was Stuart.'

'Stuart's away.'

'I know that. She might not.'

'What if she sees him come back tomorrow?'

'I don't know, Kate,' I said harshly.

In all the time we had been sneaking around, Kate and I had never talked about ways to avoid getting caught. Every step we had taken, meeting in dark car parks or pubs miles from home, phoning each other when we knew the other one would be alone, not telling another soul in the world, all the little measures we'd put in place to keep our secret, all seemed like natural things to do. Whether a self-preservation instinct had kicked in, or that not being caught was so obvious it didn't need to be spoken about, the conversation had never felt needed. Now, with one drunken slip up, one moment where we'd let our desire overtake us, everything we'd built could potentially come crashing down.

I lay flat on my front and army crawled across the cold tiled floor, carefully working my body around the legs of the table, stopping underneath the window.

'What are you doing?' Kate asked, her voice low, as if Mrs Wallace could hear us.

'Seeing if she's gone.'

'She might see you.'

I ignored her and slowly raised myself onto one knee and lifted my head a few inches at a time until my eyes were just over the windowsill, quickly ducking down again.

'What?'

'The light's still on.'

'Did she see you?'

'I couldn't see her. She must be at the other end of the kitchen.'

Kate silently pointed towards the hallway and then started moving across the kitchen on her stomach. 'Kate,' I said. She stopped and looked at me. 'It's your house. You can walk around your own kitchen.'

'I don't want her to see me.'

The situation would've been funny if it hadn't been so serious. Two grown adults commando crawling across a dark room at half-past two in the morning to not be seen by an old woman was laughable, apart from the consequences of her actually seeing us. I slid my body across the floor and followed Kate.

In the hallway, we sat side by side again, listening to the silence of the night. No cars passed the house, no dogs barked, or doors shut. The only sounds were our heartbeats. 'It'll be OK,' I said, trying to reassure her. 'If she saw us, then we'll just have to face the fallout. We love each other. We want to be together. We can get through it. It'll be horrible, but we can.'

'I know,' she said. 'But I liked the plan to tell Stuart when you'd gone away because it gave me some control.'

I don't know how long we sat there, silently holding hands. Eventually, Kate stood up and walked to the kitchen door, peering to the window. 'Her light is off.'

I stood up on numb legs. 'I should go.'

She walked into the kitchen and picked up my jacket. Handing it to me, she said, 'OK. I'll let you out of the back door, so you're not walking straight out onto the street.'

MRS WALLACE'S GRANDSON, Will, is my age. In the school holidays, he would come and stay with Mrs Wallace and her husband Albert. We would play football together in the street, using the brick posts of driveways as goalposts. We were best friends in those weeks when school wasn't a distraction. Mrs Wallace welcomed me into her home nearly every lunchtime, providing sandwiches cut into triangles and Penguin chocolate bars.

The Mrs Wallace who stood in her kitchen the previous night was a very different woman to the nice old lady of those days, always making sure we had plenty of juice and didn't stray too far from the security of an adult's eye. Since the death of Mr Wallace six years previously, she'd become frail and noticeably slower in movement during her daily walk to buy her newspaper. Shortly after Mr Wallace had died my dad started cutting her grass for free, taking on the task her husband had performed for so many years.

I spent most of the next morning in my bedroom, sick with worry. What had she seen the night before? Had her eyesight deteriorated the way her small frame had over the past few years? If she'd seen anything, did she recognise me or just assume it was Stuart having sex with Kate in their kitchen. Surely if she thought it was Stuart, the subject would never be raised – inappropriate for a woman of her age to talk about.

Kate and I didn't speak that day. The fear of seeing Mrs Wallace and triggering her memory trapped me in my room. As the day moved on, nothing of significance happened. The tight feeling in my stomach subsided. Mid-afternoon, the dark started to cover the street. The curtains in Mrs Wallace's house were drawn shut around half-past three and remained that way. Stuart returned home and went straight into his house, not leaving again.

If Mrs Wallace did catch me and Kate together in the early hours of that Saturday morning, there was no indication she'd reveal what she'd seen.

MRS WALLACE DIED on Sunday 5th December 2004. She was found by her daughter, Louise, who had driven to the house worried after her mum had not answered her four attempted phone calls.

As was the way with our small suburban community, people gathered on the street to share thoughts and information, compare feelings and stories. Neighbours reported Mrs Wallace had been found in her favourite chair, the morning news on the television, a plate of a half-eaten toast on the small side table, next to a full cup of cold tea.

We both attended the funeral on the Tuesday, nine days later; Kate with Stuart, me with my parents. We stood among a large group of our neighbours after the small church service and commented on what a nice tribute it was before arranging the more practical details of who was going to the burial and if anyone needed a lift.

At the graveside we stood back from the main family as the priest delivered words of ceremony and comfort, before watching the coffin being lowered into the ground. Kate and I caught each other's eye and we both knew that our secret was potentially being buried at that moment. We would never know for sure if Mrs Wallace had seen us that night, if she was the only person to know about our affair, or if she looked out into the dark with no idea what was happening just a few feet from her, over the fence and through the kitchen window.

With her gone it didn't really matter if she knew or not.

We talked about it once, three days after she died, during a brief phone call.

Kate asked, 'Do you think she saw us?'

'It doesn't matter,' I said. 'If she did, she can't tell anyone now.'

There was silence on the line for a few seconds before Kate said, 'I guess not.'

As everyone walked back along the long pathways between the graves, I caught up with Will. We'd not seen each other for a few years and surprisingly, given the emotion of the day, his face broke out into a big smile when he realised it was me tapping him lightly on the back.

'Hello, mate,' he said.

'Hi. I just wanted to say how sorry I am,' I said, shaking his hand. This was the first adult interaction we'd ever had together. I felt extremely guilty that the major part of my sorrow wasn't because his grandma had died, but that my first reaction to the news was one of selfish relief.

Writing the above words, admitting those first thoughts, more than anything that happened with Kate over those months, fills me with a sense of shame that I still feel to this day.

I STOPPED WORKING for my dad just before Mrs Wallace's funeral. The harsh winter weather and days with minimal daylight meant I'd been working reduced hours for a few weeks anyway. Since the summer months our work had changed and I think Dad was struggling find full days of work for both of us. One Thursday night, as we were plating up the weekly takeaway curry in the kitchen, I raised the idea of me finishing earlier than Christmas to allow me to get fully prepared for going away. Dad simply said, 'Sounds like a good idea,' and continued to spoon rice onto four plates.

On the Friday I finished, as we were getting out of the van, he quietly said to me, 'Thanks for all your hard work over the last few months. It's been much appreciated. It can't have been easy working for your old dad.'

I said, 'No worries. I've enjoyed it to be honest.'

And I had. The truth was, despite my initial reservations, I'd grown to enjoy the daily routine of hard manual work. The buzz from building something or turning a garden from an overgrown mess to something for the customer to enjoy was a feeling I wasn't expecting. Plus, the skills I'd learnt would stand me in good stead if I needed to look for causal work when I was travelling around Australia.

THE DAY AFTER Mrs Wallace's funeral I rang Melissa. 'You done your Christmas shopping yet?' I asked.

'Most of it.'

'I should've known.'

'Why?'

'Fancy coming to help me do mine?' I said. 'I need to buy the family some stuff and get a few things for going away.'

'When?'

'Saturday. We could go to town?'

'I'd love to.'

The following Saturday, the eighteenth, we sat next to each other on the tram, rocking from side to side as it sped towards Manchester. Stopped at Old Trafford station, overlooking the open stands of Lancashire's cricket ground, Melissa said, 'I've been doing something and I wanted you to be the first to know.'

'OK,' I said, cautiously.

There was a loud repetitive beep as the doors signalled they were closing and then a jolt as the tram moved forward again.

'I've decided to go to university.'

I probably looked a bit shocked. 'Nice one,' I said. 'To do what?'

'Nursing.'

'Wow. Where did that come from?'

'I've been thinking about it for a while, but our conversation, the one on the wall that night, when I cried. Well, that sort of inspired me. You inspired me.'

'Me?' I asked, shocked.

'Yeah. When we were talking about feeling trapped by our lives, I realised that although we felt the same, you were actually doing something about it. By going travelling, you were breaking free. I thought if you could do it then why couldn't I? I went into work on the Monday morning and thought, I really don't want to be here for the rest of my life. What can I do to give myself something more? And then I thought, *why not go to university*. So, I've started looking into it.'

'Why nursing?'

'It's something I think I'd be good at. The course sounded interesting, it's a job that will allow me to travel. Every country in the world needs nurses. I could go to Africa and work with kids or Australia and not have an issue getting a visa. It just felt right I suppose. The right fit with what I want from myself.'

I smiled at her, a full genuine smile of pride at seeing my friend taking her life in her own hands and making a decision for herself. She smiled back and swayed towards me as the tram veered right then left. She said, 'So, thank you.'

'What for?'

'Showing me there is more in the world than the suburbs of Manchester.'

KATE'S PLAN TO tell Stuart their marriage was over after I'd gone away meant my plan didn't change. Preparing for Christmas and travelling distracted me from the very real situation that in a few weeks Kate was going to leave Stuart and, whether people knew it or not, we'd finally be together. The day after I went shopping with Melissa, Kate, and I found ourselves huddled in the dark corner of a pub on the outskirts of Manchester. Despite being confident we were far enough away from people we knew, the fear of somebody walking through the pub door and catching us meant we both sat with one eye focused on the door.

'Are you excited about Christmas?'

'Sort of. My mum's using it as an excuse to make a big deal about the fact I'm going away. She's glad of the excuse to invite the whole family. Grandparents. Auntie and Uncle. My cousin Hannah. How are you feeling about it all?'

'I'm not sure. It'll be strange being at Stuart's parents.'

ON THE WEDNESDAY three days before Christmas, two days after his sixteenth birthday, I watched my brother grow up.

The Death Stars had their first gig with him as a member, in a dirty underground music club in Manchester. My parents stood at the back of the room, sipping warm lager out of plastic pint pots, desperately trying not to look out of place. I'd invited my friends and their girlfriends, plus Melissa and Stephanie.

Chris was nervous. He wasn't the cocky kid who tried to take the piss out of me at home. Instead, he stood in the tight circle of his

314

band, quiet, sipping on a Coke. He caught my eye at one point and I lifted my beer towards him and smiled. He just looked at the floor.

And then they went on stage.

Jordan, Sam, Neil, and I, plastic bottles in hand, made our way to the front. Chris nervously slipped the strap over his head and tested the strings on his guitar. The other band members quickly sound checked their instruments for the last time and then the singer moved to the front and said, in a voice slightly above a croak, 'Hello. We're the Death Stars.'

As the gig went on Chris was transformed. He started the set staring at his guitar, concentrating on all the parts, making sure he didn't make a mistake. But with every clap between songs from the small crowd in front of him, he started to feel more confident in his own ability. And so he should have. He was good. Not amazing, but good enough for me to forget it was my annoying little brother and get right into the music he and his new mates were playing. It felt so strange considering I was the first person to teach him chords on the guitar and here he was standing on stage playing it with more ability than I ever had.

After the gig, when he asked me how I thought it went, I put my arm round him proudly and said, 'Bro, that was fucking amazing.'

He smiled, knowing I was a bit drunk, but I could tell he was pleased to get some form of approval from me. I knew it wasn't the night to take the piss out of him or treat him like a child. He had stood up on stage in front of people and showed that he had talent. I respected that.

People disappeared, my parents took Chris home, and the next couple of bands played their sets. We finished our drinks and Neil, glad of the night out, suggested moving on. We went to a couple more bars, Jordan and Charlotte dancing in front of a small DJ booth in one place, me and Melissa hugging in another, her telling me she was going to miss me, me saying how strange it was that in a weeks' time I'd be on the other side of the world, alone in an exotic city. Shots were drunk, dances danced, and goodbyes shared more than once. Later, in a dirty kebab shop, I told Charlotte how much I liked her and how great she was for Jordan, and that she should look after him because he was my mate and he deserved a good woman. She laughed and I told her not to laugh at me before biting into a chicken kebab, spilling chilli sauce, and laughing at myself. Taxis were flagged and goodbyes were said, instructions of how to get home were argued over, and then I fell asleep on Melissa's shoulder and woke up outside my house, disorientated. I let slip that I'd bought her a secret Christmas present and I'd definitely see her before I went travelling to watch her open it. Outside I stood in the refreshing cold of the December night and thought how impromptu nights out were the best nights out.

I WOKE UP late to a quiet house. I made myself breakfast and drank two cups of tea before going back to my room and taking out the list of things I needed to pack. I slid my rucksack from underneath my bed and opened it, emptying it of the things that had accumulated in it from my travels around Europe. I found ticket stubs from the tour of Barcelona's football stadium and a receipt from a meal in a pizza restaurant in Germany shoved into one of the pockets. I placed them on the side in my room, clearing space in the rucksack for new mementos.

I worked slowly and methodically down my list, laying out all the items on my bed, piling clothes on top of each other, placing my passport, tickets, and other important documents together in a clear, waterproof folder. There is something very liberating about reducing your life down to the contents of a rucksack. Each item I packed deep inside the bag, including the Febreze Sarah had recommended, felt like it lifted the weight and pressures of the treadmill that is daily life off my shoulders.

I repacked three times, each time lifting the rucksack and testing its weight. On the third try I was happy I'd found the right weight for carrying my life on my back. Happy I had everything I then pulled the drawstring tightly shut, closed the top, and locked the clips, leaning the rucksack against the wall ready for leaving.

Chapter Twenty-Three

Boxing Day. I was first up, struggling to sleep with the excitement of travelling racing through me, like a child thinking 'one more sleep'. I went downstairs and surveyed the hangover from Christmas that was evident throughout our house: plates piled high on the kitchen side, waiting to go into the dishwasher, empty chocolate wrappers open on the floor in the living room, next to finished beer bottles – all serving as reminders of the excess of the previous day.

It had been a fairly normal Christmas. My mum panicked over the cooking and where everyone was going to sit. My dad tried to calm her down and spent a lot of time encouraging me and my brother to stop watching television and try to help. Our Grandparents arrived and we exchanged presents. Everyone gave me money for travelling, which helped, although I'd have to get my mum to pay it into my account after I'd gone. More family arrived and all squeezed around the dining table, eating more food than we needed to. I genuinely enjoyed myself, laughing at old stories about my mum and dad when they were kids, and playing party games and quizzes. I spoke to the lads from uni. A tradition we'd started in our first year, when we'd called each other to complain about our families and talk about how we couldn't wait to get back to Leeds for New Year's Eve. As the evening wrapped itself around the festivities, we settled into the lounge, a comfortable quiet falling over the house as we had a few drinks and watched television.

I unloaded the dishwasher and tidied up the kitchen a bit before the rest of my family got up. My mum was first down, her thickest dressing gown over her pyjamas. She filled the kettle and while she waited for it to boil, she pulled me in for a big, slightly awkward hug and said, 'I can't believe you're going away again tomorrow.'

'Don't, Mum,' I said.

'I mean it. It's been nice having you back at home. I'm going to miss you.'

She was being honest in a way only a parent can. There was no embarrassment in her words, no reason to think I'd feel uncomfortable hearing them. I was her first-born child; she loved me and she was telling me to my face. To her it was the most natural thing in the world. Now I'm older I understand. Stood in the kitchen as a twenty-one-year-old who thought he was cool, to have his mum say these things was annoying, and, well, distinctly un-cool. I wanted to race upstairs, grab my rucksack, and run to the airport.

We ate a last breakfast together as a family, slumped in front of the television watching a comedy DVD that we'd bought my dad for Christmas, drinking tea, and eating bacon sandwiches. I was more comfortable with the lack of ceremony.

THE PHONE CALL came at about half-past ten.

The noise of the low ringtone made me realise the phone wasn't in my pocket, the place I'd kept it ever since I'd started seeing Kate. I'd desperately tried to avoid a family member thinking they were being helpful by stopping the ringing and explaining to the caller I was on my way. I followed the noise, bounding down the stairs three at time, into the kitchen, and answered it. 'Hello,' I said breathlessly.

'I need to see you,' Kate said.

'OK,' I answered.

'The usual meeting place in half an hour.'

'No problem,' I said, my eyes using the kitchen window as a mirror to see if anyone was behind me.

She put the phone down.

'Who was that, love?' my mum asked, making me jump.

'Jordan,' I lied.

AS I WAITED, I realised this was the first time Kate and I had ever met in this spot in the daylight. It was a bright day with frost on the ground. I could see across to the children's play area where a few brave kids and their parents were enjoying the dry weather. They had hats and gloves on, scarves wrapped around their necks. I could just make them out as they climbed over frames, their movements hindered by their clothing.

I again leant against the red door, as I'd done so many times over the last few weeks, and tried to make myself as out of view as possible, placing my gloved hands under the opposite armpit to keep myself warm. I could feel Kate's wrapped Christmas present in my coat pocket, its edges sticking into me slightly when I moved.

Kate arrived fifteen minutes later, her black hat pulled low over her ears, hiding part of her face.

We stood facing each other for a few uncomfortable seconds. I went to kiss her, but she pulled away and took a small step backwards. Then she said, 'Do you want children?'

I'd been asked that question a few times in my life. Melissa asked me one night in Spain when we sat on the beach watching the waves flicker in the moon light and roll onto the sand. We were two teenagers in love, talking about our future together, and it was obvious she'd meant did I want her children. That wasn't the way Kate asked me. Her version of the question meant did I want children at any point in the future, with anyone.

'Yeah,' I said. 'I think so.' I was stunned by the question and after a split second, to break the tension that had enveloped us, I said, 'Do I have to decide now?'

'When?' she asked.

'When what?'

'When do you want them?'

'Why does it matter?'

'It matters,' she said.

'Why?'

'Because it does.'

'Then, yes. I want children.'

'I want children,' she said, her tone matter of fact. 'I want children soon.'

'What are you saying?'

'I'm saying that if we do this, if we run away together like we're teenagers in a Hollywood film, I've got to know that we want the same things.'

I stepped forward, put my hands on her arms, and said, 'If you want to know if I'm in this for the long haul, then I've told you, I love you and I want to be with you. I want to have a life with you.'

'I know what you've said. I need to hear it again.'

She was getting upset. Her lip quivered and she bit down hard on it. 'I want to be with you,' I said again.

She was frozen to the spot, looking at me, almost through me. I didn't feel capable of saying the words I wanted to say, so I stayed silent.

Eventually, she said, 'I can't come with you.'

There was an initial moment of calm, when the words floated from her mouth across the cold air between us to my ears. Then they exploded inside my brain. I must have offered no reaction, because Kate continued to talk, although her words felt almost inaudible for the first few seconds. I snapped into focus as she said, 'If I come with you, I'm certain it will ruin your life. We want different things. We can kid ourselves that we can fly off around the world like some kind of dream couple but eventually we are going to have to come home. Eventually, we are going to have to face up to our families and Stuart and everyone we know and admit what we did. What we've been doing for all these months. What are we going to say? That we met in the middle of Australia and suddenly realised we were in love?'

She paused. I remained motionless. 'Even if we do that, Tom, even if we admit everything and start a life together, it won't be the life that you want.'

'It will,' I said. 'I love you. I want to be with you.'

'I don't doubt that you love me. I love you. But I cannot come with you.'

'Don't do this,' I said, emotions rising up in me. 'We'll come back and we'll have each other. That's what we want. That's what you told me.'

'I know,' she said.

'I want to be with you,' I said, more defiantly. 'I didn't sneak around for all these months, risking getting caught, risking facing my family,' my voice rose a pitch on the last word and nearly squeaked, 'facing Stuart, because you're a bit of fun. We can have a life. We can be together. We just have to commit to each other. You are the most amazing woman I've ever met in my life and I want to be with you forever.'

'Tom, listen to me,' she said calmly. 'If I come with you, we'll come back eventually and maybe we'll survive the anger when we tell people we're together. Maybe people will accept it. But then what? We'll live together for a bit, maybe even have a baby or two and in about three or four years you'll look at me and you'll see a thirty-five-year-old who is making you live a life you don't want.

You'll be twenty-five and stuck. You'll see your friends going out and having holidays and living a life you can't have because of me. You'll hate me. And I don't want to be the person who makes you feel like that.'

'I choose you over all that.'

'Why do you want to travel?'

Her change of direction surprised me. 'Because I want to see the world.'

'That might be true. But it's also because you feel trapped. Trapped by what life will be if you stay. How many times have you told me your biggest fear is ending up around here, living the same life as your parents? You're scared of being trapped. If we go away together, eventually that's going to happen. It'll be before you feel ready for it. No matter how you feel now, in five years' time you're going to realise I'm right. Because it doesn't matter how we feel about each other now, it won't always be like this. And when it ends, you'll resent me.'

It was too much to take in, too much to process. I looked away from her and saw an old man walking his dog, content with the simple pleasure of enjoying the views of the park.

At that moment, all we had been through flicked through my mind, like a flashback in a film. The night we met while walking to the pub, the night she knocked on my door and we had sex in my small single bed, unable to get enough of each other, all the problems of the world melting away because we were together. Bonfire night, and my confession of wanting to be with her. In my heart, it was true. If I'd ever revealed my feelings for Kate to anyone, spoken of our situation, they would have told me I was crazy. They would have told me to end it, to forget about her. But I couldn't do that. I couldn't let her stay, unhappy in her life, unhappy in this place, stuck in the suburbs in a marriage that was dying. The world she inhabited was killing her beautiful soul.

Sometimes, in the quiet moments after we'd been together, when we were laughing at a stupid joke or her head was just resting on my chest, I felt like I was the only person who saw the real her. I felt like all the people she worked with, or lived near her on the street we shared, even her husband, didn't see the woman I saw. They didn't see how beautiful she was, or how funny she could be when she let down her guard. How passionate she was when she spoke about a subject she loved. How kind she was, or how thoughtful. I wanted to shout to the world about all these qualities and yet I couldn't. Instead, I kept them chained up in a vault inside me and carried them everywhere.

I turned back to face her. She was crying, a single trail of tears running down each side of her face.

'I love you,' I said.

'I love you too,' she said. 'That's why I have to let you go.'

'You don't,' I said, the fight draining out of me.

She hugged me and kissed me full on the lips. She moved her mouth about half an inch from mine and said, 'I'm so sorry, Tom.'

And then she was gone.

I sat down, my back against the changing room door, and cried.

I SAT ON the cold concrete floor, numb. I'd cried for about ten minutes but once the emotion had been released from me, I couldn't bring myself to do anything but stare into nothing. With one deep breath and a push from the ground I creaked into a standing position and walked home, carefully placing my feet into their steps because of the thin layer of frost on the pavements. There was a glimmer of ice on the roads too and the cars that were passing me were going slower than normal.

I turned onto my road and my heart sank.

There were two ambulances parked across the road, doors wide open. A car, young Paul's blue Renault Clio to be exact, was smashed into the space where Kate and Stuart's wall used to be. The front of the car had crunched together like a flimsy accordion. The front windscreen was smashed and small fragments of glass covered the pavement. A crowd of neighbours stood in a circle around the scene, giving enough distance to not interfere but close enough to obtain details.

I couldn't see Kate.

My mind raced, counting backwards, questioning how long it would have taken her to walk home, how long the ambulances and their crews had been at the scene. I didn't have any basis for my guess, but they didn't look like they'd just arrived.

Several members of the gathered crowd looked distraught. Hands were covering mouths and people were holding each other, devastated by the sight they were witnessing on the other side of the wall. I couldn't see what they were looking at, my view blocked by the angle I had. Paul's dad was tightly holding his wife as she cried controllably into his chest.

I still couldn't see Kate.

Something snapped inside me and forced my legs to work faster. I jogged down the road but stopped as a bright orange stretcher was lifted from behind the wreckage. It was impossible to tell who lay on it. All I could see was a black winter hat and a bloodied face, the person's body covered by a blanket. I could tell by the way the paramedics were treating them they were alive.

Paul's mum turned to face the scene and collapsed, screaming. His dad held onto her. He was trying to comfort her, but the fear in him was obvious. I couldn't tell if they were crying because their son was on the stretcher or his actions had caused someone else to be on it.

I moved to the crowd, ready to ask someone who had been hurt, practicing the question over and over in my mind, to not give away my fear it was Kate.

As I reached the edges of the crowd, she appeared in my view; a blanket loosely wrapped around her, Lorna Keane's arm around her shoulders. Kate's face was covered in shock, but there were no obvious signs of damage, no blood or cuts.

We looked into each other's eyes for a brief moment.

If I'd known that would be the last time I'd see her, I would've held the moment for longer. I would have smiled or remembered what she was wearing, what her hair was like. I would have taken in every detail of her face and committed it to my mind forever. Instead, as I watched Lorna lead her towards the second ambulance I walked anonymously past the crowd and down my driveway.

IMMEDIATELY, AS I entered the house, Chris said, 'Have you heard what's happened?'

'Yeah, I saw the ambulances outside.' Hoping my disinterested voice would convince him I didn't want to talk.

'Not outside. In Thailand.'

'No, what?'

'There's been a tsunami. Loads of people have died. It's all over the news.'

I moved quickly down the hallway into the living room where I saw a massive wave racing towards a beach on the television. The water crashed onto the sand and continued at speed, over a wall and into a beach front resort. It was only when I saw a car floating in the water that the scale of it hit.

I, like many people I've spoken to since that day, sat there glued to the news coverage. I watched footage of devastating waves, images of the sheer destructive power of the sea, looked at maps of the area it was affecting as sombre reporters informed me it wasn't just Thailand impacted. We sat as a family, captured.

My mum was crying. 'What an awful day,' she said. 'First young Paul, and now this.' She began to get angry, 'I told you that boy was going to hurt someone driving like that. I bloody said it, over and over. Kate is very lucky she managed to spot him losing control of the car when she did and jump out of his way, otherwise she'd be dead now.'

'What did you say?' I said, unsure I'd heard her correctly.

'Kate Young. She just managed to jump out of the way as Paul's car mounted the pavement and hit the wall. She's bloody lucky she spotted him otherwise he would've hit her. She could've been killed.'

The weight of the words hung in the air.

'Will what's happened stop you going away?' Chris asked.

I know he was referring to the tsunami but as I answered, 'I don't know,' I was thinking about Kate.

Epilogue

Kate was right; we wouldn't have worked. With the experiences I've had since, and the life I have now, I understand that.

I flew to Thailand as planned, my mum stressing the importance of being safe. Disorientated by jetlag and the size and the noise of the busy city, it was easy to be distracted from Kate. I spent the first couple of days trying to get information about the affected areas of the country. Obviously, my plans became insignificant as I was provided with details of people being trapped on islands, unable to leave the scene of their nightmares.

I extended my stay in Bangkok to acclimatise. I visited temples, ate food from the street vendors, and went out drinking with people from my hostel, most of whom were in similar situations to me, their plans to hop around the islands of Thailand unworkable. I ended up travelling with a few of them into Cambodia and Vietnam, spending time on the beaches there. Lying in the sun all day with nothing to do but swim and sunbath, I couldn't fight thinking about her anymore. I'd close my eyes and her face would appear.

During this time, early in the new year, my attitude to the affair with Kate changed. There wasn't one exact moment, but being so far away from her I was able to have some perspective. She was right; I was trapped. I did fear not being able to escape from it. But I came to the conclusion that she was trapped, too. I'd recognised that in her and I wanted to rescue her. That's the word that sums up how I felt about her. I loved her, however stupid it would seem to other people if they knew about us, and because of that love I wanted to rescue her.

In those moments we shared, for those months I was home, we needed each other. She needed something to pull her out of her unhappiness. I needed something that wasn't normality.

But those needs weren't enough for us to change our lives forever.

Once I fully understood the reasons for our relationship – the clear truth of why we had done what we had, why we had taken the risks and the chances – I was able to move on. I was able to travel, to enjoy myself, to live.

I climbed up Sydney Harbour Bridge in Australia and jumped out of a plane in New Zealand. I sat on a beach in Fiji and read a ridiculous number of paperback books. I got drunk with people I'd just met and had some fun with a few girls. I flew to LA and met up with guys I'd shared a dorm room with in Australia. We hired a car and drove the Pacific highway to San Francisco.

On our second day in the city, we went on a tour of Alcatraz. On the boat back from the prison I got talking to a girl called Maria. She was travelling alone from Warwick, visiting a friend of hers who lived in San Francisco. She was twenty-three, a year older than me.

We got on pretty well and she and her friend offered to show us a few decent bars.

We clicked. We spent the next few days together, seeing the sights of the city and getting to know each other. Those few days in San Fran, followed by the drive we took to Vegas and the three nights we had there, were the seeds of a relationship that has continued to grow to this day. In Vegas we put two hundred dollars on red on the roulette wheel and won, spending the money on the best room we could in the MGM Grand. When we said goodbye in San Francisco, we knew we'd meet up again.

That happened less than a week after I landed back in England. I came home via New York for Christmas, almost a year after I'd left. I spent New Year's Eve in Warwick with Maria and her friends. Within six months I was living there permanently in her parents' house. I got a job working for a local bank, saved up some money, and went back to university to retrain to become a PE teacher. I tell all my sixth formers to go travelling. They all look at me like I'm mad.

I proposed in Berlin on a city break, and we got married a year later in Warwick. Jordan was my best man. Fortunately, he didn't tell the story of the student whose halls I left in Manchester without ever finding out her name. Sean, Matt, and John were my ushers.

Jordan is now an assistant store manager for the same supermarket chain in Manchester, with full salary and company car. He's still with Charlotte and they've got a little girl, Lucy. He claims he doesn't see the point in getting married, but Lucy asked him recently why 'Mummy has a different second name?' so I would guess it won't be long.

Neil isn't with Lisa anymore. They moved into their own flat while I was travelling but within a year Neil had moved back in with his parents. He sees Alex for two nights and one weekend day each week. Although we've not fallen out, we don't really speak anymore.

I see more of the lads from university these days than I do my mates from Manchester. We get together at someone's house about once a month. Our wives and girlfriends all get on well. We've had a couple of New Year's Eves away together in rented houses. Drinking until the early hours, reminiscing about long hours in pubs in Leeds when all we did was drink and talk about how great everything was going to be when we got older. Sean has asked me to be the best man at his wedding to his fiancée Rachel, next year.

Melissa is still an important part of my life, although now from more of a distance. She qualified as a nurse in Manchester and started work at a local hospital. After a year or so, on my recommendation of the city, she moved to Sydney for a year to work out there. She met an English doctor, Josh, who worked in the same hospital. They returned to England engaged. Maria and I went to their wedding. I like Josh. He's a nice guy; a bit serious at times, but I've never seen Melissa happier. They have one child – a boy, Thomas – and Melissa has recently announced she is pregnant again. For Melissa and me, the bond we shared when we were teenagers will never end. We speak on the phone every few months, sharing news from our now separate lives. It's always easy, always comfortable, like it should be for good friends.

The only word to describe my brother is cool. He's grown taller than me. He's all skinny jeans, trendy haircuts, and Jimi Hendrix T-shirts. He is twenty-three years old and lives in a shitty flat in London he shares with three others. He went to uni there to study music production and now gets bits of studio work to pay his rent. His band (not the Death Stars) is his true love. There are five of them, including two of the lads he lives with, playing gigs, writing songs, working hard to get noticed.

Chris and I have a better relationship now than ever before. When I came back from travelling, he'd grown up, more so perhaps in the year I'd been away than in the three years I lived in Leeds. Although our lives keep us apart, the age gap between us feels like less of a problem. We share the same taste in music and he's always ringing me recommending new bands to listen to. We talk a couple times of week, the banter more grown up and jokey than when we lived under the same roof. It's something I'm happy about.

My mum and dad are still ticking along. My dad is still working hard landscaping. He complains about his knees more now but I don't think he'll ever retire. He'd miss the fresh air, the graft, the sense of earning and providing he gets from running his business on his terms. He rings me regularly for advice about his computer, frustrated because he can't use it. I offered to pay for an Introduction to Computers course for him one Christmas, but he just said, 'What the bloody hell do I want to sit in a classroom for?'

My mum is semi-retired. She likes planning weekends away in different parts of the country, reading books and, to be honest, I think she enjoys the peace and quiet at home now Chris and I don't live there. She and my dad come and stay with us once every few months and we all go out, including Maria's parents, for a curry or Chinese. Our mums drink too much red wine and drop hints about grandchildren. My dad just smiles and says, 'You enjoy your life. Plenty of time for that.'

As for Kate, I haven't seen or heard from her since Boxing Day, 2004. My mum told me in a phone call home from LA that she'd moved out and filed for divorce. I felt a knot in my stomach, expecting that my mum would go launch into a speech about how disappointed she was to find out I was involved in the marriage break-up, but actually she was just sharing a bit of gossip from the street. By the time I got home Stuart had sold the house and from what neighbours tell me, Kate moved to Edinburgh for a new job. I hope she found the happiness she was searching for.

About two years ago I was back in Manchester for Jordan's birthday. I stood in the Boathouse having a drink, with Maria, Jordan, and Charlotte. A hand tapped me on the shoulder and I turned around to find Stuart facing me. He smiled and said hello. I introduced Maria and he introduced the women he was with. He had put on weight and his hair had a sprinkling of grey throughout but he looked well. I noticed he wasn't wearing a wedding ring. He shook my hand, said it was good to see me and that he'd leave us to our evening.

'Who was that?' Maria asked.

'Just an old neighbour,' I said.

Acknowledgements

Thank you to my wife, Gemma, for all the years of saying: 'Stop talking about it and do something'. She assumes the role of my biggest critic out of a desire to see me improve and succeed. I can't thank her enough for her love, patience, and support.

Thank you to Mrs Keast, my former drama teacher, whose feedback on a script for one of her lessons helped me discover that writing was something I enjoyed doing and was potentially good at.

Thanks to my Eight Albums (eightalbums.co.uk) partner, Matt Johnston, for all the hours listening to story ideas, and for the on-going conversation about how to balance a 'normal life' with a creative one.

Firm handshakes to: Justin Scholes, for his constant encouragement, Lawrence Evans, for making me believe that people would want to read Tom's story, and finally, Mark Barry, for being a fantastic source of advice, guidance, and inspiration.

Printed in Great Britain
by Amazon

11332652R00193